THE BOSS'S WIFE

OTHER WORKS BY S. L. STEBEL

NOVELS
Spring Thaw (Walker and Company, 1989)
The Widowmaster (with Robert Weverka)
The Collaborator
The Vorovich Affair

BIOGRAPHY
The Shoe Leather Treatment

TRAVEL
Main Street 1971 (The Vanishing Americans)

PLAYS
The Way Out
Fathers Against Sons

THE BOSS'S WIFE

A Novel

S. L. Stebel

Walker and Company
New York

First published in the United States of America in 1992 by
Walker Publishing Company, Inc.

Published simultaneously in Canada by Thomas Allen & Son
Canada, Limited, Markham, Ontario.

Library of Congress Cataloging-in-Publication Data
Stebel, S. L.
The boss's wife : a novel / S. L. Stebel.
p. cm.
ISBN 0-8027-1198-7
I. Title.
PS3569.T33815B67 1992
813'.54 — dc20   92-2546
CIP

Printed in the United States of America

2 4 6 8 10 9 7 5 3 1

For the women in my life:
Jan, Patricia Ann, and April

Acknowledgments

This book would not have been possible without the seminal work of the father of us all, James M. Cain; the impeccable, always available ear of Charles Rome Smith; the enthusiastic encouragement of that encyclopedic reader of mysteries, Maggie Bradbury, and her husband, Ray, as well as that of my agent, Don Congdon, keeper of the faith; the verification of generational matters by Brendan Schallert; the computer expertise of Ted Pedersen; and last, but hardly least, Peter Rubie, whose skilled manipulation of the creative tension between author and editor materially enhanced the story.

THE BOSS'S WIFE

ONE

At the hour before dawn when dreams often turn into nightmares, those few pedestrians on the hilly, litter-strewn downtown streets of what was once considered the City of Angels stumbled past the earthquake-resistant steel girders rising seventy-two stories from the two-block-square, eight-story-deep excavation, too drunk or fatigued to give more than a passing glance to the beat-up panel truck parked near the construction headquarters shack.

With NOBLE 9 SON, ELECTRONIC COMMUNICATIONS CONSULTANTS hand-stenciled on the truck's side panels, they assumed the truck belonged there. Even had they paused to watch the lithe figure in starched white coveralls and yellow hard hat unspool insulated wire from the truck to the construction shack's porch, their assumption would be that the workman was anxious to get a start on the day's work.

The workman's athletic leap up on the porch rail to fuss momentarily with the telephone connection under the eaves was accomplished so swiftly even the overweight security guard hastening back with coffee and donuts from the nearby 7-Eleven noticed nothing out of the ordinary.

Back inside the truck, the workman, Jack B. (for nothing, a hopeful joke on his father's part) Noble took time to lock the panel door and murmur soothingly to his part Labrador, part Rhodesian Ridgeback dog, Roger. The dog drowsed fitfully between the seats while Jack turned to the laptop computer set up on the fold-down shelf over the bunk bed and plugged in the telephone jack to the computer's internal modem.

In spite of his uncalled-for anxiety, Jack smiled when he got a dial tone. He'd never lost his golly-gee-whiz awe at the rewards possible once he'd mastered complex computer software. Anyone dedicated and skilled enough, with patience and the right passwords, could break into the most sophisticated computer network. Not forgetting to factor in luck, of course, Jack reminded himself, glancing reverentially at the pinned-up newspaper photos of brilliant hackers who'd run afoul of the law, tripped up by a moment's carelessness.

Carefully, Jack punched in the memorized numbers. A few rapid heartbeats later there it came, up on the highlighted screen, MetroBank Central Data Processing, letters glowing urine yellow in the ghostly dark, followed by the expected question: Password?

Jack hesitated, fingers poised over the humming keyboard, delaying his connection to the power that would surge through his system, enlarging his thinking capacity a thousandfold, enabling him to calculate odds and probabilities with a speed that seemed faster than light, providing him the kind of oxygen-deprived, mountaintop rush that neither alcohol, drugs, nor even sex could approximate.

What was he waiting for? He'd planned until the factor of risk was close to zero. Any risk larger and he wouldn't for a minute have considered tapping the till, certainly not at the bank where he worked. But before anyone was the wiser, every borrowed nickel would be put back.

He tried to repress a mouse of anxiety gnawing at his confidence, the hated remnants of a conscience imposed upon him by the nuns. Money was the devil's lure, they'd said, ruler-rapping his knuckles to underscore the point. But they'd never experienced the pressures Jack now faced. Nor did they understand that money had no moral quotient. Money was just the real world's way of keeping score.

From the streets above, in that haze at the peripheries of his concentration, Jack heard a honk and tire squeal. Work traffic was beginning. The hour, according to the flashing digital clock in the corner of his flip-top screen, showed 6:26 A.M.

And counting.

Taking a breath, Jack entered the code that was supposed to have been erased when the system became operational, opening a "back door" that no one but he — the system programmer — knew still existed. Now safely inside, he typed in the password, Diogenes.

Finally, *finally*, the word Enter appeared. Shaking off unwanted thoughts like a dog water from its fur, Jack typed List All Certificate of Deposit Accounts.

A moment later there they were — Treasures of Xanadu, the Golden Apples of the Sun, enough money to purchase Nefretete's Jewels! One moment the pulsating screen was blank, the next numbers appeared, conjured from air, etching themselves in his memory and along the computerized spreadsheet on his laptop screen.

Cert. #	Date	Term	Rate	Amt.	Int. to Acct. #
36-6725-00	9_2_91	1 yr.	8.25	$350,000	14-000-80
55-8247-11	9_5_91	1 yr.	8.75	$500,000	14-327-80
36-4510-24	9_6_91	1 yr.	8.05	$100,000	14-021-80
24-7771-01	9_7_91	1 yr.	7.25	$ 50,000	14-563-80

Jack put the flashing cursor on the column marked Int. to Acct. #, then transferred the numbers of the first three CDs — ignoring the $50,000 account as too small — into a separate holding file, securing it from scrutiny by entering a new password, Home Sweet Home. From a hidden file, Home Castle, he brought up the savings account numbers to which, in the previous quarter, he'd redirected the CD interest.

Carefully typing in how much was owed to each, Jack put back the exact amount necessary to match what had been taken. Bank statements wouldn't be mailed until next quarter's end, giving him almost three months before he had to face any day of reckoning.

6:31 A.M. Five minutes. Each minute on-line his chances of getting caught increased exponentially. Reading from a signature card, Jack quickly typed his new account number into the computer. Tagging it with an *, he ordered the system to Transfer int.

Waiting for Computer Central to confirm, Jack calculated the interest total thus far: seventy-five thousand dollars, give or take a few cents. Seventy-two thousand five hundred to pay back what he'd borrowed the quarter before, plus twenty-five hundred on top of that, sent to his personal account, every penny allocated to fill desperate needs.

Transfer Confirmed happily blinked from the screen.

6:34 A.M. Elapsed time eight minutes. A lot swifter, and without the potential for blood of an old-fashioned robbery. But it wasn't robbery, Jack chided himself, just a loan.

He signed off with the initials R. J. There were sixteen vice presidents with those initials among MetroBank's several thousand employees in the western United States, not counting those who'd moved on. In the unlikely event the transfers were accidentally stumbled upon, it'd take an investigator years past the statute of limitations to narrow it down to nobody.

6:35 A.M. Better get moving. Within minutes crews would begin arriving.

[3]

A quick look making sure the security guard was still concentrating on breakfast, Jack switched the computer's modem into voice mode. He punched in the number. It rang. Rang again. Rang a third time. . . . Jack was about to hang up when a sleepy voice answered.

"Sunset Years Manor."

Jack picked up the telephone handset. "Could I speak to William Noble, please?"

"Told you it was for me," the familiar, anxiety-ridden voice rasped, after an interminable wait. "Jack?"

"Hi, Dad. I only have a minute. Things going better?"

"Loan come through?"

"Any day now. There's been a glitch in my credit rating, but. . . ."

"Son, level with me. This too big a stretch? This ain't the worst place I ever lived—"

"I told you," Jack interrupted, heart aching at his father's attempt to put a good face on a situation the old man despised, "I'm on the edge of a big score—we'll be borrowing each other's razors before you know it."

"Main thing is, son, not to get overextended. Don't follow my example. If I'd exercised more caution at certain key points in my life things would've worked out different. For you and for me. With a normal upbringing you wouldn't've had to watch your old man piss away the family residence, like he has everything else worthwhile in his life—"

"Stop worrying, Dad. Everything's rosy. Sorry, gotta go, talk to you tomorrow." Jack, moist-eyed, hung up before his father could continue his litany of self-flagellation.

Though time was rapidly shrinking, Jack took a moment to control his emotions. It grieved him to see that optimistic, generous-spirited individual reduced to a frail, vulnerable old man racked with guilt over having been forced to become, during much of Jack's early life, an absentee father. How could that honey-tongued salesman have known he'd sold the idea of marriage to a wandering-eyed woman not cut out for the grungy reality of motherhood?

If anyone had been at fault it was himself, Jack thought. He'd been a clinging, needy, love-starved child.

6:39 A.M. Pushing painful thoughts of his early years aside, afraid they'd degenerate into self-pity, a condition he despised, Jack quickly packed up the computer. Securing the too-small hard hat on his head, he opened the door panel and hastened back to the construction shack.

[4]

The security guard, mouthing crumbs off the wax paper, looked in his direction. With a casual wave, Jack stepped up on the shack's railing and disconnected the phone connection. Stepping down and walking backward toward the truck, he rewound the wire back onto the spool.

Heaving the spool into the truck, Jack grinned at the guard, patted his stomach, then got into the driver's seat. He scratched the drowsing Roger and turned the key. When the truck's engine caught at first grind he blessed his foresight in having the starter rebuilt.

Jack sped up the rutted road leading to the street above as fast as the chattering first gear would allow. He bounced past the fenced gate just as an air horn blasted the dawn, announcing a trailer truck delivering the day's first load of steel.

TWO

The Sports Cafe was in a rundown section of Santa Monica Boulevard not far from downtown L.A., distinguishable from shabby storefronts on either side by its red, yellow, and green neon depicting a tipped martini glass with a tumbling olive, a foaming beer stein, and a rack of billiard balls rolling in all directions. BREAKFAST, proclaimed another red neon sign, and then, one at a time the words SERVED ALL DAY appeared, illustrated by a stack of yellow pancakes tossing in the air.

A few minutes before eight was early enough to find a parking space in front. A now wide-awake Roger snapped at the rundown but polished heels of Jack's brass-buckled, Gucci-look-alike loafers as he stepped out of the truck, computer snugged under his arm, feeling less comfortable in his discount-store knockoff of an Armani double-breasted suit than he had in his coveralls.

He still owed those happy immigrants from mainland China $125, and the suit was already showing signs of wear. But it was shower-steam pressed and clean as he was, courtesy of the new Westwood Recreation Center. He'd even managed a few laps in the Olympic-sized pool before being told by the snotty, sleek-muscled lifeguard that the lanes were reserved for master-class enrollees.

Biting back a retort, he'd hung his head, but whistled while he shaved in the shower, to the disgruntlement of those eye-on-the-main-chance upwardly mobiles who mistakenly thought performing morning ablutions in public was the stunt of a show-off instead of someone with no other choice.

Hey, he could have told them, this bravado's phony, a cover devised by the shy, repressed yet somehow persistently optimistic creature hiding inside. But they wouldn't have believed him — not someone on the slippery edge of thirty, hair skull-tight in a ready-for-action pompadour, with only a whiskery trace of the ponytail trimmed so he could join the gainfully employed. His right ear was absent its undetectable-to-the-naked-eye-flawed diamond, and he wore his coat unbuttoned to show off the blue-flame French silk power tie, knotted with a casualness that bespoke an affectionate contempt for the uniform of the fast track.

The only cloud in a day that gave every indication of turning out sunny was the frustration he'd encountered at the neighborhood bank branch where he'd opened a pseudonymous account. When he'd tried to withdraw a mere thousand dollars there'd been an unaccountable delay before the teller found Roger Jonas. On the first two tries the teller's computer had come up blank, and only when Jack insisted he try once more had the Jonas account appeared.

Though such electronic difficulties seemed increasingly common in "El Lay" these days, it had given Jack heart-clutching pause.

Inside the Sports Cafe, the smell of malt from the bar was fighting a losing battle with the fatty bacon and sausage sputtering on the back grill. The area around the billiard table was smoky dark and stale from last night's cigarettes. An aproned man with the veined nose of someone long in his profession stood behind the slick, polyurethaned bar squinting at the morning paper, looking up through bloodshot eyes as the door squealed open and shut.

"Up early, ain't you, Rooster?"

"Hey, Carl — got the weekend line there?" Easing his computer down to the bar, Jack opened it, flicking the switch on.

"Not so loud, you tryin' to get me busted?"

"Someone here I don't see?" Jack asked, giraffeing his neck elaborately in all directions.

"You wanna engage in extracurricular activities you gotta use discretion."

"Read 'em and weep." Jack unfolded the computer screen, swiveling it so both could see, and booted up Football.

In a moment up on the screen appeared:

```
Bears (-3) Packers
Raiders (+3) 49ers
Vikings (+10) Redskins
Eagles (-1) Cardinals
Giants (-6) Steelers
```

Pick, Jack typed.
Raiders-Bears-Redskins-Cardinals-Steelers
came the response.

"Interesting." Carl checked the choices on the computer screen against those in the newspaper. "You've gone one hundred percent *contra* the line."

"It's a lock."

"Your machine smarter all of a sudden?"

"Smart as the information it gets. I factored in match-ups, deducted for gimpy players, added for veterans off the bench who can pick a team up—"

"Vegas does that too."

"—and wherever the computer came in with a standoff I programmed it to consider pride, poise, and desire."

"Only suckers talk intangibles."

"Three hundred says the computer's got it right."

"You got three hundred, pay your tab."

Managing with some difficulty to subdue the smart-alecky side of his nature, Jack resisted popping each twenty as he counted out five stacks of one hundred each before sliding them across the bar. "Two for the tab, three for the bet."

The bills disappeared under Carl's newspaper as the door behind Jack opened. A brown-mustached young man about Jack's age, in a C & R Clothiers three-piece suit, sauntered in. "Hey, Carl, I see you added another neon to your collection. Business must be booming."

"This place look crowded to you, Harry?"

Harry shot his cuffs and peered happily at the computer screen. "You know the kind of business I mean. Hey, Rooster—these picks anything to crow about?"

"My mother named me Jack—I think in honor of her memory you oughta use it, counselor." Jack tucked five twenties into Harry's vest pocket. "What I owe you."

"Put me down for a bill, Carl."

"In a minute, Harry." Carl made room for the tray of bacon, eggs, and coffee deposited on the bar by a waitress with purple nails and mascara to match. Powder obscured any hint of her original complexion. Her hair had been bleached to the consistency of straw. Stitched over the pocket of her faded purple knit shirt was her name, CLAIRE, stretched so far by unconstrained breasts underneath it was barely readable.

Claire smiled at Jack. He hastily averted his eyes, hating that his face reddened.

"Bring me the same, okay, Claire?" Harry said. "And try to make that illegal you got cooking back there understand not everyone likes burnt bacon."

"Long as you're up." Jack cleared his throat. "You mind bringing me a buckwheat pancake to go? And something for Roger? Please."

[8]

"Not good for your digestion you eat on the run."

"Better than not eating at all." Jack concentrated on folding his computer back into its carrying shape.

Claire hesitated, then inserting herself between Harry and Jack, lowered her voice. "I hear you got no roof over your head. That you got evicted for not paying your rent."

"You heard wrong," Jack lied, politely. "Now that I'm building my own house I want to live close to make sure it's built right."

Claire looked at Harry and Carl in turn, raising eyebrows that had been tweezered into lines as thin as parentheses, and returned to the grill.

"You actually started building?" Harry asked.

"Soon as the construction loan comes through."

"Our last bone's in the soup," Claire called from the grill, "and the hamburger patties are still froze. Think Roger'd eat a pancake?"

"That'll do fine, thanks," Jack called back.

"That dog's diet would stagger a goat," Harry said, as Roger rose, tail wagging, to greet Claire returning with a platter of pancakes. She slid the platter under his questing nose.

"He only hangs in because of the treats," Jack said. "It's what keeps him loyal and true."

"Were you born cynical, or was that your major in college?" Claire asked.

"Some woman dumped on him at an early age," Harry said.

"It *vas* mine kindergarten teacher, doctor," Jack said, wondering if once after too many beers he'd let slip something about his mother. He filched a strip of bacon from the plate Carl had pushed aside, putting what remained of the eggs and potatoes on the floor for the panting Roger.

"Men who complain about women just haven't met the right one," Claire said.

"I don't recall complaining."

"Meaning you've met the right one?"

"Meaning I'm not looking."

A bell dinged from the grill. Claire, making a face, left, returning a moment later with a bag and two large plastic containers.

"I appreciate this." Jack took the bag. "But I don't drink coffee."

"I know that," Claire snapped. "Orange juice's in one, milk in the other. Keep your strength up to fight off those chicks you claim you don't want."

"Kind of you," Jack murmured, reddening again as he accepted the containers. He slipped a twenty from his pocket and handed it to her.

[9]

"You strike it rich?"

"You could say that."

"Even if I believed you, my treat."

"Bet it with Carl on my computer picks," Jack said, refusing to take the twenty back. He snapped his fingers for Roger, who gave one last lick of each plate and followed him to the door.

"I hope your computer knows what it's doing," Harry called. "That's my ex-wife's alimony I bet."

"Safe as money in the bank," Jack replied.

THREE

Each of the windowpanes, black as corporate hearts, on the fifty-six floors of the MetroBank headquarters tower facing east from Bunker Hill mirrored the morning sun. Panes of adjoining towers caught and remultiplied those suns, shining pitilessly in all directions, blinding cursing drivers on the streets below—except for Jack, who'd tinted every window of his vehicle, including the windshield. It was illegal, but necessary for survival in this overdeveloped, drought-stricken, nerve-jangling city.

Braking opposite the driveway to MetroBank's parking lot, Jack rolled down his window. Ignoring the honking, he hung halfway out, importuning the short-tempered drivers approaching from the other direction with a prayerful, zenlike palming of his hands. A red-lacquered CRX driven by a tousle-haired, dark-glassed brunette sucking up an orange juice from a plastic container stopped and waved him across, middle-finger upraised and circling to encompass all those leaning on their horns.

Blowing her a kiss, Jack inched his panel truck through two lanes of traffic into the brick-walled parking lot.

The black-mustached security guard wearing a badge marked LUIS grinned as Jack stopped. "Wha' hoppen to your car?"

Opening the door, Jack pushed the suddenly affectionate Roger out. "Repossessed. But I got a great deal on the truck."

"I chure hope so." Luis hooked a leash onto Roger's collar, running his hand down the dog's ridge of fur.

"Appreciate your concern, Luis." Jack handed over two twenties. "This square our account?"

"More'n enough. Keep Roger'n me in burritos for a month."

"Easy with the beans, he's getting windy." Jack gave Roger a head scratch and, because it was closer, drove against the wrong way arrows to the slot marked JACK B. NOBLE, DATA PROCESSING MAN-

AGER, waving an apology to the BMW, probably carrying a loan officer, that braked to avoid him.

Carrying his computer as casually as if it contained only catch-up bookkeeping instead of his gateway to freedom, Jack headed for the rear entrance, then paused by the slot reserved for his boss. It was empty, blocked by a MetroBank maintenance cart. A heavyset black man in faded coveralls was painting out Warwick's name.

"You think Warwick will appreciate having his parking slot changed without his permission, Mr. Shafer?"

"He in no position to appreciate anything now."

"They wouldn't fire Warwick!"

"Didn't have to. Found him in his garage behind the wheel of his Chrysler with the motor runnin' and a hose from his exhaust pipe pumpin' fumes inside."

Jack felt his blood run cold. Warwick dead? It wasn't possible. There'd been rumors he was under pressure to resign, something about making room for a major shareholder's relative, but the feisty Warwick would have fought that to the end.

"What'd the police say?"

"What police got to do with it? Man's got a right to off himself."

Warwick a suicide? It didn't track. But, Jack reminded himself, all we really ever know about anyone is what they choose to tell us.

Saying a little prayer for Warwick's soul, Jack moved on through a day that had suddenly become somber. He would miss Warwick, who'd recognized that those who programmed computers were cut from a different cloth, and had given him free rein. No telling what kind of controls a new man would install.

Still, one boss was much like another, Jack reassured himself, shrugging off his unease. Few top management people knew enough about computers to interfere.

Inside the building, Jack quickened his step to keep from being trampled. Employees shouldering in from other entrances crammed the marbled corridors. The squeak of sneakers and the tattoo of spike heels ricocheted off the waxed floors.

"Cock-a-doodle-do!"

Though his face grew hot, Jack didn't turn. Holding his computer overhead he managed to squeeze into an express elevator as the doors whispered shut. The sudden, overpowering mix of perfumes, powders, fragrant soaps, and colognes made him momentarily giddy. Then he became extraordinarily conscious of a young woman's buttocks pushing back and cushioning his groin.

"Sorry," Jack murmured, to no one in particular. But he was

unable to move as the elevator, and, as seemed inevitable, his sexual organ, rose.

"Watch it, ladies, Rooster's aboard," said a man whom he couldn't see in a voice he couldn't place. Several men chuckled. A woman snickered.

"Any groping going on, don't blame me," Jack said before he could stop himself, then ducked in embarrassment as the retort was acknowledged by laughter.

At the twenty-fifth floor the elevator eased to a stop. Most of the passengers, including the young woman in front of Jack, got off. As he feared, she glanced back over her shoulder. Reluctantly he met her eye just as the doors slid shut, and she surprised him with a smile.

At the fifty-third floor, face still flaming, Jack got off behind several hip-gyrating young women who looked at him sideways from eyes as startlingly rimmed as those of parakeets.

"Morning." It would have seemed impolite not to acknowledge them.

Freshly lipsticked mouths widened into smiles. "Morning, Mr. Noble," they chorused, chirping birds of a feather.

"You know better than that—Jack does me fine."

"Don't you prefer Rooster?" asked one, bolder than the others, nipples breaking the silk as she tucked an already tight shirt deeper into the band of her thigh-hugging skirt.

"It's not appropriate." Were they actually *clucking* under their breaths? The teasing was a sexual challenge, he knew, a come-on that dared him to react. But it wasn't something he was about to do. He didn't even know what it was about him provoked such reactions.

A wispy girl whose watery eyes seemed enormous behind thick glasses hurried to walk beside him. "Mr. Noble, I was wondering could I get an advance on my check."

"No can do—against bank policy."

"But it's an emergency!"

"Can't you borrow from a friend?"

"None of my friends can come up with a hundred and fifty dollars!" She seemed about to break into tears.

Distressed, Jack reached into his pocket and pulled out his remaining bills. Three hundred and sixty dollars. How could money diminish so fast?

"Can't you put off whoever's dunning you a few more days?"

"Oh I don't owe anyone—I'm entering a beauty pageant in Huntington Beach, and the deadline's today!"

[13]

Jack stared. "Why would you want to let a bunch of lewd strangers give you the once over?"

"Men can look all they want as long as they don't leer or make stupid comments. It's wonderful to be genuinely admired."

"You've done this before?"

"I've never got up the nerve before."

She held out her hand. Her nails had been chewed to the quick. Acknowledging it was her decision to make, not his to judge, Jack handed over a hundred and sixty.

"Use the extra ten for diet colas. On me."

"This is really, really wonderful of you. Thanks a bunch—I'll get it back to you payday, I swear!"

At a cordoned-off, recessed area, the young woman joined other women and men slipping into body-contoured chairs before computer screens and keyboards. The wall digital clock read 8:56. Jack stepped up on the raised platform overlooking the computer pool and slid his computer out of sight underneath his desk.

Sitting with a sigh, Jack felt immediately comforted. In the front row facing him was his good and undemanding friend, Nancy, perfectly coiffed, cinnamon-haired, with a complexion fresh as if washed in milk, wearing a starched shirt softened by a flowing scarf. Smiling to show teeth that did not seem to need the retainer, Nancy stood. Her tailored slacks, however severely cut, couldn't hide the shapely contours beneath.

"You don't look any the worse for wear. Where'd you sleep?"

"Got a panel truck with a fold-down bed."

"Using what for money?"

"Guy's letting me pay it off."

"Lucky. But it can't be as comfortable as my couch."

"There's no way I could sleep knowing that you were snugged in with your teddies just a few feet away."

"There's an answer for that."

"It's not the right one, Nancy. Not now. Not yet. Heard about Warwick?"

"What about Warwick?"

"He's no longer with us." Why was he reluctant to tell her what had happened? "Hold the fort a minute?" Forcing a smile, Jack hiked to the exit door. Slipping through, he took the stairs three at a time until he reached the top floor.

Making sure his coat was buttoned and his tie in place, he strode jauntily along the executive corridor to what had been Warwick's corner office. The door stood open. A man in spattered coveralls held a wooden brace under a brush with which he was meticulously lettering the frosted glass with gold leaf. SAMUEL J HAR was as far as he'd gotten.

The ceiling suddenly trembled. There was a muted, but thunderous clatter. Windows rattled. The employees on the floor worried only for an instant; it wasn't an earthquake, the company helicopter had landed.

While the helicopter's rotors wound down, the door to the roof opened. Four middle-aged men Jack did not recognize, all somewhat stooped and wearing dark suits, strode down, peering about through what seemed identical wire-rimmed glasses. They were each carrying black plastic attaché cases that looked as if they'd been purchased at the same discount price club.

Auditors? Jack wondered, and his heart sank. Of course there'd be auditors. When a man as high in the hierarchy as Warwick died under mysterious circumstances, management would immediately start looking for a discrepancy in funds.

The fourth man hung back, holding the door. Jack recognized at a glance that the burly, middle-aged man who strode down a moment later was someone used to power. The bold burgundy stripes of the shirt under a very expensive brown cashmere suit were something only a top-level executive would dare wear. Jack barely had time to wonder why the man was carrying his own bags — an expensive attaché case in one large-fisted hand, a bulging briefcase in the other — when he was unexpectedly distracted by what was tucked under the man's arm.

It shouldn't be. But it was. A high-powered, laptop computer.

Jack became suddenly anxious. He'd counted on his new boss being computer illiterate. Somehow Jack managed a nod and forced a smile as the five men strode past.

The painter still hadn't finished.

"No one told you I want the period in?" The voice was smooth and strong as raw silk.

The painter hardly looked up. "It's corporate style to leave them off. . . ."

"Put the period in."

"That got the painter's attention. "Yessir."

And then the new boss — Samuel J period Harris — ushered the others into his office and pulled the door shut without so much as a glance at Jack. But Jack could swear the man had somehow — maybe when they'd passed in the corridor — managed to give him a complete, combed head to polished toe, once-over.

It wasn't possible. But Jack felt as if he'd been x-rayed and identified as someone Harris already knew to be untrustworthy.

FOUR

The clock numerals turned up 9:00 A.M. just as Jack, slightly out of breath, anxiety level increased tenfold, returned to his platform.

He clapped his hands. "Okay, my little chicks—let's get with it. The only chatter I want to hear is from your keyboards."

Jack was in no mood to acknowledge the soft *clucking* that rose from the desks below. However much he wanted to attribute a misguided conscience to that feeling of incipient disaster, Jack couldn't avoid the realization that his work situation, which he had counted on to remain stable, had changed. And not for the better.

Nothing he could do about it now. Worry had never solved a problem yet. All he could do was try to handle whatever developed when—or more optimistically *if*—it came.

Checking to make sure his "chicks" were all concentrating on work, Jack switched on his computer terminal and entered 1-900-Sports Book. Somewhat calmed by this routine procedure, he punched the Enter key and settled back in his executive chair to wait for the communications software to connect him.

Before he could relax, however, his calm was demolished by what appeared on-screen next:

SPORTS BOOK UP-TO-THE-MINUTE WIRE

First String AFC Injury Reports
Los Angeles RAIDERS . . . Marcus Allen, hb,
hamstring, J. Schroeder, qb, knee, Howie
Long, DT, ankle . . .

As he tried to absorb this information—was it too late to change his bet?—his intercom buzzed. Jack fumbled for the intercom button. "Hen house, Noble here."

"This is Mrs. Nelson." Warwick's secretary, usually serene, was speaking quickly, under pressure. "Mr. Harris wants all department heads in his office. Immediately."

"Did Warwick seem depressed to you?"

"I wouldn't dawdle if I were you." Mrs. Nelson rang off.

Jack's feeling that this was not turning into one of his better days grew into a certainty. Telling himself that he was overreacting—every department head had been summoned, after all, and maybe Carl hadn't placed the bets yet—Jack stood and leaned over his desk. "Ms. Buford? Ms. Buford! Take over my desk?"

Nancy looked up. "My, you *are* antsy this morning."

Nancy took her sweet time putting her desk in order. He couldn't complain; tidying up the work station whenever a worker left was a rule he had instituted himself.

When Nancy finally stepped up on the platform, he made an elaborate show of sliding his chair under her shapely seat. She met his embarrassed glance, smiled—then saw what was on his screen. "Isn't that a little risky on company time?"

"Do me a favor—call Carl at the Sports Cafe and tell him I'd like to put my bet on hold. Oh, and tell him Harry wants to do the same. And when this report finishes downloading, I'd appreciate your transferring it to my personal computer."

"What if someone notices I'm working on private stuff?"

"Anyone who'd care's going to be tied up in a meeting." Managing a careless smile, Jack pantomimed a fighter's victory handshake, then once again headed for the staircase.

By the time he arrived at the top-floor corridor, other department managers, dressed in somber suits, were emerging from elevators, looking tense.

Momentarily relieved that he wasn't the only one with problems, Jack found himself double-timing a few steps to pick up momentum, then sliding the remaining length of the superbly waxed corridor to reach the office door first.

Opening the door with a flourish, Jack held it for the other managers. The two females frowned, as if he'd challenged their capability.

"Sorry, sorry. I was brought up wrong, I know. The result of a Catholic education. The nuns were terribly old-fashioned when it came to manners." Winking at the men, Jack stepped inside ahead of them.

The office had been rearranged. The secretary's desk had been moved forward. It was no longer possible to walk directly into the large rear office without first confronting her.

Mrs. Nelson, senior secretary in years as well as experience, was looking damp and distressed as she held the inner door open. To Jack's knowledge, that door had never been closed. And as Jack, failing to persuade Mrs. Nelson to enter first, followed the others inside, he heard the door shut with a snap behind him. Obviously, Mrs. Nelson hadn't been invited to join the gathering.

The conference table was surprisingly bare, without the ruled tablets and sharpened pencils Warwick had always made sure Mrs. Nelson provided. Wasn't anyone going to take notes? Didn't the new boss know that at MetroBank off-the-record meetings weren't permitted?

So far, Harris hadn't even acknowledged their entry. He was engrossed in unpacking his briefcase — his computer, Jack noted, nowhere in sight. Stacking file folders neatly to one side, unfolding a "week-at-a-glance" embossed leather desk diary, placing a sleek, gold-nibbed pen ready to hand, Harris finally pulled out a gold-framed photograph before snapping the case shut. As if — contrary to what they'd been told — time was no object, he carefully wiped the photograph's protective glass with his breast-pocket handkerchief, then positioned it just so on his desk.

From where Jack was sitting, he could see that the woman — no doubt Harris's wife — was a beauty.

"I'm Samuel J period Harris," Harris said, without so much as a smile, approaching the table. "Your new executive vice president. I've looked at your personnel records, but I've been so busy examining auditing reports I haven't matched face to name. If you wouldn't mind identifying yourselves, starting with you?"

"Betty Haskell, commercial loans." As disconcerted as if Harris's pointing finger and cocked thumb were a real gun, she tried, but couldn't manage, a smile.

"Arthur Wonder, treasury bills."

"Hal Briggs, corporate securities."

"Thelma Musante, money markets."

"Joe Brankowski, new accounts."

"Jack Noble, data processing. Can you tell us what happened to Mr. Warwick?"

"Haven't you heard? Mr. Warwick, for reasons best known to himself, has committed suicide." Though there was no humor in Harris's seemingly pupilless steel blue eyes, Jack could swear that he was amused.

"No farewell note or last-minute phone calls?"

Harris's hesitation was barely discernible. "None that we know of. Look, I'm not a man who believes in pussyfooting around. Let's put all our cards on the table. We'll probably find his reason somewhere in the audit. There's been a leak in funds. A large leak. A multimillion-dollar leak. Money unaccounted for. Management thinks there's a glitch in the system. I don't. I think someone has been siphoning MetroBank funds. Possibly Warwick. Who couldn't have managed it without the help of someone very clever. I tell you straight, if there's a culprit here to be found, I'll find him!"

"Him?" Jack wondered, as casually as he could with heart pounding so hard it seemed it might break out of his chest. A multimillion-dollar leak? That left him out. Except—what if an extraordinarily thorough examination of the records accidentally turned up that temporary small loan he'd arranged for himself?

"Or her, fair enough." Harris shrugged. Again, though there was no surface evidence to show it, Jack could *feel* Harris's amusement. "The reason I'm taking you all into my confidence is so you'll know how to handle the rumors bound to be circulating when the auditors start work. Which will be the moment this meeting is over. Fact is, at the moment, we have no proof Warwick did anything. The party line is we're preparing for a possible merger. Clear?"

During this last, the intercom on Harris's desk had buzzed. And buzzed again. Making a face, Harris returned to his desk and picked the phone up, jabbing the intercom button. "I told you no calls, Mrs. Nelson!" Harris waited, listening. "Oh. She on the line now? Well, wait five minutes, then get her back."

Returning, Harris remained standing. "Where were we?"

"Putting our cards on the table." No one else seemed willing to speak.

"Right. Comments?"

"Mr. Warwick was as honest as they come," Jack offered when again no one replied.

"If that's so, the audit will confirm it," Harris said, lips twitching. "And show us who's stealing. In any case, Warwick is gone, and I'm stepping into his slot."

"When's the funeral?" Jack asked.

"Services are private," Harris said. "I'm sending flowers with everyone's name on it, plus the company's making a donation in Warwick's name to the Institute for Clinical Depression."

Harris strode to the door and held it open. "I expect everyone's cooperation in finding the leak. Those who can't, or won't, consider yourself expendable."

As each of the shaken managers walked past, Harris identified them aloud: "Ms. Haskell. Mr. Wonder. Mr. Briggs. Ms. Musante.

Mr. Brankowski. Oh, Noble—hang on here a few minutes longer, will you?"

Jack, though his stomach turned, managed a smile and returned to his seat.

"Smoke if you want," Harris said, shutting the door.

"It's a vice I can do without."

"There are others you cannot?"

"None I can't handle."

Harris sat across from Jack. He pulled out a flat silver case engraved with his initials and selected a flat brown cigarette. "You don't mind if I do? Every time I try to quit something aggravates me, and it's either smoke or take it out on my loved ones. You have any loved ones, Noble?"

"You mean relatives?"

"I know you're a bachelor now. But sometimes employees who are looking to better themselves don't want to show instability by listing prior marriages—or any, say, involvements, where they may be living with someone. . . ."

"I live alone. Unless you count my dog."

"You're an amusing fellow."

"Sorry. It slips out before I can stop myself. . . ."

Jack stopped as the intercom buzzed. Harris went to his desk. "Yes?" he said, picking the phone up. "Good. Put her on." Harris rearranged the photo facing him. "Darling?—Yes, I know, I found out when I tried to open it—I thought I'd forgotten the combination before it dawned on me that it wasn't my case . . . I'm sorry. Well I didn't do it on purpose! I was in such a hurry to get to work I grabbed it without even looking. . . . Now? Well I can't now. I know it's inconvenient. . . . No, not at lunchtime either, I'm going to be working right through lunch. . . . Well if it's so important for you to have it now I'll send someone over with it. Of course someone trustworthy. Right. Delivered to you personally. I'll make absolutely sure it's placed right in your own sweet hand. Love you. . . ?"

Harris's voice trailed off. Jack felt a surge of sympathy. The man's wife had obviously hung up before he'd gotten so much as a thank you or good-bye and God bless. Harris turned his back and walked to the windows. What was the man doing? Was he actually touching his eyes with his handkerchief? Impossible. The man couldn't be weeping.

"I beg your pardon," Harris said, replacing his breast-pocket handkerchief as he turned back, eyes moist. "I've been under a bit of a strain—and now my wife's upset because I took her personal effects bag by mistake when I left her at the airport to come directly here. Women. They can pick the worst times to be irrational, can't they?"

"That's been my experience." Jack was thinking of his mother.

Harris had brought a folder from his desk. He leafed through pages until he found what he wanted.

"You've got quite a bit of sick leave coming?"

"I like to let it accumulate – in case there's an emergency."

"I'd appreciate it if you would take your leave now."

Jack stared. He hadn't thought it possible for there to be any more surprises.

"Your department's key to the audit. I think the auditors would appreciate not having to worry about anyone looking over their shoulders."

Jack remembered to breathe. "I think I ought to at least be available. In case there are any questions. And I could set up a program that would evaluate and hold the data so that the backlog wouldn't be overwhelming – "

"Already taken care of. Saw to that before I left Phoenix."

"What if I really get sick and I'm stuck without any time left – "

"Look, if it would make you feel easier about it, we'll make it a paid leave – a kind of bonus vacation time."

It was pointless to argue – and could, instead, raise questions that might not otherwise get asked. "Starting when?"

"Starting now."

Jack reluctantly nodded.

"Good man." Harris stood. "Appreciate your cooperation."

"Sure. Though it would have been fun to help prove that Warwick didn't get all that money."

Harris smiled, but said nothing. Jack shrugged, furious with himself for having gratuitously defended Warwick, thus calling attention to other possibilities, then rose and started for the door.

"Oh, by the way," Harris said. "You live north of the city, don't you? I thought – if you have nothing better to do – you might drop my wife's personal effects off at our new condo."

"Happy to be of service," Jack lied.

FIVE

The rectangular case still had a PNX airport tag tied to the handle. It was a handsome piece, of hand-tooled black leather, well cared for except for the smudges on the brass combination lock.

Now, with Roger dreaming in the backseat, as Jack drove north up Vermont past Sunset, through a crowded shopping district of window-cluttered foreign stores toward the gracefully aging/slowly decaying—he couldn't tell which—Los Feliz–Griffith Park district, his glance returned to the case again and again.

He couldn't imagine what personal effects would be important enough for Harris's wife to raise such a fuss about. Stopped by a red signal, he checked out the SPECIAL OF THE DAY: LASAGNA of the shabby Italian restaurant on the corner, saw that the marquee of the PussyCat Theater proudly announced the return of the award-winning *Deep Throat*, then casually thumbed the case's latch.

Locked tight.

Stop that, he told himself as he felt his fingers caressing the raised buttons of the combination lock. He floored the accelerator as the light turned green, hoping to leave temptation behind. Whatever was in the case was none of his business.

Michael's American Restaurant, the landmark he'd been told to look for, was just ahead. Turning right, Jack drove to the end of the tree-shaded block, where blue and white flags were snapping in the late-morning breeze. A banner indicated that all but two units had been sold.

A cobblestone driveway curved up an incline to the steel and glass tower. Raised gold letters on a marble facade identified the building as the Regent Tower. Roger, awakening from his nap, growled deep in his throat, then started barking.

A doorman who seemed uncomfortable in a uniform more appropriate for a third-world general was holding the copper-braced glass door for an elegantly gowned woman carrying a tiny, bug-eyed dog that seemed mostly fur.

"Shut up, Roger!"

Jack heard a tire squeal. A tan Lincoln Town Car wheeled around him, stopping at the canopied entrance. A dark-skinned parking attendant in a drabber version of the uniform slid out, holding the door for the woman. Jack drove past, parking the truck next to a Mercedes sedan.

"Stay inside, dammit. Restrain yourself." Jack got out with the case, slamming the door against Roger. As the Lincoln started past, Roger flung himself against the tinted glass in amorous despair.

"Love at first sight," Jack observed to the woman, who on closer look seemed older. She evaluated him too, then, with a wistful smile, drove on.

"You driving that truck?" the doorman asked. "Passenger cars only here."

"I'll only be a minute. Delivery for Mrs. Harris in PH three."

"I'll see she gets it."

"Sorry. My boss told me it has to be delivered personally. If she told him otherwise he'd have my ass."

The doorman considered this, then going to an intercom, pressed the button several times for PH 3.

"She's not answering."

"Keep trying. She's expecting me."

"Well if she's there who knows what she's doing—in the can, on the phone, and I ain't got all day." The doorman hung up. "You don't wanna trust me with the case, fine. But get that truck outta here."

A gray Cadillac came wheeling up the drive from the garage. The doorman rushed to hold the passenger door for a well-dressed older couple.

Unsure what to do, Jack returned to his truck. Placing the case under his legs, he drove back to the street. Should he find a parking spot and wait? But who knew how long it would be before she'd be ready to receive visitors? Or she may have slipped out, unobserved, and God knew when she'd return. The easy thing would be to leave the case with the doorman—except his new boss's instructions had been absolutely explicit.

Jack transferred his growing irritation from his own uncertainty to her seeming thoughtlessness—if she was going to be unavailable, why hadn't she left a message with the doorman?

Swearing softly to himself, Jack headed back the way he had come, seeing no option but to return the case to the office.

The drive back took much longer than he expected. The streets were so crowded with late-morning shoppers that by the time he turned into the bank's parking lot, it was noon. A lot of the executive slots were empty. But Warwick's stall now held a black Cadillac Coupe de Ville, so new its license plates were paper. And his own slot was filled with a gray Mercedes limousine marked with an auditing firm's logo:

KLEIN, HOWARD, PESCATELLI, MCCLAIN 9 PARTNERS, CERTIFIED PUBLIC ACCOUNTANTS, NEW YORK, WASHINGTON D.C., CHICAGO, KANSAS CITY, RENO, PHOENIX, LOS ANGELES. It bore Nevada plates.

Nervy, Jack thought, pulling his van into a limited-parking service slot, behind a catering truck from the Pacific Dining Car, an expensive downtown steakhouse. Making sure Roger had water and kibbles, Jack picked up the case and walked to the Lincoln, putting his face against its tinted window.

The interior was luxurious, with hand-tooled leather, a divider window, and a burled-walnut bar in the back under a TV screen. A cellular telephone and fax machine were uncovered, ready for use.

This audit was apparently important enough to bring out the head of the accounting firm, Jack mused. Without thinking, he ran his fingers over the decal. The glue underneath was lumpy, as if carelessly—or recently—applied. The car must have been rushed into service as speedily as Harris had initiated the audit.

Shrugging away his unease, Jack walked into the building. Few people were in the corridors. He took an express elevator to the top floor, bracing himself against his boss's displeasure.

The executive floor was deserted. Good, Jack thought, relieved. He'd be able to leave the case with a note explaining he'd been unable to deliver it, thereby avoiding another probing scrutiny from his boss's knowing eye.

A young man in starched white coveralls marked with the steak-house insignia suddenly emerged from Harris's office, leaving the door slightly ajar. The auditors were seated at the conference table. Presumably, Harris and whoever owned the limousine were seated with them, digging into the meals that had been delivered.

Jack pretended to busy himself at a desk as the young man passed him on his way to the elevators. But the moment the elevator doors shut behind him Jack quickly removed his shoes, slipping one into each pocket. Hugging the wall, he took the long way around, approaching the office from its blind side.

When he reached the closet pillar, Jack stood behind it, listening. He could hear voices, but not what was being said.

Leaving his hiding place, Jack inched closer. Finally, ear so close to the doorjamb he worried about casting a shadow, the words became plain.

. "We don't have much time. A week, maybe ten days, max!" An unfamiliar voice, harsh.

"We're moving as fast as we can." Harris, deferential. Jack became confused. Why was Harris kowtowing? Didn't the auditors work for him? "Some things can't be rushed. Human behavior can be predicted only up to a point. But if I'm any judge, I'd say the lure is going to prove irresistible to him."

The man must fancy himself some kind of armchair psychologist.

"It's too elaborate." Another voice, effeminate, but wasp-mean. "I don't like it. My motto is keep things simple. Your fish doesn't take the bait, we're back to square one."

"He surfaces, he's hooked, take my word for it." Confident to the point of arrogance, Harris was still silkily soft-spoken and extraordinarily polite.

"It's the time element worries me." Mr. Harsh again. "We gotta button it down before the Feds come in."

Feds? Jack worried, palms beginning to sweat.

"Tell the senator to keep stalling them."

"He's done all he can."

"It'll work out fine. Trust me."

"Hate to tell you how many funerals I've gone to guys said that to me."

Silence, except for the sound of eating. Chilled, Jack eased back. He turned and skated his stockinged feet away along the polished floor as fast as he could, pulse pounding. He felt absolutely certain it was vital that no one know he'd returned.

The elevator took forever to arrive. When the indicator light showed it approaching the floor, Jack stooped behind a desk.

Two department managers got off, engrossed in conversation. As soon as they passed, Jack slipped inside the elevator and leaned on the button for ground floor. After an interminable wait the doors slid shut and he was at last dropping toward safety.

In the sanctuary of his panel truck Jack took in a shuddering breath, then realized with a shock that he still held the case.

Swearing so loud a surprised Roger barked in response, Jack hastily started the motor and sped out of the lot. He wanted to avoid the possibility that any of his co-workers, returning from lunch, might see him. They could let it slip to Harris he'd been lurking about.

With all that talk about Feds etcetera it was best if his boss considered him an insignificant nuisance, out of sight, out of mind.

He'd deliver the damned case and make himself scarce. Then for all he cared they could trawl the data system forever. They'd never catch him, he'd been too careful.

At the first gas station he came to, Jack pulled the truck up next to a phone booth. Why wasn't he surprised his boss had an unlisted home number? But the information operator, patient as a saint, provided him with one for the Regent Tower.

"Mrs. Harris?" the desk clerk wondered.

"The Harrises just moved into Penthouse Three!"

"Oh, right. Don't have a cow."

At first ring, the phone was picked up. "Yes?" Her voice was throaty, and anxious.

"Mrs. Harris? Your husband asked me to deli — "

"I expected you an hour ago!"

"I was there, the doorman called you, you didn't answer — "

"I must've been in the shower. Dammit! Well now you're here, bring my case up."

"I'm about a half hour away. I did a few chores, and then my truck broke down. . . ."

A lengthening pause. Then, "We're wasting time talking — get here as fast as you can."

"Right."

She'd hung up. A puzzled Jack returned to the truck. She was terribly anxious; his boss had been right about that. How valuable could "personal effects" be?

Jack lifted the case. It wasn't all that heavy. Maybe it contained items of jewelry, a few medications, possibly makeup she was especially fond of. Dropping the case on the seat beside him, Jack sped off once more, uncomfortable that he'd been forced to lie and wondering, in spite of himself, if that troubling conversation he'd overheard at work was anything he should be concerned about.

When he got to Los Feliz, running along the spacious boulevard at the well-mowed edge of Griffith Park, near the turnoff for the Harris condo, Jack, increasingly uneasy, pulled the truck to the curb.

Allowing the motor to run, he placed the case in his lap and examined the lock. All the raised button numbers seemed clean, at least to the naked eye. He caressed each number, trying to *feel* which of them, if any, seemed less stiff than the others.

He couldn't be sure. Numbers 5, 12, and 15 seemed somewhat looser, easier to push. Even assuming he had identified three correctly, most combinations used five numbers. He would need to identify at least two more.

Dangling from his key chain was a Swiss Original Army knife.

Turning the motor off, Jack slid his knife off the chain. Nestled among the blades was a small but powerful magnifying glass. Congratulating himself for having now found a use for the knife's every tool, Jack held the glass over each number in turn.

Numbers 5, 12, and 15 were smudged, however faintly. Under magnification numbers 22 and, finally, 36 revealed portions of lines partially filled with a barely discernible grease, oily residue from repeated fingerings.

Assuming, Jack thought, that the number most heavily smudged was first in the sequence, and the least smudged last, that would make 5 first, 12 and 15 tied for second, 22 fourth and 36 clearly last. Jack grinned, delighted with himself. He was making progress.

The next step was obvious. By trying the middle numbers, whose order he wasn't certain of, in varying sequences with those that seemed clear, he was bound eventually to hit upon a combination that would open the lock.

The problem was, Jack reminded himself, there were hundreds of conceivable combinations. It would take hours before he hit upon the right one. With Mrs. Harris already beside herself with worry, he couldn't delay much longer.

Once again, however, Jack found himself caressing the combination lock's buttons. Having got this far, he should at least try a few sequences. Where was the harm?

Eagerly, Jack punched in 5, then the numbers 12, 22 and 36. The latch remained tight. He tried 15 after 5, followed by 22, 12, 36. The latch didn't budge. With diminishing enthusiasm, he tried 22 after 5, followed by 15, 12, 36. The latch seemed as impregnable as the vault in MetroBank's basement.

Give it up and get a move on, the disappointed Jack told himself. His mind was nearing overload. It was becoming increasingly difficult to retain the sequences he'd already used.

What if, he suddenly asked himself, the owner of the case might have a habit of wiping her hands dry before opening the lock? Then 36 might be cleanest because it was first, followed by 22, 15, and 12, with 5 containing most buildup, because by the time that last number was reached the fingertip skin would be extruding oil again. On that remote possibility, Jack reversed the sequences.

More out of frustration than anything else—he'd never yet seen a lock combination that went from small numbers to large—he ran the numbers sequentially: 5, 12, 15, 22, 36. The chances of this working were so infinitesimal he was almost reluctant to test it.

He wasn't fast enough getting his hand out of the way. The latch, springing free, stung his thumb.

Jack shouted triumphantly. When a long shot did pay off, the feeling was near indescribable. No matter how hard anyone worked, or how carefully they planned, luck added a wonderful *spritz* to an otherwise flat life.

Slowly, his grin faded. The lock was open. Nothing to prevent him looking inside—except that he felt the presence of Sister Theresa, ruler in hand.

But the long-nosed Sister Theresa was powerless to get at him now, wasn't she? And this was hardly Pandora's box.

Jack lifted the lid.

He hadn't known what to expect. But he had difficulty absorbing what he was looking at. The case was packed tight, corner to corner, bottom to lid. Stacked in neat rows were crisp new twenty-dollar bills. If each stack contained twenties top to bottom . . . there had to be twenty-five thousand dollars here!

Was this an elaborate trick designed by his boss to see if he were dishonest enough to filch any money? It couldn't be, he told himself. They couldn't possibly know he'd be curious and clever enough to open the case. Could they?

Jack dropped the lid. Hastily, he thumbed the latch into its slot. Hesitating only a moment, he tested to make sure it was locked. Then jamming the key back into the ignition, Jack started the motor and pulled away from the curb—flinching as a honking pickup truck swerved to avoid him. Still in a daze, he was only remotely aware that the other driver yelled "shithead."

Jack tried to calm himself. Harris's wife was frantic to get her case back. Wasn't she? Lucky for her, Jack couldn't help thinking, he'd been the one chosen to make the delivery. It'd be easy to slip a bill out of any number of stacks, with no one any the wiser. He'd hate to think how much she could have lost if the case had been opened by someone dishonest.

Jack tried to imagine the thin-lipped Sister Theresa smiling. She'd be proud of him. And he'd be eternally grateful if it turned out she'd helped him avoid a trap.

Finding a parking place down the block, Jack left a window partially open to provide ventilation for Roger, then taking the case, walked back on the opposite side of the street until he spotted the Regent Tower's garage entrance.

The parking attendant and the doorman were engrossed in watching a tow-truck driver hook a chain to the axle of the Mercedes. Jack hastened down the ramp into the dimly lit garage. If there

[28]

was something fishy about the money, he didn't want anyone witnessing him delivering it.

He spotted the service elevator near the back. Walking close to the carelessly stuccoed wall, thinking that gaps around the pipes provided a haven for rats, he passed the slot for PH 3. It was occupied by a creamy white Jaguar XJ-S convertible with Arizona plates.

The security gate on the elevator was open. Riding the padded interior to the top, Jack stepped into a corridor with a carpet that seemed woven from rope. But the lack of give underneath told him it had been inexpensively padded.

Number 3 had a name plate with MR. 9 MRS. SAMUEL J. HARRIS scripted in gold. The door was ajar. Jack lifted a brass lion's-paw door-knocker and let it drop.

"Come in!"

She was standing at a full-length gold-framed mirror propped against a freshly painted, off-white wall, vigorously rubbing her darkened, because damp, lemon yellow hair with a burgundy towel. A sea green silk skirt and matching blouse clung like foam to her shapely body.

She was even more spectacular than he'd guessed from her photograph: tall as Jack, even in her bare, highly arched feet. The blush in her cheeks was heightened by the heat of her bath.

Her eyes, suddenly meeting his, were a startling gray and impenetrable as winter fog. Was she wearing contacts? he found himself wondering.

"Sorry about missing you. . . . Stupid painters left a wet brush on a shelf—took forever to get out of my hair." Seemingly uncaring or unaware that her blouse was partially unbuttoned, she adjusted her skirt, giving him a fleeting glimpse of a creamy thigh, and came toward him with the sinuously graceful stride of a predatory animal.

"You are Mrs. Harris?"

"Who else would I be?"

He averted his eyes from her cleavage as she took the case. She exuded an unsettling aroma of what he imagined must be a terribly expensive bath oil. But when she walked away he watched her, marveling at her surefooted grace—she'd been a tennis player in her youth, he guessed. Or maybe a dancer. And guessed too that she was at least ten years younger than Samuel J. Harris.

The few pieces of furniture were encased in plastic. At a partially uncovered table shoved carelessly under an unshaded window—that streaming sunlight would surely blister the glossy finish—she put the case down and examined it for a long moment, as if making sure it hadn't been tampered with, before punching in the combination.

Though she made an effort to hide the case's contents, it was awkward and not completely successful, as if she hadn't much experience in being secretive, Jack observed.

"Everything okay?" he couldn't help asking.

When she snapped the lid shut and turned back to him, he took in a sharp breath: the sunlight had made her clothing transparent, revealing a body, surprisingly without undergarments, that could have served as a model for those ancient sculptors who had glorified the female form.

"Just fine." She seemed startled he was still there. "Can I get you something?"

". . . a soft drink would be nice," Jack heard himself saying, though he'd planned to make himself scarce once he'd delivered the case.

"I'll see what we have." She was obviously under stress, but reflexively polite, perhaps an attribute of the well-born, Jack told himself. She went over to a corner bar, and he watched her stoop to open an under-the-shelf refrigerator, careless about the slit in her skirt, which slid down her thigh. Her skin seemed never to have been exposed to the sun. "Club soda'll have to do it, I'm afraid." She returned with a glass filled with ice and a bottle. "Want something in it? Sam's got a full bar."

"No, thanks." As she bent to pour the sparkling liquid her breasts stretched the open blouse. Her perfume filled his nostrils. "This will do just fine."

She looked at him distractedly. Had she guessed his admiration? If so, she didn't seem offended.

"You're young to be a banker."

"I don't think of myself as a banker. I manage computers—the bank's data processing system."

She gazed at him a moment longer, as if debating whether to ask him anything else—or had lost track of the conversation. Now that she had her case she ought to be relaxed, Jack thought. Instead she seemed inordinately tense.

Before he could think what he might say to relax her, she suddenly picked up the case and carried it into the next room. Moments later she was back.

"This enough for your trouble?"

He came back to himself—she was offering him a twenty-dollar bill!

"No. Thank you, no," He backed away, feeling the heat in his cheeks and ears.

"My husband take care of you?"

"It was a favor," he mumbled, and stumbling backward out the door, he pulled it shut.

He took a moment to get his breath. Then, feeling inept, incompetent, and thoroughly humiliated, he ran for the elevator.

His face was hot as fire. It was his own fault. He'd overstayed, and she'd treated him like an insensitive underling — or worse, as if she'd guessed at the lustful images that had flooded his mind. Oh, Sister Theresa, why didn't I pay more attention? he implored himself. Sister had warned them to beware of such situations. He hadn't believed her. How could someone so cloistered know so much about the world?

By the time Jack reached the garage he'd calmed himself enough to rethink his earlier assumptions. Instead of the money in the case being bait, as he'd wildly surmised, a farfetched test of his honesty, he was now certain it was a stash his boss's wife had squirreled away without her husband's knowledge.

How, he asked himself, had she managed to accumulate twenty-five thousand dollars without her nosy, on-top-of-every-conceivable-situation husband finding out? More importantly, how could a woman of such stunning beauty and mature self-control be enticed into marrying a high-strung bully like Harris in the first place?

By the time Jack reached the street, his curiosity had become near overwhelming. Though Mrs. Samuel J period Harris perfectly fit Sister Theresa's description of Temptation Incarnate, there was no question in his mind about what he must do. It was pointless to argue with himself about it.

Sliding into the truck, he adjusted the side-view mirror for a clear view of the Regent Tower driveway. Then removing his tie, Jack took off his suit jacket and vest, ruffled his hair, and slipped into the coveralls that made him practically invisible. No one would look twice at an unkempt man in coveralls driving a beat-up panel truck.

She was clearly in a hurry to do something with the money. He'd follow her until he found out what.

The way the day had turned out, he had nothing better to do anyway.

SIX

Jack was pouring water into Roger's bowl when the white convertible Jaguar came purring up from the underground garage.

Leaning out the panel truck's door and peering through tree branches that shielded him from view, Jack glimpsed her striding out under the canopied entrance. Though she was wearing lethally provocative spike heels, she was as surefooted as someone wearing sneakers. She must be in some kind of hurry to have finished dressing so fast.

Jack nodded to himself as she refused the doorman's offer of assistance. He wouldn't want that much cash out of his hands either. She smiled mechanically at the parking attendant holding the car door, and put the bag inside before sliding behind the wheel.

While the puzzled doorman scratched his brow — no doubt wondering how that precious bag had gotten delivered — she lowered the convertible top. Then, wheeling the sleek car into the street, underinflated radial tires squealing, she surprised him by heading in a direction opposite from the way his truck was facing.

Where was his head? Jack thought, ducking back inside. He'd been mesmerized by her. As he went to switch the motor on, he realized he still held the plastic water jug. Slinging the jug into the back, Jack started the motor and jammed the gear into reverse. Ignoring the shuddering transmission, and the lurching Roger's startled yelp, he backed all the way to the corner.

Just in time. Her Jaguar barely paused at the Los Feliz stop before making a left turn. He raced to the boulevard, then had to wait for a gap in traffic. She was no longer in sight. He sped the wrong way against a left-turn lane to find an opening, changing lanes twice before spotting her a few cars ahead on his right.

Why had she slowed? Pulling up on her, confident he was only a shadow behind his tinted windows, he saw a map unfolded over her steering wheel.

Slowing, Jack allowed several cars to get between them . . . only to watch her speed across a crowded Vermont Avenue intersection on a yellow light, leaving him trapped behind a new red-lacquered Honda CRX.

At the green, he honked, and as the beat-up Chevy on his right lagged, he swung around the smaller car, earning a baleful look from its teenaged driver in Vuarnet sunglasses. How was it that only illegal immigrants and the terribly indebted drove used cars anymore? Racing ahead, Jack found her drifting again in the right-hand lane, a car phone at her ear.

Who would she be calling in a city new to her? An appointment she'd been unable to confirm?

Again he fell a few car lengths back. At Western Avenue she turned south. By cutting in ahead of an iridescent steel blue Beamer unwilling to challenge his truck he made the turn before the signal changed.

Again she'd slowed. What had happened to that sense of urgency? Jack checked his watch. One forty-five. Maybe an appointment had been delayed. He'd bet his few remaining shekels she was not going to the bank employing her husband.

If she were killing time, he could understand her exploring Wilshire. They passed formerly elegant department stores whose clientele had aged with them, set amongst grand hotels being converted into condominiums. They slid past renovated mansions on a once-splendid Highland Avenue, lined with palms inspired by a movie-land Egypt, across Crenshaw, stylish in past times but now a shabby boulevard of gas stations and car dealers, and along the fenced boundaries of the WASP-founded, city-fathered Wilshire Country Club. Was she heading there? Executives of MetroBank were entitled to membership.

She continued on, however, toward privately owned, sculpture-fronted bank buildings and the gold-leafed home offices of insurance companies and brokerage houses, floor after floor of silk-shirt-sleeved smooth talkers with necks crooked from shouldering telephones, who'd be eager to give her advice about where to park her money.

It occurred to Jack, belatedly, that she could have transferred money from Phoenix — wire transfers were practically instantaneous. Cash meant she was paying off some personal debt where she — or her creditor — didn't want records kept.

Jack couldn't imagine what kind of debt that might be. A

woman of her demonstrable class would have legitimate reasons for paying in cash, he told himself. She hadn't necessarily come by that money illegally.

At La Brea Avenue, winding snakelike from the smog-ridden Hollywood Hills down through well-maintained neighborhoods being swallowed up by wealthy immigrant Asians and prosperous blacks, she moved again into the left lane and stopped for the signal. He began to worry. He hoped she wasn't planning to turn, accidentally or not, toward territory that was unsafe, beyond the power of the hard-pressed law to control. A depressing thought suddenly crossed his mind: cash was needed for the purchase of drugs.

She couldn't be a dealer. Not in a strange town. And she didn't seem an addictive type. Though these days it was difficult to tell—more than one seemingly straight chick in his henhouse had suddenly done a 360-degree roll: calling in sick, arriving late and leaving early, until their computer workups looked like gibberish, and it turned out they'd been using toilet breaks to inhale nose candy.

When the signal changed he sighed with relief. She was staying on Wilshire, rolling into the so-called Miracle Mile, a genteelly shabby, once-upper-middle-class district renewing itself with renovated storefronts and new restaurants.

Suddenly, her Jaguar made a U-turn in the middle of the block, infuriating oncoming drivers, catching him by surprise. She slid the Jaguar into an alley Jack hadn't even known existed.

Anyone would think she'd grown up driving here, Jack muttered, and raced around the block.

What was she doing? These shops sold cut-rate merchandise. Stopping near the alley's exit, he waited for her car to emerge. Finally he eased forward. She'd parked the Jaguar and gotten out, carrying her personal effects case and a large purse. Opening the Jaguar's trunk, she dropped the case inside.

What was she up to? Had she transferred the money to her purse?

Across the street, a florist's truck vacated a yellow-painted space. Jack gunned his truck in a U-turn and skidded into the space. A uniformed driver, large and scowling, jumped out of a waiting UPS van.

"Roger!" The dog leaped eagerly into the front seat. "Attack!" Roger flattened himself against the side window as the angry driver grabbed the door handle.

"Sorry," Jack mouthed, pretending to have difficulty restraining his dog. From the glove compartment he pulled out a well-used EMERGENCY ELECTRICAL WORK sign, flashing it at the other driver, who had paled. Cursing, the shaken driver stalked back to his truck. Gears clashed as he drove away.

"Attaboy, Roger." Jack placed the sign on the dash, then hugged the dog. Wiping off saliva from Roger's affectionate tongue, Jack made sure there was adequate ventilation before locking the dog in.

He hastened down the alley, keeping a wary eye out for the UPS truck's return. When he arrived at her Jaguar she was nowhere in sight. She might have gone into the back entrance of any number of stores, though none seemed the kind someone of her style would patronize.

Then he spotted the double-barred windows and saw the discreet sign: STANTON COSTUME JEWELERS, APPOINTMENT ONLY.

Jack hastened to the street, then sidled down the storefronts to the jewelry store. A stocky, black, armed security guard stood in the doorway.

"Happen to know which bus goes to Santa Monica?" Past the guard's shoulder, he could see Mrs. Harris inside, being shown trays whose items he couldn't make out by a swarthy, fawning proprietor.

"You on the wrong side of the street. Santa Monica's that way."

"Thanks."

Strange, Jack thought, hastening back the way he'd come. With a rich husband, why would she buy imitation jewelry? Unless she's hocked something Harris had given her, and was replacing it with what looked like the real thing before her husband found out?

All in the realm of possibility, Jack told himself, letting Roger out of his truck. But why couldn't he shake the feeling that something about her didn't compute?

SEVEN

Walking Roger past the Jaguar, Jack casually depressed the trunk's lock to see if by chance she'd left it open. Disappointed, he returned to the alley exit, tweezered a tick from the dog's muzzle, and observed a meter maid writing the Jaguar a ticket. He resisted the urge to protest. He was brushing Roger to soothe him when Mrs. Harris returned.

Her scarf was now pinned to the jacket lapel with a glittering bauble that, if real, would be worth more than twice his monthly salary. And on her wrist was a watch that glittered with diamonds. He'd seen shops that carried such jewelry, expensive as sin, along Rodeo Drive in Beverly Hills; how had she known she could buy them here for half the price?

She spotted the ticket. She tore it in two without bothering to read it, casually tossing the halves into a nearby trash basket. Interesting, the startled Jack thought. A woman married to a stickler like Harris wouldn't deliberately flout the law. Unless . . .

Jack remembered how distraught Harris had been when she'd called him. With a leap of pleasure so small he was hardly aware it was there, he decided they were having marital difficulties. If true, and if she was preparing to leave him, she wouldn't care about tickets. And the cash might be her stake for starting a new life.

They didn't look like they belonged together. Though older than Jack, she was more than a few years younger than Harris, about the age Jack's mother had been when she'd abandoned him, afraid (or so his father had said) she was wasting her best years in a stagnant marriage. As he couldn't imagine that restless, swollen-lipped young woman in the wedding photograph as his humorless father's wife, let alone the mother who had (briefly) suckled him, so something about Mrs. Harris seemed incompatible with his new boss.

She put the top up before driving away. Afraid of disturbing her hair? With little firsthand knowledge of women, Jack remembered avidly reading someone — Steinbeck, most likely — who'd said you could do anything to a woman as long as you didn't muss her hair. The possibilities of that "anything" had intrigued Jack since.

With a start, Jack came out of his musings. She had wheeled the Jaguar to the curb, next to a motorcycle cop trying, unsuccessfully, to remain inconspicuous.

Mrs. Harris smiled in a manner Jack found himself resenting, and asked the cop a question. The cop, plainly admiring, gave her the benefit of his manly profile as he jerked a gauntleted thumb right.

Jack, caught in the traffic flow, moved beyond them. At La Brea, the corner was partially blocked by a DPW crew attacking the pavement with jackhammers. The din rattled his eardrums. A miniature dust storm stung his eyes.

The car behind honked. Irritated, Jack resisted the urge to flip his middle finger, wanting to attract neither the cop's nor his quarry's attention, and waved the driver around.

A Porsche raced by him with a roar — followed a moment later by the motorcycle cop. A delighted Jack — sometimes justice was served — waved at the pulled-over Porsche as he turned the corner and idled by.

He had lucked out. In his side-view mirror he watched her negotiate the same turn, seemingly too distracted to care what those dust particles were doing to her car's sparkling new finish.

When she passed he fell in behind. A block further she pulled the Jaguar alongside a street-corner newsstand. She honked for the attendant, a slim Pakistani engrossed in a sports event on a miniature TV.

The attendant limped to the car window. Listening, he nodded, then brought her a newspaper from a rack marked OUT-OF-TOWN NEWSPAPERS. As soon as she pulled away Jack, who'd risked double-parking behind her, pulled into the vacated space.

"I want the same paper she got."

The attendant brought him a *Phoenix Sun.* "Say," he began, suddenly raising his brows. "How. . . ?"

"Thanks." Jack handed him twenty, waiting impatiently for change before rumbling away.

At Wilshire, she headed west again. The traffic had increased. The midday haze was starting to brown from developing smog. Jack began to worry about losing her. Cars were double-parked, forcing others to drive around them. Past restaurants, shops, corner shopping malls, high rises under construction and towering bank buildings, they came into an area of beautifully designed new buildings marked Museum Town Houses.

Across the way stood the County Art Museum, on land geologists insisted would not sink, next to the La Brea Tar Pits. Adjacent to the park she entered a parking structure.

Jack's eyes were watering. He sneezed. Wiping his leaking nose on Roger, who had inched up into his lap, he parked in a loading zone. Making sure his EMERGENCY ELECTRICAL WORK sign was displayed, and keeping an eye on the pedestrian exit, he slipped out of his coveralls and into worn Levis and a faded sweatshirt imprinted with a flasher opening his raincoat before a sculpture captioned EX-POSE YOURSELF TO ART.

Just in time. She was coming out a side entrance – empty-handed. Jaywalking across the street she dashed between stalled vehicles, refused to acknowledge a whistle from an admiring truck driver, and entered the park.

Tying a sweat-stained bandanna around his neck, and putting on a pair of ski glasses tinted yellow, Jack closed the door on a whining Roger and trotted after her, wondering why she would choose – or agree – to meet anyone at the tar pits. Every thousand or so years, the primal ooze disgorged the bones of extinct creatures, not exactly a setting to consider the future optimistically.

But not even glancing at the pits, she strode lithely up the steps into the museum. He waited for a hand-holding young couple in ripped but expensive jeans to go in ahead.

Inside, his glasses gave the room a yellowish tinge. But he kept them on to maintain his disguise.

Not spotting her among those wandering the echoing foyer, Jack walked toward a directory announcing exhibitions, then noticed an arrow indicating membership applications. Walking in that direction, Jack, relieved, saw her standing at a circular counter marked MEMBERSHIP INFORMATION. An angular woman in an ill-fitting gray silk suit and wearing a badge marked MUSEUM DOCENT sat behind it. The docent, pale lips stretched into a forced smile, didn't seem to like Mrs. Harris, no doubt resentful of her confident bearing and radiant beauty. It was remarkable in a woman her age, Jack thought, estimating Mrs. Harris to be perhaps thirty-nine.

Why had he assumed she was rendezvousing with anyone? She was seeking out attractions in her new community.

Jack couldn't resist passing behind Mrs. Harris close enough to smell her perfume, a scent so exotic he imagined it being made from pale crushed roses in a very special old Cognac.

"This museum has no relationship whatsoever with the Phoenix museum," the docent was fluting. "Even if it did have it certainly would not apply to the transfer of docent membership. Should you desire to apply, however, you are welcome to do so, keeping in mind that the waiting list for docents is impossibly long."

Jack didn't hear Mrs. Harris's response. He stopped at a desk across the way marked TOUR THE EXHIBITS BY CASSETTE, RENTALS HERE, where a mini-leather-skirted young brunette with Betty Boop bangs almost tripped over herself getting to the counter.

"Help you?"

"These worth it?"

"So I hear. Wait five minutes, I'll give you a personal tour."

Jack's face burned. He just couldn't get used to whatever it was that attracted women to him. The envious Harry claimed there'd come a time when he'd regret not taking advantage of it. He doubted it. He was afraid that, like his dad, he could never live up to such fevered anticipations.

He pretended not to notice the brunette's eager smile. "Where's fast forward?"

"You gonna run through the exhibits?"

"I'm on my lunch break."

"Here."

Out of the corner of his eye, Jack saw Mrs. Harris leave the docent desk and go past a pillar marked FRENCH IMPRESSIONISTS.

"Got one for French Impressionists?"

"What I majored in. Hey — there's a twenty-five-dollar deposit."

"Can I leave my watch instead?"

She seemed impressed by its brand name. "Don't tell anyone."

Jack faked a smile, though somewhat ashamed about misleading her, then followed the direction Mrs. Harris had taken, snugging headphones into his ears as he went.

Apparently giving only cursory glances to the spotlighted paintings, she was already at the far end of the room, empty except for the profoundly bored security guard. Only the determined click of her heels disturbed the hush.

Maybe she *was* meeting someone here, Jack thought, quickening his step as she entered the adjacent gallery, trying not to be distracted by the art. The skewed landscapes, smeared colors vibrating like heat waves under August suns, figures distorted into triangles and cubes, as if the artists had squinted first one eye and then the other to gain alternating perspectives, seemed to demand his attention. Jack promised himself he'd return at first opportunity. He had to discover what there was about it that excited him.

Hastening into the next room, Jack became caught up by a

painting of a storm-tossed boat so real he could almost feel the surf pounding, and came within a step of stumbling over Mrs. Harris. Seated on a bench, contemplating a painting on a side wall, she seemed to possess the same coiled energy as the nearby sculptures.

Jack skirted her bench, fussing with the cassette player's controls. She glanced at him only briefly, too immersed in her thoughts to be fully aware of his presence. Was she really crying? Something about that momentary look, soft as a moth's wing, seemed to brush Jack's soul, and he shivered.

What was she looking at with such yearning? He stood behind her and followed the direction of her gaze. A young woman in a wide-brimmed garden hat bent over a little girl carrying a bouquet of brilliant red roses.

What did she see in that painting that affected her so? Was she an artist herself, examining brush strokes and color, grieving because her own talent didn't measure up? Jack fast-forwarded the tape, periodically stopping it to hear a female voice describe various paintings, knowing he had the right one when he heard a description of Mary Cassatt's *Mother and Child*.

As he concentrated to understand what was being said about Cassatt, an impressionist equal to but acknowledged later than the men of her era, the hand-holding young couple strolled in. Mrs. Harris, her contemplation disturbed, got up and left.

Jack took a closer look at the painting before following. Did she identify with the mother? Or the child? Was her biological clock ticking? Or given the way she was taking matters — whatever those matters were — into her own hands, was she resentful of the subservient role she'd been forced by men to take, more specifically, by a man like her husband?

She wasn't in the next room. Not in the adjacent room either. Where had she got to? Hastening under an exit sign, he found himself in a corridor. She was entering a down elevator. Was it worth the risk of going in after her?

The staircase. Taking the marble steps down three at a time, Jack dodged through people in the foyer, trying to get out before the elevator disgorged its passengers.

"Stop that man!" It was the brunette. "He's stealing a tour cassette! Hey!"

Jack kept going, red-faced more from exertion than shame. He'd put too much into this to be delayed by discussions about paying.

They could keep his fake Rolex. A gift from his father when he'd graduated from Loyola, it had only sentimental value. Sentiment, in his life to date, hadn't been worth ten cents on the dollar.

EIGHT

Jack became so engrossed examining the badly lit photos in the *Phoenix Sun* of the socially prominent Mr. and Mrs. Harris's farewell party, while listening to the soothing voice on the Art Tour Tape, that he almost missed seeing her Jaguar come booming out of the parking structure. By the time he got his truck started, she'd blended into the Wilshire traffic.

She seemed suddenly confident about where she was going. He noted she was using the car phone again. Was she being given directions by someone?

A block behind, Jack watched helplessly as she suddenly swung south on Fairfax, beating the signal. Adrenaline surging, Jack spotted an alley and swerved his truck across oncoming traffic.

To the strangely-muted sound of squealing brakes and blaring horns he bounced into the narrow alley, and saw, too late, that it was one way. Praying no car would meet him head-on, Jack reached the near-empty street on the other side unscathed. Flooring the accelerator, he raced toward Fairfax.

Roger howled in joy. Jack had to elbow the dog aside to make the turn. And there she was, pulled over by a bus stop, where those too old, young, or poor to choose alternatives to the city's not-very-rapid transit were no doubt giving this stranger in a strange land conflicting directions.

Jack pulled over. Roger continued to howl. Jack put both hands on the dog's muzzle to calm him. When the ambulance screamed past he frowned. Something was wrong with his hearing—he'd been unable to distinguish the siren from Roger's howl.

Her Jaguar pulled away. About to follow, Jack became aware of a shadow rapping at his side window. A motorcycle cop. Heart sinking, Jack rolled the window down. He watched in amazement as the cop's lips moved without sound. Had he gone deaf?

"Could you speak a little louder?"

Reaching in, the cop removed the earphones from Jack's head.

"Forgot I had them on."

But the cop was already roaring away.

Swearing at himself for his carelessness, Jack caught up with her at the entrance to the Santa Monica Freeway. Mrs. Harris now headed west to the San Diego Freeway at a moderate pace, then surprised Jack by melding into the rapid flow of traffic without any hesitation whatsoever.

Untypical, he thought. Out-of-towners were usually terrified by the devil-take-the-hindmost attitude of L.A. drivers. She entered the Marina Freeway boldly as well, moving immediately into the fast lane, holding her own all the way to the highway's end, where cars spilled out on crowded streets paralleling the condominium-cluttered bay.

She drove directly into the marina, past sail markers, pleasure-boat builders, and restaurants that seemed designed for Oriental potentates. She finally pulled into a parking lot being resurfaced by a smelly tar truck. Two attendants, beach bums by their blistered look, jostled each other getting to her car.

Jack idled by. She was opening the truck. Yes—and, finally, taking out her personal effects bag. Letting out a breath he hadn't realized he was holding, Jack eased into a red zone at the end of the block and placed the *emergency work* sign on his dash.

Roger began whining. "Okay, okay. But stick close." Jack let the dog out. Roger dashed to the hydrant nearby, and after an exploratory sniff, lifted his leg.

"I thought only comic strip dogs did that!" A stocky young woman wearing circular earrings, hair streaked blond, and face dark as oiled leather had turned from a window displaying Scheherazade-like garments made from parachute silk.

Jack felt his smile freeze as Mrs. Harris left the parking lot heading his way.

"Roger. You should be ashamed. I've taught you better manners than that!" Jack hastily bent over the dog, unwilling to push his luck by allowing Mrs. Harris a straight-on look at him.

The leathery young woman bent to pat Roger as well, haltered dress gaping to reveal that she disdained brassieres. "He's only doin' what comes naturally."

"I can't believe he's letting you touch him—he gets very nervous around females—just like me—maybe because we haven't met that special person. Is she the one, Roger?"

Roger woofed twice.

"He wants you to walk with us."

"I'm on my way to the bus stop."

"We'll keep you company . . . Deirdre?"

"Deirdre? How funny. I can't even spell that. JoAnne."

"Randy," Jack said.

"I'll bet you are."

"No." Jack cursed the inner imp that had pushed that paradoxical name to his lips. "I mean yes, I have all the normal urges. But I keep them under wraps. You have nothing to fear, m'dear."

"I look scared to you?"

Disconcerted, Jack linked arms with the amused JoAnne just as Mrs. Harris, carrying her personal effects bag, passed them. He hoped what she saw was a young couple, enamored of each other, walking their dog.

Mrs. Harris paused in front of a saloon whose handsomely wrought stained-glass windows depicted a hamburger, french fries, ketchup, and beer. Her hesitation seemed to Jack as fraught with significance as Caesar's before the Rubicon. He turned his attention toward JoAnne, hoping his so-called charm would not choose this moment to desert him.

"Join us for a late lunch?"

"I'm supposed to meet a friend in Beverly."

Jack fished a quarter out of his jeans. "Tell her you'll be late."

"Where'd you have in mind?"

"That place looks good."

"I'll call my friend later."

The interior was dim, lit by multicolored hanging fake-Tiffany lamps displaying the same motif as the windows. Rattan-imbedded ceiling fans rotated cool air. Leaving a wistful Roger at the entrance, they walked to a sign reading PLEASE WAIT HERE FOR HOSTESS.

The hostess, an exceptionally tall young redheaded woman, was escorting Mrs. Harris into a room at the back. She returned at a near-incredible speed, raising sawdust in a skidding stop. She was on roller skates.

"Smoking or non?"

"Back there looks good."

"Those are reserved."

"Please. JoAnne and I just fell head over heels and need someplace private. It must happen to you a lot?"

"Maybe I can manage something."

They followed the grinning hostess, carrying menus, as she rolled to the back room. Mrs. Harris was standing at a booth, facing a squint-eyed older man who had the mournful complexion of someone who lived on the roots of colorless vegetables. The man leaned forward, looking to greet her with a kiss. Mrs. Harris, turning her face aside, as if his breath smelled of rotting flesh, slid into the booth, keeping the bag next to her hip. Grinning mirthlessly, the man sat too, pushing a half-finished steak aside.

"Mind if we take this one?" Jack urged JoAnne into a booth where he could watch that unlikely couple without being noticed himself.

"You're very forceful," JoAnne said after the hostess handed them menus and skated away.

"I like the view here — we can watch all the folks and try to guess what they're saying to each other."

"That's your idea of fun?"

"Like that couple across from us. They don't seem to have anything in common. Why would they be together?"

"I wouldn't have a clue."

"He looks like he forecloses mortgages and she — "

"Looks like a kept woman."

For some reason this annoyed Jack. "Think so? Seems more the creative type to me, an artist maybe — "

"No artist I know can afford clothes like that."

A young waitress with legs like a hockey player coasted over to Mrs. Harris and filled her cup from one of the two pots she was carrying. Mrs. Harris was having nothing else. The waitress skated to them.

"Great lookin' earrings."

"Thanks. They're condoms. See?" JoAnne pressed one and a sheathed condom popped out. She put it back.

"Neat. Anything to drink?"

"Decaf please."

"You?"

Jack hadn't been able to take his eyes off the earrings. "I avoid all stimulants." Jack attempted a smile.

". . . ready to order?"

"Give us a couple minutes," Jack said, though his stomach growled.

"Mormon?" JoAnne asked, when the waitress left.

"Buddhist." Jack forced himself to remain calm as he watched Mrs. Harris's companion lean across the table and say something that caused her to flinch.

"So am I! Nichiren Shoshu?"

"Zen."

Clutching her bag, Mrs. Harris started to slide out of the booth. Her companion reached across the table and grabbed her wrist.

Jack had gotten up.

"Where you headed?"

"He's hurting her."

"I don't see her complaining."

Jack sat back down. Mrs. Harris was now slumped in the booth. Her companion, standing, had yanked the case from her grasp. "Slut!" The man had hissed the word, but Jack heard it clearly. He felt shamed for doing nothing as the other strode away with her case.

Mrs. Harris sat a moment longer, head bowed. When she stood and turned to walk past, Jack saw that her eyes, those forget-me-not, frosty blue eyes, were melting into tears.

"Christ." Jack glanced at the wrist where his watch had been and stood up. "I just remembered. I'm supposed to see my doctor for a blood test. Look, you stay, order whatever you like, then call a cab — it's on me!" He pulled twenty from his pocket and dropped it on the table.

"A blood test?"

"I've been having a little trouble urinating. . . ."

JoAnne shrank from his outstretched hand. Jack tried his best to look hurt, then walked to the opposite booth. He used a napkin to pick up what was left of the steak.

At the entryway, he teased Roger outside with the meat. Mrs. Harris was nowhere in sight. Her companion, however, was just pulling away from a parking spot in a tan Chevrolet that Jack identified, from the sticker on its rear bumper, as a Budget Rent A Car.

Hastening to his truck, Jack allowed Roger to leap inside. He was about to jump in himself when he noticed his left-front tire. Flat.

"Shit." No way he could follow. Jack ran his hand over the worn tread, feeling for a nail or chunk of glass. Nothing. Probably a slow leak, he thought.

Now what? Jack looked about. Where had Mrs. Harris got to? He doubted she would be in a mood to go shopping. She hadn't given the money up easily. Why would a woman married to a well-paid bank executive, and the daughter of a leading shareholder, according to the Phoenix paper, owe that kind of money?

Unless it wasn't a legitimate debt, but some kind of payoff. But how would a classy woman like that even *know* such a disreputable-looking man? Disturbed, Jack walked past the restaurant in the opposite direction, checking shops on both sides.

He almost missed the sign, small and posted between two of the buildings: BEACH ACCESS.

Without hesitation, Jack took the indicated path. He came out from between the buildings onto a sand strip that sloped down to a band of water that lapped the shore between two rock-built, break-water jetties. Except for a few gulls, there wasn't another soul in sight.

Jack headed toward the water. At low tide it was possible, he suddenly realized, to walk to the other side of the jetties and be hidden from view.

Someone had preceded him. There were high-arched footprints in the oozing sand. He followed them to a partially hidden cove. Her clothes had been carelessly strewn on a pile of rock.

Jack sucked in an anxious breath. What was she thinking? He looked to the water. There was a chill in the air—and in his soul. Unless she had ice in her veins, this was too early in the year for swimming.

NINE

The oil-streaked waters of the bay stretched to a horizon layered with smog. The vista, in the middle of this workday, was empty, except for a stationary rowboat with two overalled figures bent over fishing lines. A fish surfaced, causing Jack's heart to jump with it, then disappeared, leaving the water, though not Jack, tranquil once more.

In the distance beyond the boat Jack suddenly spotted movement. Squinting against the glare he eventually made out something swimming toward the open sea.

Panicked, Jack stripped to his shorts. What was her destination? "Stay!" he ordered the frisky Roger, and plunged into the water.

The cold took his breath. He persisted, flailing as much to warm himself as for speed. As he churned through the murky waters, part of himself couldn't help wondering why he bothered. With her head start, it was near impossible he'd reach her in time. If she wanted to kill herself, for reasons he couldn't even guess at, what business was it of his?

"Yo!" With an enormous froglike kick Jack came out of the water hip-high to yell at the two men in the boat. "Swimmer in trouble! Yo!"

He went under, then surfaced again, blowing like a whale. The salt stung his eyes. He blinked them clear, saw that the two men had heard. His relief lasted only until he realized they were rowing toward him.

"The other way! That way! Out there!" He beat at the water in frustration. Backs to him, the two men continued to row. The boat moved in spasmodic jerks, the rowers bending to it eagerly but at cross-purposes with each other, casting occasional glances over their shoulders to make sure of his location. "I'm okay! It's her that's in trouble! There, there, can't you see her *there?!*"

If he hadn't ducked and gone under, one of the oars might have caught him behind an ear. He came up sputtering. Before he could take in breath to say more, he was grabbed under each armpit and hoisted, splay-legged, into the boat.

"Take it easy, man, you safe now."

The two men were black. Jack, chest heaving, sprawled next to a bucket of squirming live bait. He raised his goose-pimpled arm to point. "It's her needs saving — she's trying to do herself in!"

"You know that for a fact?"

"Absolutely!" Jack lurched to his feet.

"Stay still now, you hear? You rockin' the boat." Facing about, the two began determinedly rowing in the direction she was swimming, toward the open sea.

Jack couldn't be sure, but when she passed the channel marker she seemed to be losing strength. Had she paused momentarily on one of her alternate beats and observed them before resuming her faltering crawl? If she had, what must she be thinking?

As they pulled up on her, she stopped swimming and turned to face them. Jack's eyes met hers. He thought he saw anger, not fear. Did she recognize him? Then she raised her arms as if consigning her soul to the heavens and disappeared under a wave.

In a frenzy, Jack launched himself over the side. This time the water seemed warm. When he reached the spot where she'd been, he frantically gulped in air and dove under.

Salt stung his eyes. He couldn't see anything in this murky sea. And then, as his breath ran out, his blindly searching hands touched her yielding flesh.

Kicking for traction, Jack flung an arm around her motionless form and, lungs aching for oxygen, used his free arm to windmill them toward the surface, a part of his mind transfixed by the way her slippery limbs intertwined with his.

They surfaced near the boat. Jack sucked air into his burning lungs. The younger man held an oar out. Jack grabbed the slick aluminum, trying to keep Mrs. Harris's head above water as her sleek form cleaved to his. Slowly, slowly, they were pulled toward the boat.

As the older man reached down to help, Jack felt Mrs. Harris stir, as if trying to slip out of his grasp. With a mighty effort, he lifted her to the grabbing hands and fell back, gulping in brackish water as he went under.

Sputtering as he surfaced, Jack managed to climb in with help from the older man. The younger man was helping Mrs. Harris lean over the boat's gunwale. Finally, in a great gush, she spewed out water and vomit, then fell back to the boat's bottom, half-unconscious.

[48]

"That better." With extraordinary politeness, the old man threw a ragged blanket over her glistening nakedness. "Rest now. Don't try to talk."

"B-borrow your towel?" Jack asked through chattering teeth.

"You don't mind the grease on it."

The younger man—were they father and son?—threw him a dirty towel.

"T-thanks. P-preciate it."

They drew closer to shore. "That your dog?"

Roger was racing from one end of the strip of sand to the other.

"Yes."

"Don't mind my sayin' so, he got more sense than you two. Here, this'll warm you."

Jack took the offered bottle. Whiskey, a brand he'd never seen any advertisement for. He coughed at the rawness, and nodded gratefully as warmth spread through him.

"Rub-a-dub-dub."

Only the older man laughed. Then, dripping whiskey on his index finger, he rubbed it over Mrs. Harris's lips. Jack envied him her grateful murmur.

By the time they reached the shore's shallows, she'd managed to sit up. But she kept her back to him, hunched into the blanket, gazing out toward the horizon, now illuminated by the setting sun.

"Sorry to interrupt your fishing."

"She gone be all right now?"

"She'll be fine."

Returning the towel, Jack scooped a wriggling minnow from the bait bucket and stepped into the sea. It was only calf-deep, but the cold immediately went to the bone. Shivering, he reached up to help her.

She ignored his hand, and despite the two fishermen's protestations, handed back their blanket. Then stepping over the side, unconcerned about her nakedness, she strode toward the rocks where she'd left her clothes, as surefooted and queenly as if she ruled a native habitat.

For the first time Jack noticed she was wearing panties, sheer, clinging to the split in the firm, wet flesh of her buttocks.

Roger bounded after her. She stayed him with an imperious finger, then disappeared behind the pile of rock.

Roger returned at Jack's whistle and stood, paws on Jack's shoulders, swallowing the minnow Jack had palmed in a single gulp. Jack buried his face in the dog's fur, grateful to embrace someone who couldn't guess at his embarrassment.

"What's taking her so long, Roger?"

Even with his clothes on, he couldn't stop shivering. But no point in berating himself. Whatever was distressing her—the money, or the disreputable man who'd taken it from her—wasn't his doing. And if her despair had turned into anger, he could understand that, too. Anyone planning a swim to eternity wouldn't feel grateful to whoever interrupted her.

She came out from behind the rock, fully dressed, carrying her purse. She marched straight up to him.

Jack thought for a moment he'd been wrong, that she was going to thank him. She reached inside her purse, pulled something out, and pressed a cold, round cylinder into his neck.

"Okay, sailor. Talk to me. Why are you following me?"

Jack's heart turned to stone. He shuddered, picturing what a bullet could do to his brain. Why would a woman of her breeding be carrying a gun?

"I'm not. I come to this beach to walk my dog. I saw you were in trouble, and—"

"Don't con me. Tell me what you're up to before my nerves get the best of me and this harmful object goes off."

"Can't you put that thing down?" Jack pleaded, hoping to buy time. "I can't think with a gun at my head—"

"That's the general idea. Talk."

"You looked upset." Jack put all the sincerity he could muster into his voice. "I have an intuition about people. I decided to follow you, just in case—I suppose it sounds stupid—"

"It does sound stupid. If you can't come up with something better than that. . . ."

"I can't think of anything better. I mean, it's the truth."

"I'm going to fire this gun and holler rape and when the cops come I suggest you have a better story than the one you're trying to lay on me now."

"I saw the money in your personal effects case."

"You saw—?" She removed the barrel from his neck. "Comb your hair out of your eyes, Sylvester."

Jack did as she asked. He put a smile on his face. "The name's Jack, ma'am."

She didn't return his smile.

"You. The kid from the office." Her surprise seemed to have driven out any vestige of anger.

"I wouldn't say I was a kid, exactly. I'm almost thirty."

"You have that much mileage on you?" She looked him over,

partially lowering her gun. "I would never have guessed. You're practically in mint condition."

I'm deteriorating fast, Jack wanted to say, but bit his tongue, not willing to risk offending her further.

"What else did you see?"

"You giving money to the bad guy in the cafe."

The gun lowered still further and a look of pain came over her face. "You are a curious fu—fellow, aren't you? But I don't see where what I do or don't do is any business of yours."

"I work with MetroBank security." Jack wondered what she'd been about to call him, and whether he dared make a grab for her gun. "There's been a very large leak in bank funds. All employees and their spouses are under scrutiny. With the amount of cash you laid on Mr. Congeniality, the bank authorities will want to ask you where it came from."

"You wouldn't—you couldn't put me through that!"

Her desperation made Jack uncomfortable. But he was in so deep he couldn't think how to back out now. "Afraid I have no choice."

From the top of the strip, a young couple carrying a blanket walked toward them. Mrs. Harris turned to look and Jack swiped the gun out of her hand. She lunged as if to fight him for it, then slumped and leaned against him as the young couple passed. The young woman grinned at them, a conspiracy of lovers; then the couple disappeared around the pile of rock.

Mrs. Harris pulled away, causing Jack momentary regret.

"I'd like my gun back."

"And have you use it on me? Like the man says, I may be dumb, but I'm not stupid."

"It's not loaded."

Jack examined the small automatic, found the catch in the yellowing ivory handle, and slid the well-oiled magazine out—empty. He handed it back.

"What good's an empty gun?"

"Most people wouldn't be dumb enough to risk finding that out."

Jack flushed. She couldn't be referring to him? "Including the man you gave the money to?"

She flinched. "It's not what you think. And it has nothing to do with my husband."

"It's not for me to say."

"But you're on the wrong track!" She seemed beside herself with worry. "Look—we'll catch our death—I can see you shivering—

[51]

let me buy you a drink? Least I can do, your having saved my life. And I'll try and explain what I can to you."

Jack eyed her closely. Was she being sardonic? Or genuinely grateful? Finally, he shrugged. What difference could it possibly make? "Sure. But my treat. I don't want you thinking I can be bought off."

TEN

After depositing Roger in the truck, they returned to the saloon, causing raised eyebrows on the part of the hostess, who, after a wondering look at their disheveled appearance, sat them in a dark portion of the bar. The waitress brought them each a towel.

"Thanks." Mrs. Harris used the towel vigorously on her hair. "Shot of rye, with a beer back?"

"Just beer." Jack made a scarf out of his towel, wondering where she'd learned to drink what he'd always thought of as a macho man's choice.

When the drinks arrived, before the waitress could pour, Mrs. Harris placed her beer bottle vertically inside her glass. Lifting the bottle in one continuous motion, she filled the glass without spilling a drop. The only other person Jack had seen do that was Carl, the bartender at the Sports Cafe.

"Nifty."

"That?" She saluted him, then gulped the contents of the shot glass, following it with a swallow of beer. She tongued foam from her sensuous lips, causing Jack to drift into reverie. "It's something I learned when I was . . . younger." She seemed lost in memory.

"You were going to explain to me about the money?"

She came back to him. "I made some bad investments. I was desperate to become financially independent—Sam keeps me on such a tight budget—and when the investments fell out I made the mistake of borrowing money from . . . from . . . that awful person."

"You couldn't go to your family?"

She hesitated. "They cut me off years ago."

"What about your husband?"

"The investments were kind of . . . shady. We had to pay off some politicians. Sam's career with the bank means everything to him! If he ever found out I did something like this behind his back—" She looked at him with those wonderful, forget-me-not eyes. "He has a terrible temper. I'm afraid of what he might do."

Jack could believe that. He took a moment, pretending to consider what she'd told him, then, "I'm not the one supposed to make these decisions. And if it turned out you weren't telling me the truth . . . but what the hey! This job's not my life's work. What the bank doesn't know won't hurt them."

She took in such a deep breath that she shuddered. "You're unbelievably kind. And I am telling you the truth." She let out her breath. "As far as it goes."

Though an inner voice warned him not to pursue this, Jack felt that he had to ask. "There's a problem with that money?"

"No, that money's from a trust fund Sam never knew about. It came due when I was thirty-five."

"What else then?"

"It's nothing that concerns the bank. Or you. Better for you not to know about it."

"Let me be the judge of that."

"Didn't your mother teach you never to meddle in other people's troubles?"

"My father did the teaching. Said to always be helpful and kind."

"And how often did that get you more than you bargained for?"

"I've never had cause to be sorry."

"Yet." She gave him a look he couldn't read. "I'm being blackmailed."

Jack held her gaze with difficulty. She'd more or less convinced him her problems had to do with investments. This sudden turnabout made him feel foolish.

"Why would you tell me that?"

"You're very nice. You took me at my word. I couldn't be comfortable with myself knowing I hadn't told you everything."

Blackmail explained why she'd handed that disreputable character money. Money her husband knew nothing about. Jack swallowed beer to lubricate his throat. He ought to be telling her that he'd been lying too. Instead, he said, "I can't imagine you doing anything you'd have to pay someone to keep quiet about."

She studied her drink. Her voice was so low he could barely make out the words. "You're very sweet. And very naive."

His face grew hot. Now, tell her that he'd lied to her now, he told himself. But he heard himself saying, "I'm no more trusting than the next guy. And no more trustworthy either. But I know when I meet someone who's straight."

"That a vote of confidence?"

"You need my vote, you've got it."

"If Sam felt that way, I wouldn't be in this predicament."

"A wife should be able to confide in her husband."

"If you try not to look at me so . . . so close, maybe I'll be able to explain . . . why I can't."

Though he didn't want to take his eyes from her, Jack forced himself to concentrate on removing the label from the sweating bottle of beer.

"I wasn't always the person I am now. What I mean is," she corrected herself hastily, "when I was young I was pretty wild. I was the kind of girl men took to. I could never get enough attention. I depended on men's admiration. So when this . . . photographer . . . asked me to pose I jumped at the chance. Those pictures wound up . . . on the kind of calendars you see in auto shops. . . . You promised not to look at me!"

"Sorry."

"You lovebirds want anything else?"

Both of them looked at the waitress, startled.

Mrs. Harris suddenly stood. "Thanks, but I've got to go. This ought to cover it?" She started to peel off a twenty.

When Jack pushed her hand away and paid, she left.

"That's it?" Jack caught up to her as she reached her car in the gathering dusk. "Calendar art? You expect me to believe you'd pay someone off to keep quiet about that?"

"I don't expect you to believe anything!" As if sorry for her outburst, she put her hand on his arm, the touch electrifying him. "But you're right. That was only the start. I find it . . . difficult to tell you more."

"I can handle it."

"This guy claimed to be a *Playboy* photographer. He dazzled me with visions of millions of men looking at me with their breath coming short and their tongues hanging out. . . . One thing led to another. . . ."

"I'm listening."

"He got me to do beaver shots. Don't look at me. *Please.*"

Jack rocked back on his heels and watched traffic. "What issue were they in?" he asked, trying to make it casual.

"None. When I saw the pictures I wouldn't sign the release. But the bastard wouldn't give me the negatives, kept track of me all these years, and when it looked like I was in Fat City with Sam, said he'd show them to my husband unless I came up with two hundred and fifty thousand dollars!"

It was hard not to look at her. "They that bad?"

[55]

"Sam would think so."

"I can't believe that he wouldn't under—"

"You haven't seen the pictures!"

Thank God he hadn't spoken the words aloud. But then, reading his mind, she said, as if disgusted, "You'd like to, wouldn't you?"

He blushed, hoping it couldn't be seen in the dusk, and stammered, "N-not for the reasons you think. I just can't imagine them being as bad as you say. . . ."

"Take my word for it." She yanked her car door open, then, hesitating, said "Please?" in a manner that melted his heart before getting in and driving away.

ELEVEN

Jack found it difficult changing his tire in the dwindling daylight. By the time he left it for repair at the gas station at the mouth of the canyon it was early evening. Dusk, gray as a mourner's shawl, was shrouding the contours of the Santa Monica hills.

For the first time since he'd owned his lot the twisting ride up the narrow road failed to excite him. He was filled with a sense of foreboding. The day, which had started out well, had turned into a near nightmare of unwelcome surprises. Meeting this woman who disordered his senses, the last woman in the world he would have believed he could become infatuated with, a woman unavailable to him by virtue of marriage, age, and social status, he felt as if all his carefully laid plans were in danger of going suddenly awry.

The timbers on his partially framed house loomed against the darkening sky like the ruins of an abandoned temple. In the dark, confused state of his mind, that skeletal structure reflected more of the grave than what he'd planned to flesh out his dreams. He'd been so confident of getting the loan that he'd started building without it, trenching the foundation personally, ordering top-of-the-line materials, wanting his house to possess integrity from inside out, unlike those built by speculators for strangers.

Buildings were as good or bad as the society around them, the Jesuits might have said. Jack, not given to philosophical musings, would have scoffed at the idea that his passion for quality was a reflection of his Catholic teaching. Because he and the other boys, in bedside whisperings after lights-out, had scoffed at the nuns' relentless reiteration of dogma, he did not realize how deeply the attitudes they'd propounded were ingrained in him.

Parking where he meant the garage to be—the lumberyard, after repeated demands for payment, had cut off his credit—Jack let Roger out. While the dog zigzagged from corner to corner marking his territory, Jack walked to the berm at the lot's edge, where he stood brooding over the view.

At this distance the city seemed serene. The headlights of the cars speeding along the lighted thoroughfares were glittery as trained fireflies. The surrounding hills, blackened from last summer's fire storms, took on, in this lowering dark, the texture of velvet. Even the swaying lights of ships at anchor in the bay, which he knew to be oil-leaking, rust-covered freighters, seemed in his imagination to glow over sleek decks crafted from the timbers of exotic climes.

What was preventing him from chucking it all, signing on as a deckhand, and sailing to the earth's far corners? Stability had never been his strong suit. Trying to take responsibility for his dad as well as himself did not seem to be working out too well. Being kept away from the bank made him feel helpless, subject to proceedings he couldn't control.

Behind him, from the steep, winding road, he heard the whining engine of a small Japanese car straining to make the grade. Then headlights flashed, illuminating his abandoned house, chasing the shadows from his mind. The rotary-engined Mazda drove onto the lot, parking behind his truck. Roger began barking.

"Roger, stay!"

The dog's tail whipped the air. Nancy, though dressed as she had been at work, had improved her makeup and combed out her hair, which now hung to her shoulders.

"On your way to a party?"

"Help me with this." She was struggling with a large cloth-covered basket.

"What's in here, hot bricks? My arms just popped out of my shoulder sockets."

"Well, Mr. Curiosity, you're welcome to look."

Lifting the cloth he saw containers of warm food, droplets of steam clouding the plastic covers, along with a sweating bottle of chilled blush wine. Eye of the Swan. Which reminded him, perversely, of Mrs. Harris.

"I know you're broke, and with payday not till Friday . . ."

"How'd you know I'd be here?"

"You weren't at your usual hangout." She flashed a matchbook marked SPORTS CAFE. Then she leaned toward him, delicate nostrils flaring. "Been cleaning fish?"

"It's a long, boring story."

"Let me be the judge of that."

"Can we eat first?"

[58]

They spread the cloth on the table inside the truck. She unrolled glasses from cloth napkins, then pulled candles out of her shoulder bag, lighting them while he opened the wine with the corkscrew on his Swiss Original Army knife. The flickering candles highlighted her chestnut hair as she began apportioning salad, a herb-redolent baked chicken, and rice.

"Very healthful." He was ravenous.

"It's important to eat balanced meals."

"I wouldn't argue with that."

"You know that bachelors are more susceptible to disease than married men."

"I don't doubt it."

She was looking at him, damp-eyed, over the rim of her glass. He'd already started eating. Putting down his knife and fork Jack suppressed a sudden apprehension and picked up his own glass. "Cheers."

"To us."

"Friends forever."

She pursed her lips, not liking that overmuch, but clinked glasses with him. They drank. She watched him eat.

"I knew you didn't have lunch."

"Don't pretzel sticks count?"

"They have pretzels at the Sports Cafe?"

"Come to think of it, they don't. What happened at work after I left?"

"Nothing to speak of."

"The auditors didn't come up with anything?"

"Nothing they told me about."

"None of them went rushing in to Samuel J period Harris waving their skinny arms and hollering eureka?"

"Don't be silly."

"Harris didn't come out and give the chicklets a little pep talk?"

"How'd you know that?"

"Lucky guess."

"He taught us some shortcuts."

"He know computers that well?"

"He's a whiz. Almost good as you."

Jack took an unhappy moment to absorb this. "What else?"

"Told us that if anyone was aware of the slightest discrepancy it was important to let him know. *The tiniest blemish on a piece of fruit can lead to rottenness at the core.*"

"Guy has a way with words." Jack's throat was dry. His glass was empty. He poured himself another.

"I wouldn't mind more myself."

"Sorry."

"You're worried about something."

"The guy doesn't like me."

"Oh, Jack, don't be paranoid. He said it was obvious you were a dedicated worker."

"He talked about me?"

"Not really."

"How'd my work habits come up?"

"When he was explaining to us why you weren't there."

"He didn't think I would have told you that?"

"Now, Jack. He wanted to make sure we understood you hadn't been all that keen on abandoning your chicks. In fact he told us you had protested more than somewhat. *A clear indication that you were a dedicated etcetera.* Don't look so put out—he meant it as a compliment."

"Maybe you're right. He's really a brick."

"What's bothering you?"

"If they find the leak in our files I could get blamed."

"Hardly likely."

"Don't be too sure."

"Jack, they're looking for big-time stuff. Not small fry."

"Thanks."

"Not that you won't be important some day."

"Appreciate the vote of confidence."

"Jack . . ."

"I'm listening."

"Never mind."

"I'm *listening.*"

"It must be cold sleeping in the truck."

"Roger keeps me warm."

"You'd rather sleep with a dog than me?"

"What a question."

"I guess that's my answer."

"Nancy. Sit down. Please." Her hand was warm and vibrant in his, her perfume light and elusive as flowers in rain. Her dark eyes were bright, her mouth inviting. Jack felt himself leaning toward her, like a plant toward light.

Her lips were wet with wine. His hand found her firm breast. Her fingers explored the back of his neck. His hand slid down to her narrow waist, over her flat stomach, cupping her silken bush, which became suddenly moist. She moaned softly, in a voice he did not recognize.

His eyes snapped open. Who was this? He'd been imagining himself embracing someone else! He pulled away, feeling himself shamed by an act of betrayal, though whether of Nancy or Mrs. Harris he couldn't be sure.

"What is it?"

"You know I care about you."

"But?"

"My life's very complicated right now."

"You involved with some other woman?"

Jack wasn't sure why he hesitated. Of course he wasn't involved, and it was pointless to hurt Nancy's feelings by admitting to something that if it existed at all was only in his own mind. "No."

"You think I'd be a burden to you?"

"That's not what I'm saying. A distraction."

"Maybe just what you need."

"What about what you need?"

"Sweet. What if I told you I'd be getting what I want?"

"I don't see how."

"Take my word for it."

"Nancy, I don't want to take advantage of you."

"Why should you be different than every other guy? Never mind. Forget I said that. Look. If I'm willing to settle for whatever you've got to give, why deny me? I haven't been with a guy since we met, and for a year before that, what with every bachelor in this town either gay, or bi, or some stud out for number one. . . . Let me confess something—when I thought about what I was going to say to you, I went out and got an AIDS test."

"That's very reassuring." Jack hoped that the candlelight would hide his sudden color.

"You making fun of me?"

"Not in a million years. I think you're a super chick, Nance. Always have. You're smart, you're pretty—"

"At least you've got your priorities straight."

"I admire the way you lay it all right on the line."

"But."

"I'm not in a position to make a commitment."

"You hear me asking for one?"

"But don't you see . . ."

"What? *What!*"

"A commitment is what I want to make. And I can't even think

[61]

about something like that until I get my house built and get my dad out of that home—"

"You telling me you'll gamble on football but you're not willing to take a chance on things working out for us?"

"I don't take chances unless the odds are in my favor." Jack said. And believed he was telling the truth.

TWELVE

It was still early when Jack got to Los Feliz and backed his truck into an alley beyond the Regent Tower. Settling down in his seat, pulling his Australian bush hat down over his eyes, he shared the greasy donut with Roger, trying not to ask himself why he was here, knowing that whatever answer he'd come up with wouldn't be rational.

He hadn't slept well.

Nancy, eyes glittering with tears, had fed the affectionate Roger leftovers, careful to keep chicken bones from him, then, refusing Jack's offer to help, packed up her basket and headed for her car.

"Keep in touch?"

She'd nodded. Jack, afraid if he said more he might negate any understanding they may have achieved, watched silently, admiring her as, carefully brushed head held high, she got in and drove off without a backward glance.

"Stupid bastard." He berated himself, suffering a feeling of loss. Something of value may have just slipped out of his grasp. And all over an improbable, certainly momentary infatuation. Though he tried to reassure himself that a decision about a future with Nancy was only postponed, not denied, Jack mourned a missed opportunity that might never come his way again.

Later, tossing in his bunk, Jack began worrying about the audit, too. How well had he covered his tracks? Again and again he went over the way he had transferred the interest between accounts. For the life of him he couldn't see any slipups. Still, he felt fevered with anxiety and frustration.

Eventually, Jack fell into a troubled sleep, only to wake with a start, gasping. What was wrong now? Why was he short of breath? Sitting up, he gradually became aware that the sheet was wet. His sexual organ, still throbbing from some imagined sexual encounter, was gradually subsiding.

He'd been dreaming. About whom? The indistinct features of his compliant lover began to take shape.

She'd been swimming toward the horizon, as before. Endlessly swimming, arms churning, toward a continually retreating horizon. He'd caught up to her. As she'd turned, he'd reached for her, embracing air. And she'd turned again, and again he'd reached until, taking pity, she'd allowed her supple body to become enfolded in his eager embrace. The two of them gradually sank beneath the water, slippery legs and arms entwined, belly to belly, crotch to crotch. . . .

Jack's face became hot. Desire and embarrassment fought for supremacy. He'd needed sexual release, that was obvious. But why dream of a married woman instead of the younger Nancy, or the girl with the condom earrings, or any one of the miniskirted, long-legged, hormonally charged, butt-twitching chicklets in his henhouse?

Don't sweat it, the chagrined Jack told himself, getting up to find a towel. Dreams were irrational. Any message they might contain, supposing there was one, would be indirect. He'd dreamt about sex because of general frustration, he thought, toweling his sticky self dry, and dreamt of Mrs. Harris because she was unavailable. And because she was an enigma.

Spreading the towel over the wet spot before slipping back under the covers, Jack, who'd never considered himself an introspective young man, made an effort to understand what was going on with himself. Why did Mrs. Harris trouble him so much?

She was an intriguing woman, no question about that. But something about what she said, he couldn't put his finger on what, seemed out of sync, like a recording played at the wrong speed, or a photographic image printed off center. He felt compelled to find out more. He couldn't stand leaving any kind of riddle unsolved.

Unaware that he was justifying a decision already made, Jack relaxed enough to fall asleep again, this time deeper than before. Later, during the night, he dreamed of swimming after his mother. But when, at first light, Roger's cold nose awakened him, he remembered only the first dream.

Still somewhat groggy, Jack hosed himself down, using water from a neighbor's hillside sprinkler line he'd tapped into to irrigate trees he'd planted alongside his lot's boundaries, then put on his Gap sweats and Nike Air Max running shoes.

Roger made short work of the dried kibble, and seemed eager to get started on their morning run. But the sound of increasing traffic from the city below made Jack anxious.

Whistling Roger back inside the truck, Jack pulled his visor down against the morning sun and discovered a twenty-dollar bill, folded into a heart, pinned behind it.

"Bless you, Nancy," Jack thought, pushing away the guilty twinge over not having dreamed about her, and headed down the twisting road to the gas station at the canyon's mouth.

A tanker was blocking two of the islands, forcing him to circle and park near the oil-change bay. He hailed the Hispanic attendant.

"Fix my tire?"

"Chure. All it need *es aire.*"

"Air?"

"What I said, *aire.*"

"No nail or glass?"

"*Aire.* Somebody play joke on you."

"Probably a slow leak." The annoyed Jack slid the panel door open. "Put it inside while I get some breakfast."

At the food counter manned by a sorrowful-looking Cambodian, Jack bought two glazed donuts and a large coffee for himself and a plain donut for Roger, who swallowed it in one gulp. As he started to leave he heard a yell: two teenaged boys with ripped jeans grabbed handfuls of candy and gum, shouldered him aside, and sprinted away from the station.

The Cambodian came halfheartedly around the counter and chased them a short way, then stopped, shaking his fist. Customers and attendants looked on impassively.

"Look at it this way," Jack commiserated, "they eat all that themselves, their teeth will rot and they'll get diabetes."

The Cambodian glared at him and went inside.

Jack was about to drive away when the attendant leaned in his window.

"Five dollars."

"For *aire?*"

"For diagnosis."

"You a doctor?"

"Tire doctor."

Jack grudgingly smiled and handed over the five, in too much of a hurry to waste time arguing.

Now here he was, staking out his boss's castle. What did he expect to accomplish? Didn't he know when he was well out of it? Why couldn't he admit to himself that this fascination with Mrs. Harris was adolescent, obsessive, and irrational? He'd possessed her once, sexually, carnally, in his dream; be smart, he commanded himself, let that be an end to it.

Jack was about to leave when Harris drove out in the sinfully black, new Cadillac Coupe De Ville with Arizona license plates. Harris drove dangerously fast. He was that kind of man, Jack thought, enviously, unafraid of pushing past his limits, whether of speed or capability.

Jack wiped his fingers on Roger's fur and swallowed the dregs of his bitter coffee, wondering whether losing his taste for sugar was a sign of maturity. His radio was tuned to KLSX, hard rock from the early seventies, but suddenly the pulse-pounding, amplified, steel-shrill beat of Led Zeppelin had lost its power to move him.

I'm out of here! Jack told himself, and actually had his hand on the ignition key when he saw her striding out under the canopy. She wore a yellow tank top and jogging shorts, with the very latest in Nike running shoes on her swift-moving feet. Jack's heart leapt, and all good resolutions fled his mind.

"Sorry, Rog," Jack said, locking the dog inside. "But I can't have you slowing me down."

He kept pace with her on the opposite side of the street, staying as light on his feet as he could to avoid any slap of his shoes that might echo across to her ears. He was impressed that she'd broken into a full-fledged run. He couldn't help wondering, however, at the slight awkwardness in her gait. She ran far up on her toes. Endearing as it was, if she persisted that meant she'd be enduring shinsplints or muscle cramps.

He was lengthening his own stride to keep up when he realized with a shock that she was crossing the street. And heading in his direction! Before he could wheel about, she'd sprinted hard and gotten in front of him.

"You — didn't — believe — me!" Her chest was heaving, sucking in air and spitting the words at him. "You — were — stringing — me — along! You're — planning — to — turn — me — in!"

"No!" Jack was aghast at this terrible misunderstanding. Fighting for breath himself, he stood tongue-tied, unable to think of any explanation that wouldn't make it seem worse.

"Come — with — me!" She grabbed his arm and yanked him down the street, back toward her condominium.

What was she planning to do? Jack asked himself, horrified. He pulled his arm out of her grasp. She wouldn't think of calling the bank, surely, to verify his standing? Or the police, to complain of harrassment?

"Look," he began, but the look of contempt that came over her face silenced him.

"What're you afraid of?"

Unable to answer, Jack followed her without another word.

She took him in through the garage entrance. He had difficulty keeping pace down the corridor. Inside the condominium, still cluttered with unopened moving-company storage boxes, he waited while she went into the bedroom, returning almost immediately with a large manila envelope that she thrust into his hand. As he opened the envelope, she parted the window blinds and stared at the smog-enshrouded hills. He pulled out a sheaf of five-by-seven glossy black-and-white photos.

He felt the blood drain from his face and his sinuses constrict. They were the kind of pictures he'd never gotten used to, no matter how many men's magazines published them as a matter of course.

She wore a variety of hip-length teddies, and her hair then was long and brown, rich as polished cordovan. She'd taken the obligatory poses to an extreme — standing in a bedroom doorway she caressed her large-nippled breast with one hand, while with the other stroked the provocative crease underneath her buttocks; with a raised leg turned toward the camera, and the hip-length material falling away from the inside of her muscular thigh, her careless hand barely hid the promise of fleshly delights; "Gateway To Paradise" had been hand-printed on a glossy showing her kneeling on a wrought-iron chair, pouting back over her bare shoulder to the camera, the arch of her lovely spine carrying his thunderstruck eye, exactly as the art appreciation tapes had explained good composition would, over her rounded thighs and around to the magical gates that would part with the properly invoked "open sesame"; seated in an old-fashioned kitchen chair with one leg over the handcrafted wooden arm she revealed a pubic growth luxuriant as any tropical garden from within which her vagina, swollen as a split mango, peeped ripely into view — and in each and all of these poses he found himself, fevered and pale simultaneously, ashamed and prurient, drawn again and again to her eyes, which seemed to glisten with a carnality all the more monstrous for being innocent.

Then she added two photos to the pile. In the first, taken from the side, she was straddling a Great Dane, leaning forward along the dog's back; in the second she was lying supine, the Great Dane straddling her. The dog's penis was erect.

Looking up from the photographs, Jack felt giddy. With light from the partially opened window blinds pouring into the room she seemed to swell and shrink into and out of focus. The floor, like the deck of a boat, slanted first one way and then another. Out of the corner of his eye he glimpsed a white-painted wrought-iron chair. As casually as he was able, he put a trembling hand on it to steady himself.

"Cat got your tongue?"

"I feel"—Jack was short of breath—"privileged to have seen these." What he felt like was a Peeping Tom. Or a man who thought he'd witnessed the unspeakable.

"You're embarrassed."

"It's not why you think."

"Oh?"

Desperately, he cast about for a reason. "I'm traveling under false colors."

"I don't understand what you mean."

"I'm not with MetroBank Security." Almost immediately Jack felt better. "You didn't have to show me these—I had no business looking at them. I'm sorry. I don't know what else to say."

She looked at him thoughtfully, then held out her hand. He handed the photographs back, careful not to touch her, afraid she would notice that his skin was hot. She replaced the photographs in the envelope.

"Still think I can show them to Sam?" she asked, as if what he'd told her had made no impact whatsoever.

Disconcerted, Jack cleared his throat, grateful that something, her sense of courtesy, or an innate kindness, prevented her from chastising him. "It happened before you were married, didn't it? He loves you enough, he'll get over it."

"I still haven't told you everything."

Jack waited, in some despair.

"You thirsty?" she suddenly asked, heading for the kitchen. "People who fry their breakfasts use too much salt."

"A Coke would go down okay."

"Just water or beer," she called, apparently looking in the fridge.

"Whatever you're having."

She returned with two opened bottles of Heineken. Half-mockingly, she saluted him and drank. "Here's to Dutch courage."

He followed her to a plastic-covered couch, where he sat in an easy chair, also covered, opposite her.

"The guy who took the pictures . . . there was no way I could pose like he wanted without getting smashed. It turned out he had a lot of hidden talents—he was able to style my hair, kept pouring me wine, oiled my nipples until they stood out hard and straight as nails—I got turned on in spite of myself. But when he came on to me I told him I was saving myself for my husband. He said that was sweet. When I woke up the next morning I was in Nevada, married."

Jack found himself holding the chilled bottle against his aching temple. Hastily, he pulled it down to his lap. Had she noticed? That

Mona Lisa–like smile bordered on a kind of affectionate contempt, but whether for him or herself he had no idea.

"He took advantage of you."

"I blame myself. But I wouldn't let him touch me again. And I wouldn't sign the release. He swore he'd get even. And he can. I'm still married to him."

Jack wanted a swallow of beer, but was afraid his hand would shake. "Can't you have the marriage annulled?"

"I was so ashamed. I didn't want to admit to anyone that it had even happened. Then as time went by and I never heard word one from that sleazy sucker I began to hope — convince myself — that he might be dead. By the time I met Sam I thought of myself as a widow. Not that I introduced myself to Sam that way. Sam's dream was to marry a virgin."

So much for his assumption, Jack thought, that Mr. Samuel J period Harris was a man of the world. "You have to tell him now."

"And get thrown out on my ear?" She studied Jack. "You don't get it, do you? I don't give a damn about Sam. I've wanted to leave him for the longest time. But I waited too long. Now if he finds out my marriage to him doesn't count I'd be lucky to get away from him with the clothes on my back. I'd be back to square one — no money, no way to earn any. Only this time it'll be worse. I'm on the far side of thirty. All I have to show for it are some lousy memories and a bunch of near pornographic pictures . . . who'd want me now?"

His throat was so dry he barely got the word out. "Me."

She looked at him, eyes preternaturally bright. "Pictures turn you on?"

"You do. From the first time I saw you."

She stood. "Don't think I'm not appreciative. But I'm in quicksand — you don't want to go down with me."

Jack carefully put the bottle down in a crystal ashtray on a wood-inlaid end table. Pushing to his feet, he found himself standing close to her. A lavender fragrance, probably from her morning bath, filled his nostrils. "I'll help you get out of this."

"Don't talk nonsense. You don't have any money."

"I'll think of a way to get some."

Somehow, though neither of them had seemed to move, there was no more space between them. She was looking directly into his eyes. "I guess I'm as big a sap as you are. I want to believe you."

"Believe me."

"Promise?"

"Cross my heart."

Her mouth was more active than Jack would have believed possible. Her breath was sweet with malt. He was shy at first, assuming that she was offering her lips as nothing more than an affectionate thanks for his unthinkingly spontaneous, crazed offer of help. But when he felt her fingers pull at his neck hair and her darting tongue part his lips, it was as if he'd been plugged into a high-voltage socket.

Of a sudden he had difficulty breathing. He could feel her muscular breasts flatten against his chest. Somehow she had taken a step forward where there was none and locked her pelvis against his.

Either they were swaying or the room was; it was as if they were engaged in a kind of dance where only the muscles of the torso could be used. When her knee slid between his legs, he grew so excited he became suddenly afraid that his heart was about to explode.

Her mouth took the last of his breath. Then her wet lips slid off his and nibbled at his ear. What was she saying?

Words of lust sang in his imagination. Somehow his hand was at her breast. Her burning hand covered his; she guided his fingers to her zipper and tugged it down.

Her flesh was hot. He bent to the visible pulse in her neck. She took a deep breath; his mouth was suddenly over her breast. His teeth locked on her rigid nipple.

She moaned and backed a step, pulling him with her, her hand at the back of his head to keep him steady. Backing another step they were at the couch. He heard the plastic crackle as she languished backward, carrying him down on her.

In some remote part of himself, on behalf of the cautionary nuns, and the AIDS epidemic, and the botched job he'd made with Nancy, not to mention their understanding, Jack tried to call a halt. But his skull was expanding as if he were on the downhill grade of a runaway carnival ride. His eyes and his privates bulged. He couldn't stop even if he wanted, which he didn't, not with all of his senses roaring into overload, not with this sexy, forceful woman pulling frantically at his clothes. Putting both hands under her hips he yanked her jogging shorts down. As he'd imagined, she wore nothing underneath.

"All you're going to do is look?"

He sighed.

"Darling. Yes!"

He was plunged into a warm, undulant sea. Why did he feel at once triumphant, and lost?

But what did it matter? Jack asked himself, and concentrated on the matter at hand.

THIRTEEN

The phone rang, bringing a euphoric Jack bolt upright with fear. Had that passionate, once-in-a-lifetime, rocket-to-the-moon interlude been part of a dream? No, he'd dozed off happily enough, then imagined himself drifting toward a giant waterfall that plunged hundreds of feet to boulder-strewn rapids below. . . . He awoke with a pounding heart, just in time, only to discover that his newfound lover had left him naked and alone.

Where was she? He finally located the sound of rushing water as coming from the bathroom. It stopped, pipes in the building gasping with the throttled pressure, as if struggling against an early demise.

The ringing phone was abruptly picked up. Hearing her husky voice answering in some agitation from the bedroom, he yanked on his shorts and tiptoed to the door.

"Yes? . . . Well, I didn't hear it, Sam, I was in the shower. . . . Of course they have showers at the gym, but if you don't mind, I prefer my own. . . . Well I didn't expect you to call at the exact minute— it's only a quarter of and the movers aren't due until noon. . . . Of course I can get dressed in fifteen minutes, you don't seriously think I'd parade around half-nude in front of some working stiffs. . . . Of course I can handle it—you worry too much, Sam, it'll be the death of you!"

Jack stood in the doorway. Wet tracks on the creamy pile carpet led from the bathroom to the phone by the pink-canopied bed. Droplets of water still clung to her skin, hair piled atop her head, a velour towel wrapped around the lithe figure that had so recently given him such unexpected, previously unimaginable pleasure.

As she banged the phone down she saw him. Her face changed so quickly from something unidentifiably frightening to a cautious look that he was immediately on guard himself.

"He's very jealous."

"Yes."

"Suspicious of everything I do."

"It's not going to be easy getting away from him."

"No."

"I don't know your name."

"Jennifer."

"That's what your friends call you?"

"Jenny."

"You won't mind if I call you that?"

"It doesn't really matter. That was hello—and good-bye."

Jack couldn't believe he'd heard correctly. Was this the woman who only moments before had been encouraging him in ways that made him blush to remember?

The phone rang again. She picked it up, half turning away, as if hoping to regain the privacy he had somehow violated.

"Yes? . . . They're early. Give me five minutes, then send them up." Cradling the phone, she looked at Jack as if not quite sure who he was or what he was doing there. "You'd better get dressed. And stay out of sight until the movers are gone. Then I'll drive you back to your truck."

Jack, bewildered and upset, burned to ask what had gone wrong. He had a feeling he ought to apologize, though he couldn't imagine for what. Somewhat sullenly, he went back into the living room and started putting on his shirt and pants. As he reached for his socks a doorbell rang.

"Minute!" she called, and came out dressed in worn Levis, scuffed cowboy boots, and a faded blue turtleneck that had probably once matched her eyes. Putting a cautionary finger to her lips, she continued on into the kitchen.

Tiptoeing after, Jack hovered near the kitchen doorway. He heard a screen door opening. "Mrs. Harris? Phoenix Movers. Where you want it?"

"Here would be fine. But make sure there's a plug."

"One under the sink."

"The cord reach?"

"Should."

There was grunting, a shuffling of feet, and a thud.

"Is it running?" she asked after a moment's silence.

"Pretty sure it is, ma'am. Probably the thermostat's got her shut down. We had her plugged in all the way on the truck, like the shipping order stated."

"Good. Thank you. For your trouble."

"Thank you, ma'am."

The door opened, closed again. Jack hastily backpedaled. When she didn't return, he changed direction and went through the kitchen to a small service area, where he found her kneeling with her ear at the motor ventilating grill of a large white horizontal freezer.

"What's in there, caviar? Vintage champagne?"

"Venison. Sam's a great hunter."

Jack thought of his boss's cold eyes. "I believe it."

"This sound like it's running to you?"

Jack put his hand on the panel, felt the motor's vibration. "Sure." He flipped the padlock on the lid. "You're right, he's not very trusting, is he?"

She got to her feet. "You haven't finished getting dressed."

"What's the rush? Now that you've had your way with me, you tossing me aside like a piece of used Kleenex?"

"That supposed to be funny?"

"I was hoping it would be. I don't know how else to . . . why should I make it easy for you to get rid of me?"

"What makes you think it's easy?"

"Then why . . . I thought you and I . . . we . . . had something special going. . . ."

"I thought that too, for a lovely little while. . . ." Her eyes had softened, and for a moment he thought it was going to be all right between them again. Then she started, as if reminded of a distasteful reality. "Look. I let myself believe you could help me out of this jam. Don't think I don't appreciate your wanting to. But there's no way you can get your hands on enough money to let me buy Al off. . . ."

"Why would you be so sure of that?"

"Well, look at what you're driving, for one thing."

"I happen to be the owner of view property."

She stared. "You own it free and clear?"

"Almost. I used it as a down for a construction loan. Since they canceled the loan, I can use it to borrow more. . . ."

"You'd put your property in hock to help me?"

"If I had to," Jack heard himself saying, though his stomach suddenly turned. "But maybe I don't need to," he went on, mentally apologizing to his father for even momentarily breaking faith. There were other options available, he reminded himself. "How much to keep your ex—your other—Al—off your back for a while?"

She gave it thought. "Fifty thousand."

Jack couldn't help himself, he blanched. He immediately recovered, unwilling to show any doubt or hesitation whatsoever. "I might be able to manage that. Though it'd be a stretch. What about trying to stall him with twenty-five?" This wasn't the time, Jack thought, to be tiptoeing back through the data system for too much more.

"You can lay your hands on that much cash without selling your lot?"

"Piece of cake." Hand hidden, Jack had crossed his fingers.

"How?"

"I'd rather not say."

"Do yourself a favor. Walk away while you're still whole."

"Not a chance." Jack walked over and put his arms around her. *"Now that I've found you I'll never let you go. . . ."*

"Don't be a sap," she began, until, still singing, he closed her mouth with his. She responded for a moment with the same almost desperate intensity she had demonstrated before. Then just as suddenly, she pushed him away. "Not here. Not now. Sam might decide to check on whether his freezer's running okay."

"Or whether is wife is?"

"That too."

"Sorry. I haven't earned the right to be jealous, have I?"

She must have seen the hurt in his face. "It's been difficult to refuse him. I want to. I would. But Al being around complicates matters, doesn't it? If I turn Sam off he'll want to know why."

"Must be awful for you."

"Don't take it so hard — you don't really have any stake in this."

"Don't I?"

"I'm too old for you."

"For me to say, isn't it?"

"Oh, Christ, Jackie, don't I have enough problems without you tempting me with impossible dreams?"

A thrill went through him. "Okay, Jenny," he said, but his heart sang. "Let's just take it a step at a time."

Neither of them spoke on the elevator going down, or for a long while on the slower drive back to his truck. Once out of sight of the Regent Tower he rose from his cramped hiding place on the floorboard under the dash, and switched her car radio on, looking to see if she minded. But she was concentrated on driving, lost in her own melancholy. The buttons were not set properly, no doubt programmed for Phoenix, and he began readjusting them to bring in local stations.

"I'm giving you one all-news and a talk radio and the rest music," he said, punching in the buttons. "And KLSX, which is hard rock. . . ."

"K-what?"

"LSX." He was disconcerted when she laughed. "Oh, yeah, I'm a little slow on the upta—"

"I like show tunes and jazz."

"You ever a dancer?"

"Why would you think that?"

"The way you move. It was meant as a compliment."

"Where I grew up dancers double in brass."

"Come again?"

"You *are* young."

"Oh." He turned up the volume to cover his fury.

At the parking lot she pulled up next to his truck, keeping the motor running. "Looks like your dog really missed you."

"Damn. I forgot to bring him a snack. A piece of that venison would've been just the ticket." She did not respond. "When will I see you again?"

"You won't get while the getting's good?"

"No." Why this time did her manner chill him? "When?"

"Al has first priority."

They looked at each other.

"Oh, yes, Al." He leaned toward her and she met him halfway. But her kiss was chaste enough to please Sister Theresa.

"I'll see how much I can come up with," he said, hoping to cheer her up as he got out.

"If I can keep Al out of the picture long enough, I can get my divorce without losing everything and pay you back, double."

"I'm not worried about it."

"You will remember I warned you?" Blowing him a kiss, she burned rubber driving away.

Shaken and confused, Jack let Roger out of the car, then sat on the divider rail, waiting for the dog to choose a tree.

He wanted with all his heart to help her. Not only was he enraptured, smitten, infatuated, and bewitched, but her plight had aroused feelings of chivalry and compassion he hadn't even known he possessed.

At the same time, in that part of himself shaped by the absence of women during his formative years, Jack couldn't help wondering, in a combination of anticipation and fear, about what he might have let himself in for.

FOURTEEN

The Silverlake Reservoir glistened like burnished metal in the midafternoon sun. Impatient, but curious, Jack glanced from side to side as he traveled east on this hilly section of Sunset Boulevard, passing antique stores, Cuban *bodegas*, taco stands, cabinet makers, Thai restaurants, ironworks, plumbing supplies, an occasional bar, Catholic thrift shops — and not a MetroBank branch anywhere to be seen. Was bank management so upscale, arrogant, socially isolated, and ignorant they were unaware of the commercial possibilities of this burgeoning immigrant community?

When Jack spotted Rampart Avenue he impetuously took a hard right, remembering that the best chili-dog stand in town was only a few blocks away. Whether that hollow in his gut was hunger or anxiety it was crying to be filled.

And there across the street from *Tommy's*, a hut and two satellite kitchens on a parking lot at Beverly Boulevard rapidly dispensing hot dogs, hamburgers, and chili to long lines of customers, sat a newly installed MetroBank branch, complete with fake Colonial after-the-ancient-Greek columns. The architecture was an attempt to borrow integrity from the past, forgetting, Jack thought, that it was transitory and subject to decay.

Jack fingered the bills in his pocket. He had barely more than a hundred dollars left. He'd need more to last him before he could prowl the bank's system again. He'd withdraw money from his personal account. Now? His mouth watered at the smell of pickled peppers and frying onions. A desire to fortify himself before he began a process that was going to be arduous and painful made his decision for him.

Swinging into the tree-shaded lot across the street, Jack parked next to several low-riding, aluminum-shocked, glistening black-as-wet-tar Chevy's with racing stripes. The cars were surrounded by mahogany-skinned young men dressed tip to narrow snakeskin toe in black except for the scarves, blood red, wrapped Apache-style around foreheads. Hanging on muscular arms were young women wearing the flared skirts, spike heels, and sultry looks of flamenco dancers.

"Don't worry about the dog." Jack smiled pleasantly, careful not to look at the women, and making a point of not locking his doors. "He's harmless. But I have to keep him inside until we find out whether the thief he attacked comes down with rabies or not."

"Man, you got that backward, ain't chu?" came the delayed response.

"Yes, well, the cops didn't seem to know that. Cops they get these days aren't exactly deep thinkers."

A few chuckles and a giggle followed Jack. Tommy's, Jack knew, had been tacitly accepted by the gangs as a neutral zone. The large-framed black security guards helped, of course, as did the fact that city cops and county sheriffs and state highway patrolmen off the nearby freeway ate there. But no one wanted to ruin a place where the food was so good and so cheap. A fight over turf had erupted once, people had been hurt, but so far as Jack knew the incident had never been repeated.

He stood in a long but fast-moving line with cement-powdered masons, sawdusted carpenters, swollen-necked white-collar executives, string-haired students wearing USC T-shirts, weather-beaten gardeners, and hollow-eyed, runny-nosed young lads, black and brown, who were probably drug dealers, judging by the gold chains and bracelets, just gotten up for their first meal of the day. In the midst of this crowd, Jack suddenly felt incredibly lonely, heart and head full of longing for the arms of his newly beloved.

The intensely passionate interlude seemed so far past he had difficulty believing it had actually happened. But he'd been irrevocably changed. That clumsy youth burning for but afraid of sex had been initiated into mysteries of pleasure so breathtaking he had to believe he'd become one of an extraordinarily privileged few. He was now a man who knew — apparently — how to please a woman, if Jennifer Harris's mewling and manicured nails in his buttocks were any indication.

What was she doing now? Thinking of him? Realistically, given her state of mind when they'd parted, she was not likely to be dwelling on his prowess as a lover, but would rightly be worrying over whether he could actually help keep the criminally minded Al from ruining her life.

What had possessed him to promise what might be difficult, if not impossible, to deliver? Pride? Arrogance? Trying to give himself a stature he didn't yet possess? That was one aspect of himself that hadn't changed, he thought morosely. He still wasn't mature enough to keep from mouthing off. His tongue continued to move faster than his mind, ambition outstripping reality.

Behind him Jack became aware that the two men in Raiders satin jackets were arguing. Why did the Raiders' owner keep insisting on going long with a missile-armed quarterback when the 49ers had proved that a mortar-ranged but scope-rifle-accurate quarterback riddled secondaries for one touchdown march after another?

What day was this? Jack suddenly wondered. Thursday? There was a TV game tonight. Raiders versus 49ers. It was an omen. He'd check the odds. If the computer found it made any sense at all, he could triple his money. Enough to keep Al quiet at least long enough for them to devise a way to neutralize him.

"Watchu want?"

He was at the counter. A Mexican with a bandit's mustache was staring. "Two chili dogs, two hamburgers, everything on them—and two root beers." Jack put down a twenty, receiving nine dollars in change. He went to the cold case, removed the root beer, scooped up some pickled hot peppers from the huge jar at the counter's end, and bit into one. His taste buds jolted awake.

Hoping that jalapenos were indeed aphrodisiacs, Jack, eyes watering, picked up his order in a cardboard food container and hastened back across the street.

As he jogged to the curb he spotted a police black-and-white out of the corner of his eye. The cop riding shotgun, smaller than Jack, got out. Jack grimaced to himself. He believed that small men who became cops had something to prove.

"Your identification, sir?"

"Why do I need identification?"

"You have crossed this street illegally."

"Gosh, officer, I guess I just wasn't thinking—it's way past my dog's feeding time and I wanted to give him his food while it's still hot."

The Chicanos next to his truck were watching, stone-faced as Aztec sculptures.

The cop didn't blink. "Your identification, please."

Jack sighed. Putting the container down, he found his wallet. Sliding his license out of its plastic shield he handed it to the cop. The cop glanced at it, then handed it back.

"Next time, Mr. Noble, use the crosswalk."

"I will, sir. You can count on it. Thank you." He picked the container up.

"Your dog eats chili?"

"Loves it."

Jack went to his truck, avoiding the Chicanos. Letting the panting Roger out, he unwrapped Roger's share of the food and put it on the ground, then sat on the low concrete wall to eat his own. The cops remained parked, watching as Roger gulped the sandwich.

"Better not litter, man," a Chicano said. "Cops, they got a feeling about you."

"They don't have to be deep thinkers to know when they're dealing with a smart-ass," a female chimed in.

The others laughed.

Jack poured root beer on Roger's seeking-air tongue. The dog slobbered it down, and stood, tail wagging, begging for more. The cops, shaking their heads, crossed several lanes against traffic into Tommy's main lot.

"You're right, I am a smart-ass. I've got to learn to keep my mouth shut. But they didn't give me a ticket," Jack couldn't resist pointing out.

"Man, they just putting on a show for us. Pretending they willing to hassle Anglos too." The Chicano spat to show his contempt.

Jack was disturbed by this. He'd noticed over the years an increasing disrespect for the law in Angel City. It was difficult making do without certain rules, observed by everyone, in place.

What bothered him now, however, was the feeling that things might be getting out of hand. Maybe this was a sign that he wasn't thinking all that clearly. It was one thing to borrow an insignificant amount, knowing he could put it back before it was missed. But pulling out a substantial sum more for Jenny also made the situation substantially more hazardous.

Fighting back a sudden urge to make a rash statement of independence as a cover for his urge to flee not only the Chicanos but Jenny as well, Jack was extra careful about putting every bit of his trash into the litter barrel. The Chicanos were amused.

Following Roger into the truck, the increasingly irritated Jack started the truck's backfiring motor. The Chicanos laughed again. Jack hesitated a moment, then, clenching his jaw, ground into reverse, the panel truck's shakiest gear, and backed up. Again, the Chicanos erupted with laughter, which Jack managed to ignore.

No sooner had he complimented himself for this first halting step into mature behavior than he found himself suddenly making the sign of the horns, index and little fingers outthrust, at the watching Chicanos. Before they could react to this profoundest of insults, he had floored his accelerator, gambling that the carburetors wouldn't flood, and roared out of the lot, bald tires squealing. In a moment he was around the corner and out of their sight.

Why had he done that? Jack asked himself, dismayed, braking and skidding into an alley that led into the rear of the bank's parking lot. What compelled him to put himself in jeopardy? Weren't there easier ways to produce an adrenaline rush?

Hiding his truck between two vehicles at the rear of the lot, Jack, still shaky, but beginning to see the humor in what he'd done, started to get out, then noticed that Roger was confused, not sure whether to follow or return to his fitful dreams. Though time was growing short, Jack took the moments necessary to put the dog at ease.

There was a Versateller machine at the street side of the building. Hastening to it, Jack punched in his account number code, followed by a withdrawal amount of three hundred dollars, the maximum allowed in a single transaction. Impatiently, Jack waited for the machine to acknowledge.

The machine remained quiet. What was taking so long? Jack was about to press the button for clear, so that he might begin again, when a message flashed on the screen.

A Hold Has Been Placed On Your Account.

Impossible. Annoyed, Jack pressed the button for clear. He must have punched in the code incorrectly. More carefully this time, he punched in his account number, then the withdrawal request: $300 w/d.

A Hold Has Been Placed On Your Account.

Jack felt a surge of anxiety. It wasn't possible for the auditors to have stumbled onto the switching of interest payments certainly not this fast. Calm down, he told himself. He was panicking over nothing.

It had to be a computer glitch. His account had been tied up through pure chance. Unfortunately chance, he reminded himself, was a factor that could screw up anyone's plans, no matter how carefully drawn.

Trying to regain his composure, Jack hurried inside the bank. He was struck as always by the needless amount of marble and an unnecessarily luxurious carpet. No wonder so many banks were going broke.

At Customer Services, a lacquer-coiffed, coffee-skinned young woman was laboriously typing new account cards. Her dangling earrings were in the shape of dollar signs.

A nameplate was upside down on her desk. As she continued to type, Jack turned the nameplate over. "Ms. Cervantes?"

The young woman continued to type. Jack walked around to the side she was facing and leaned over her typewriter, keeping his eyes from the cleavage in her low-cut brown silk dress. Even at the abysmally low pay, MetroBank employees seemed compelled to overspend on clothes, in keeping with the bank's decor. "Ms. Cervantes?"

She looked at him with the eyes of a startled deer. "I'm not Cervantes."

Jack showed her the nameplate. She took it from him.

"She's no longer with us."

"But you're sitting at her desk."

"Did you need Customer Services?"

Jack sighed. "There's a glitch in my account. I'd like you to check it for me." He handed her his passbook.

She looked at it as if she'd never seen one before, then finally stood up and started away.

"Where are you going?"

"To check your account with the computer."

"I should have explained—the problem's *in* the computer. Call downtown and find out why they've put a hold on my account."

"There's a hold on your account?"

Jack took in another silent, frustrated breath. It wasn't her fault. Banks, like most large public institutions, did it backward, hiring unskilled, unknowledgeable, low-pay people for jobs that called for precisely those skills they didn't have. "Look. I work for MetroBank. I'd make the call, but . . ."

"I'll get the manager."

Jack swallowed air, which came back up on him, tasting of onions and chili. He slouched in a leather chair while the young woman went into a glass-enclosed but curtained office. A few minutes passed. She returned with a portly woman in a pink silk suit that strained at its buttons.

"I'm Mrs. Alomayor, the manager. What seems to be the problem?"

"Hi. I'm Jack Noble. I supervise data processing downtown. It's about my personal account. There's been a hold placed on it, and I'm sure it's a computer glitch—could you check that out for me?"

"You're Mr . . . ?"

"Jack B. Noble. It's in the passbook."

"Minute." Mrs. Alomayor walked as if her feet hurt to the computers on a bench behind the working tellers.

Jack, following, watched her punch his passbook numbers into the computer. She watched the screen, then turned to him.

"There's a hold on your account."

Jack held his temper. It wasn't her fault. Bank employees weren't trained to think for themselves, just the opposite. He'd counted on precisely this lack of imagination to hide his account manipulation.

"I know there's a hold on my account. I told you that. It's probably a computer glitch. A foul-up. A mistake. Could you check with the downtown branch and have them release my funds? Please."

Looking doubtful, Mrs. Alomayor picked up a phone and punched a single button. It was the intercom for downtown, Jack knew. If he could have reached the phone without creating a disturbance, he would have done that himself and saved all this hassle.

He couldn't hear what Mrs. Alomayor was saying. She was practically whispering, keeping her back to him so that he couldn't even try to read her lips. Now she was listening, and then whispering again, and then waiting.

"Thank you." Mrs. Alomayor turned to Jack, triumphant. "I didn't think our computers would make a mistake. There's a lien on your account."

"A lien?"

"A Mr. Ahmed Hassan has placed a lien on your account."

Hassan, Jack thought, that money-grubbing SOB. Just because Jack had stayed a few days beyond his eviction notice date, his ex-landlord was putting a demand in for the extra rent. Plus the lousy cleaning fee, no doubt. And this after he'd worked his tail off scraping every accumulated bit of grit off the stove, scrubbing the walls and floors, and dusting every cranny and nook with environmentally safe boric acid to reduce the cockroach population.

Mrs. Alomayor and Ms. Not-Cervantes were watching him. Shamed to the core, reminded of just how desperate his money situation had become, Jack somehow managed a smile. He hastened out of the bank before the blood rising in his neck reached his face.

His embarrassment, however, hadn't prevented him from pocketing several blank new account signature cards on the way out.

FIFTEEN

Fifteen minutes before happy hour, the Sports Cafe was starting to fill with young white-collar workers — salesmen, bookkeepers, office clerks, purchasing agents — who had managed to slip away from work early. Jack, with Roger lumbering behind his hurrying heels, spotted Harry at the bar expounding to what looked like a matched pair of well-tailored females. Hoping that neither he nor his computer had been noticed, Jack ducked into the corridor under the sign that read EMPLOYEES ONLY.

Claire, coming out of the employees' lounge, grabbed his arm. "Where d'you think you're going, lover boy?"

"Claire, am I glad to see you. I'm in desperate need of a private phone."

"You know how Carl feels about that."

"Carl's busy."

"No telling when he'll take his break."

"Please, Claire. If I use a pay phone everyone in the place'll know my business."

"What business? I heard you were laid off."

"People get everything twisted. I had time off coming and I took it now to work on my house." But a chill had come over Jack. Who was spreading those kind of rumors?

"Oh, all right — but don't blame me if you get barred from the joint."

"A good customer like me?" Jack gave Claire a peck on the cheek, fought back a cough at her heavy perfume, and went through the door into the lounge.

"Easy on the affection, sonny," Claire called after him. "You may find you have a tiger by the tail."

Jack, closing the door, barely heard. The wall clock showed ten minutes before five. Bank employees would be too busy closing down, he thought, to be aware of any intruder prowling the data system.

He hastened to the manager's cubbyhole, making room on the cluttered desk for his computer, then plugged the phone jack into the computer. To block out call waiting, he punched the # symbol on the desk phone to keep his transmission "pure." An interruption could trigger an alert. This was hardly the time to be careless.

Password? flashed up on his screen after he'd slipped into the system through the back door.

Jack hesitated. How much to borrow? With the auditors monitoring the data bank daily, it would be terminally stupid to take more than was absolutely necessary. Of course, opening an account under another pseudonym, he told himself, using one of the new account cards he'd pocketed earlier, it'd be almost impossible for anyone to trace it back to him.

Diogenes, Jack typed, with renewed courage, then stared, in some shock.

Password Inadmissable, the screen read. Please Enter New Password.

Diogenes Jack typed again, though he knew what the response would be.

Password Inadmissable.

What was going on? he asked himself, trying not to panic. Someone had changed the password. Who? Why? Was this a result of the "new system" Nancy had cryptically referred to? Was this somehow—he flinched from the thought—a reflection on him?

The wall clock showed two minutes until five. Swiftly, Jack unplugged the jack from the computer and hooked in the phone. Grabbing the receiver, he dialed the bank's number.

The bank's recorded voice answered. Jack's heart sank. Was he too late? Jack cut the recorded message short by punching in the number of his own extension.

"Data processing." A male voice he did not recognize.

Jack was disconcerted. "I wanted to speak with Nancy."

"She in data processing?"

"Nancy Buford. The assistant manager."

"Ah. Tell her who's calling?"

"Her brother. Family emergency."

"Minute."

"This is Ms. Buford."

"Nancy. Why didn't you answer my phone?"

"New system."

"Jesus, Mary, and Joseph, no sooner is my back turned . . . Look,

I need an enormous favor." Jack's lips were dry. No use asking why the password didn't work. Obviously Nancy was in no position to talk. "You've got a friend in payroll, haven't you? My ex-landlord's got a hold on my account, and for all I know he's garnisheed my wages too. Get my paycheck for me."

"I can try."

"You've got to do better than try—that money's owed for my dad's retirement home!"

"Steady."

"I was hoping to pay you back too."

"That's not necess—"

"It's important to me!" Jack took a breath. "I want to keep the books between us balanced."

"Where are you now?"

"Sports Cafe."

"I'll see what I can do."

"You're the best, Nancy."

"You just figuring that out?"

Jack hung up, damp at the armpits and brow. Why had it been so difficult to ask a favor, especially at a time like this? They were friends. He'd been careful not to make any commitments.

But no denying he was embarrassed. He'd had to resist an urge to apologize. There'd been certain expectations on her part. Sooner or later he'd have to tell her he was out of the market, no longer in the marriage pool. But why was he even thinking about that now? he asked himself. He had more important matters to consider.

Not having access to the accounts was something he should have anticipated. Anyone with any sense would have provided himself more than one contingency plan. He swore at himself. Think. There had to be another way.

There was, he thought suddenly, faint hope rising as he stared at his computer. His football system! Though his betting program still needed fine-tuning, surely it ran well enough to bet the farm without fear of going belly-up?

Quickly booting up the betting program, then using data from the sports section he'd brought along, Jack typed in the unable-to-play members of the Raiders and 49ers. Most were second-stringers.

Game outcome? he queried when finished. A moment later, the screen showed: 49ers 31 , Raiders 27.

A four-point spread. Not as much as he'd hoped. The morning line had been seven. It was uncomfortably close.

Examining the sports section again, he found several first-stringers on each team listed as doubtful. With a sigh, Jack typed those names in too.

Again, he made the query. Game Outcome? A moment, and then the screen displayed 49ers 27, Raiders 24. That one additional point, Jack thought, at once apprehensive and elated, could make all the difference. Only the most wildly improbable chance could upset such closely reasoned calculations.

Was it worth the risk? If he won the bet, not only could he help Jenny out of her jam, but his own rapidly mounting financial difficulties would be over. At least temporarily.

Behind him then, Jack heard someone coming into the lounge. Swallowing, trying to convey an air of casualness, he put an inquiring smile on his face and turned.

It was Roger. Claire slid a plate of food in behind the dog. "You forget to feed your best friend? Poor guy's hungry as a bum." She closed the door before he could answer.

"Did I close you out, Roger? Or were you begging in the kitchen?"

The dog was concentrating on his food.

"Make yourself at home. Don't worry about a thing; I'll be finished before you know it."

Roger continued to eat, not even wagging his tail to acknowledge his errant master's voice.

Shrugging, Jack packed up his computer. He had bigger problems than worrying over whether the poor dumb creature had feelings.

Humming to himself in a hopeless attempt at a bravado he did not feel, Jack headed for the door, almost stumbling over Roger. The dog, having licked the platter clean, lay flat as a cat against the door. Using his leg, Jack moved the dog away just far enough to allow him to slip through.

The bar was crowded and loud. A Hispanic in a stained apron was replenishing the hot bean dip and chips and salsa at the steam table. Jack forced a path to the waitress station, where Carl was handing drinks to Claire. Barely acknowledging her conspiratorial wink, Jack waited until she'd gone.

"What's the line on tonight's game, Carl?"

"Forty-niners by four." Carl turned to serve a group of boisterous young men who wore the flashy plaid jackets of home products or car salesmen.

"You sure? It was seven this morning. . . ."

"Forty-niners by four."

Jack took in a breath. His heart was racing. This was barely any cushion whatsoever. If he weren't desperate he wouldn't even consider it.

"What's the deadline for a bet?"

"Five forty-five. Cash only."

"Jack! Be nimble, be quick! Over here." Harry was flushed and noisy.

Jack, waving him off, turned back to the bartender. "I'll take the Raiders and points."

"Shouldn't you be thinking of further diminishing your tab?"

"Take it out of my winnings."

"For how much?"

"My paycheck's seven fifty-six fifty. Make it seven bills."

Pulling a card from under the bar, Carl made a notation. "Where's the mazooma?"

"Nancy's bringing it from work."

"You lose this one I eighty-six you. Understand?"

"You forgetting my pending weekend bet?"

"You'll have to find a new hangout."

Forcing a smile, Jack wiped his clammy hands on a bar towel and walked to where Harry stood flanked by the two females.

"Jack, wanchata meet Wanda and Lorine."

Both women obviously patronized the same beauty shop or read the same magazines: hair in Prince Valiant cuts, eye shadow to match fingernails and lipstick, webbed panty hose of a lurid shade.

"Pleased to meecha." Wanda was smiling, at the same time evaluating him with the eyes of a loan appraiser.

"Likewise." Interested in the cut and price of his clothes, Lorine revealed tiny teeth, with which she was worrying gum.

Jack resisted the urge to take Harry to a solitary spot so he could confide in him. "You buying, Harry?"

"When don't I? Carl, bring the computer whiz a beer."

"Thanks, Harry. How's the wife and kiddies?"

"Don't do this to me. He's kidding, ladies. Tell them you're kidding, Jack."

"Slip of the tongue. What I meant to say is how's the wife and kidneys?"

Wanda and Lorine giggled nervously.

"Don't do that. I'm not married. I swear it. Claire—c'mere, Claire, tell these ladies I'm not married."

Claire, delivering a tray of drinks to a nearby table, looked in their direction. "Do they care?"

Jack laughed before he could stop himself. Claire gave him an appreciative smile. "Don't mind her," he murmured, concerned for the young women's feelings. Worry over his bet was causing him to have exaggerated reactions. "She talks to everyone that way."

"You got five minutes." Carl slid a stein of beer across.

"It's okay." Jack was not sure whether to feel relieved or upset. "It's coming in the door now." He pushed through the crowd toward Nancy. By the waft of her lovely perfume and the freshly applied lipstick, he knew that she'd spent time preparing to greet him. This depressed him more than somewhat. "You get it?"

"Fine thanks. How're you?"

"Don't fuss with me, Nance. I'll remember my manners later. Were you able to get my check?"

Reaching into her shoulder bag, Nancy rummaged about for an unconscionable time, and finally brought out a payroll envelope. "I had to get Harris to call payroll before they'd release it."

Jack was in too much of a hurry to even consider whether this should bother him or not. He opened the envelope on the way to the bar. He took the gold pen out of Harry's vest pocket and endorsed the check, pushing it over to Carl.

"When's later?" Nancy was behind him.

"Bring her the change and a beer, " Jack told Carl.

"I'd prefer a margarita."

Harry was looking at Nancy with undisguised admiration. "I'm Harry, Jack's attorney. But should any dispute arise between you, I'd be happy to switch sides."

Nancy smiled. "Has he asked you to draw up a prenuptial agreement yet?"

"Jack. Why didn't you tell me? You lucky dog . . ."

"Nancy." Picking up her margarita, Jack urged her through the crowd toward an unoccupied table. "Now you've got everybody jumping to conclusions — "

"Good. Keep the bimbettes away."

"I'm not interested in any of these women."

"I would hope not. I've always considered you a person of taste."

She was looking at him with such bright-eyed affection his heart sank. Sooner or later, he'd have to tell her he'd fallen for someone else. Not her fault. Not his either. Those kinds of things were uncontrollable. But this was hardly the time or the place. . . .

"Compliments embarrass you, don't they?"

"What's happening at work?"

"Same as yesterday. The auditors are going at it hammer and tongs."

"The auditors change the access code?"

"Harris. How'd you know?"

"I haf mine vays."

"You tried to access the system!"

"Just checking up. His new password as interesting as mine?"

"I wouldn't know."

"How could you not know?"

"It changes daily. Harris gives it to us when we come to work in the morning."

Jack frowned. That didn't sound like a spur-of-the-moment decision. "You don't suppose he got me out of the way so he could put his own system in?"

"Jack. Don't be paranoid. He has to change the system to plug the leaks, doesn't he?"

"Then why not use the company's number-one programmer to help him?"

Nancy sipped at her margarita. She had no answer for that. And with a sinking heart Jack realized that neither did he.

SIXTEEN

"You bet on this game?"

"Whyever would you think that?"

"You're so *involved*."

"I'm a sports fan." Jack stood up so he could see past the rouged-cheek-by-shadow-jowled crowd at the bar to the giant television screen hanging overhead. "Harry, what happened?"

"Forty-niners threw for another," Harry called from the midst of the applauding, whistling crowd.

"Another what?"

"Touchdown, what else?"

"Block that kick!"

"You did bet on this game."

Claire stopped by their table and pointed to Nancy's empty glass. Nancy shook her head.

Jack, watching the screen, felt his blood surge as the holder took the pass from center and bobbled it. The ball, readjusted, was hurriedly placed down just as the designated rusher from the left side of the Raiders' line launched himself at the kicker.

But the kick cleared the rusher's outstretched hands. The ball split the uprights, and Jack's heart. The score flashed on the screen: 49ers 20, Raiders 10.

"Ready to eat yet?" Claire asked as Jack collapsed back into his chair.

"I filled up on the bean dip."

"What about your friend?"

"Nothing for me either, thanks."

Claire picked up Nancy's glass, wiped the table, and left.

"What's she got against me?"

"Claire? She's just being a mother hen."

"I wouldn't call the way she looks at you motherly."

"Don't be ridiculous."

"I'm getting eyestrain. Let's watch the rest of the game at my place?"

"I don't want to miss the Raiders' comeback."

"What comeback? Looks like a blowout to me."

"That your expert opinion, is it?"

"Doesn't take an expert to see when one team's vastly superior to another."

"For your information, it only takes one injury to a key player to tip the scales in the other direction."

"That what you're doing? Praying for one of the players to get hurt?"

"Nothing serious. A sprained ankle. Hamstring pull. Concussion."

Another cheer from the crowd. Interception of a Raiders' pass. The 49ers' quarterback came trotting onto the field as if he had all the time in the world, pulling a helmet on over his golden locks, an overly handsome messenger of doom.

"Look at him," Jack muttered, hating him. "His uniform hasn't got a spot on it. Dee-fense! Dee-fense!"

"How much did you bet?"

"It's not over yet."

"How can you afford to bet anything?"

"Who appointed you my guardian?"

"I'm on your side, remember? You do remember?"

"What do you want from me, a testimonial?" As Nancy stood, gathering up her purse and scarf, Jack managed to tear his eyes from the screen. "Don't go 'way mad."

"I was hoping I wouldn't have to go away at all."

Jack wanted to reach out to her, apologize for his lousy attitude, somehow wipe that stricken look from her face. But he couldn't. That would be worse, once more leading her on, making it twice as difficult to tell her about Jenny when he did find a proper moment.

"You going to say something?"

"I don't think so. No. It's hard to concentrate when I'm having so much fun." Jack watched her go, not understanding why he should feel pangs of conscience when he was actually doing the girl a favor.

"She hurt your feelings, lover boy?" Claire was placing a beer before him.

"More like the other way around."

"Don't let it bother you. Plenty more where she came from."

"Claire. You being sarcastic?"

"How'd you guess."

"I don't remember ordering a beer."

"On the house."

Claire left, and Jack managed to put out of his mind all thoughts of how much he had hurt Nancy as he went back to watching the game. Both teams seemed suddenly unable to make first downs. His bladder was swollen. But he was irrationally afraid that the tide could never turn without him watching.

Raiders' ball. Fourth and inches to a first down at the 49er thirty-five. This was it. The moment he'd been waiting for. A touchdown and point after would make it a tie game, and he'd beat the four-point spread!

He couldn't believe what he was seeing. What were those Raiders' coaches in the polyester stretch pants doing? It wasn't possible. No one could be fool enough to wave in the field goal unit!

"You stupid clods!" Jack was on his feet. "Go for it. Your kicker doesn't have the leg to make that distance, fuck-wits!"

"Easy, kid. It ain't over till it's over." Harry and the two females had appeared at his table.

Jack groaned. The kick was not only short, but a monster lineman had deflected the ball, and now it was up for grabs amongst colliding behemoths. "Cover it!" he yelled, as a Raiders' lineman fell on the ball, only to have it squirt out from under his whalelike belly and into the hands of a 49er back, who danced it out of bounds.

Again, the golden-locked millionaire, without a worry to his name, trotted onto the field.

"These charming young ladies and I thought we might find a club and go dancing. Join us?"

"What you see up on that screen just deep-sixed me."

"I'll sponsor you." It was — what was her name? — Lorine. Probably a compassionate soul, intelligent and an achiever, not the bar hanger-on he'd categorized her. But he had neither inclination nor time to make a new acquaintance individual.

"I don't know when I've been more offended." Jack shook off Harry's hand. Picking up his computer, he was well on his way out before the pain in his bladder made him realize that not only had he forgotten to pee, but he'd forgotten his dog as well.

Now that the game was out of reach it seemed everyone had decided to relieve themselves. Jack stood impatiently in line in the men's, dancing from foot to foot, trying to ignore the sidelong glances his computer was drawing.

"You taking urine samples? Selling risk-free condoms?"

Jack didn't bother to look around as he reached the blessed urinal. With his computer under one arm, he was able to use both hands to unzip, then, groaning with relief, bracing his free arm against the graffiti-covered wall, he waited patiently for his bladder to empty. Everything in the strike zone below his belt burned, hurt, or was sore. How was it possible, he couldn't help wondering, that his penis, after its yeoman efforts in the service of love, had no visible signs of wear and tear?

Jack returned to the bar. Harry and the young women had thankfully gone. In the employees' lounge, Roger had his head in Carl's lap.

"You know dogs ain't allowed in restaurants."

"He isn't in the restaurant."

"I could use a dog. Give him to me, I'll scrub your tab."

Jack was tempted. It would be a good deal for Roger too. Here Roger would have companionship all day long. But Roger was as much his father's dog as his own, and he wouldn't be able to bear the defeated look in the old man's eyes if he had to tell him the dog had been given away.

"Can't do it. He's like a brother to me."

He'd almost reached the door when Claire, spotting him, started in his direction. Jack pointed to his wrist, was momentarily surprised to find his watch gone, then, blowing Claire a kiss, finally escaped into the welcome anonymity of the city.

The damp evening air felt blessedly cool on his fevered brow. The neon-outlined hands of the Sports Cafe window clock showed ten minutes before nine. Not even the most dedicated auditor would be working this late, Jack assured himself, his spirits lifting. He'd have the office to himself. Because he'd lost one bet was no reason to assume that his luck would continue to be bad.

The trip downtown was only intermittently difficult. By this hour the city had all but emptied. Dodger Stadium was dark, and plays at downtown theaters were well under way. The freeway traffic momentarily slowed for a three-car pileup, gawkers thirsty for blood, slowed again, seeking melodrama, for a car parked on the shoulder with emergency lights blinking, and yet again, drivers maliciously delighting at the sight of a vagabond motorcyclist being chased by a highway patrol car.

But when Jack finally arrived at the MetroBank lot, his smile reappeared. The Harris Cadillac was gone from its stall. So was the auditing firm's limo.

Jack pulled in behind a computer repairman's truck. Resisting the urge to pick up a few parts, Jack made sure Roger had water and kibble, then walked to the front of the building.

At the glassed-in lobby doors, Jack hesitated. A uniformed guard slumped in a chair at the information counter, seemingly mesmerized by the video screens of the security system. He hated having to bring the guard out of his Alpha mode, thus creating a witness to his visit. But there was no other way to gain entry.

Jack pressed the night buzzer. As the other stirred, Jack took out his identification card and flattened it against the window.

The guard, carrying too much weight for his frame, waddled to the doors. After comparing Jack to his photo ID for an interminable time, he finally unlocked the door.

Putting his ID away, Jack stepped inside. "Anyone asking for me?"

". . . forgotten your name?"

"Jonas, Roger Jonas," Jack said, only dimly aware he was using the initials of the mythical VP he'd created. He congratulated himself on his luck. The guard was still in a hypnotic stupor. "I was working late and slipped out to check on the Raiders score, and time got away from me. . . ."

The guard sniffed. "Didn't know there was a place to get beer 'round here?"

"Brought it in my lunch." Somewhat taken aback, Jack started for the elevator bank.

"You gotta sign in."

"I do that my boss'll know I've been goofing off."

"Can't help that."

Returning to the desk, Jack saw that Harris and the auditors had signed out only a half hour ago. Inspired, he signed the visitor book with his left hand.

"Sorry, Mr. Joiner," the guard said, shaking his head over the scrawled signature, "it's my ass I don't follow the rules."

Relieved, Jack smiled and went into the elevator. He rode all the way to the top, in case the guard was watching the floor indicator lights, then tiptoed down the stairs to the floor below.

The rows of desks and terminal screens between the steel pillars, ghostly under the fluorescent lights, were empty. The door of the vice president's office was slightly ajar.

Jack started that way, only to stop, chilled, as he heard footsteps ringing out on the polished floor. Leather heels with metal clips. Prudent about shoe repair? More likely, crude enough to advertise his importance by walking loud. He slid behind a pillar, pulse pounding.

Coming his way. Jack slid around the pillar, praying that whoever it was didn't see him.

On the other side of the pillar. Then past him, heading for the elevators. Jack slid around to watch: a computer technician, by his tool case and cheap suit. The technician stopped by a desk and picked up a phone.

Jack stopped breathing, the better to hear. Was the technician reporting to Harris? But the words were indecipherable. Then the technician hung up and went into the elevator.

When the elevator doors whispered shut, Jack came around the pillar and watched the descending floor-indicator lights, concerned about the obligatory checkout stop at the lobby floor, praying that the guard would not ask if the technician knew how late the beer-breathed, left-handed Mr. Jonas/Joiner intended to work.

But the pause at lobby level was brief, the guard either still half-asleep or the technician anxious to call it a day and get home.

And what was home going to be like for Harris? Jack's face grew hot. Had he found Jenny already asleep, a hastily penned note under the night lamp, topped by a bottle of tranquilizer or aspirin, pleading headache or exhaustion? Harris was the kind who might wake her anyway, jealously demanding every detail of how she'd spent her day.

And she, caught in a dreadful bind, fearful of offending him, would have to overcome feelings of revulsion at this assault on her privacy, answering question after insulting question with a courtesy that must cost her pride dearly. After which, as if that were not enough, he'd present her with certain unthinkable spousal demands she could not, at the risk of losing all, deny him.

Agitated and out of sorts, Jack began to picture them making love. No matter how he fought against it, he couldn't help imagining that silken creature being grunted over by that hairy, energetic brute, despising himself for becoming, in spite of his best efforts, turned on by the obscene images flooding his mind.

Close to tears by feelings of anguish and rage he couldn't control, let alone understand, Jack with an enormous effort cleared his mind. If he were going to help her get away from this unspeakable man, he had to stop wasting time.

Rubbing his eyes, Jack got his shoes back on, feeling as if he were undergoing an endless obstacle course. He hastened back through the conference room and into Harris's private office, guessing that someone who prided himself on his efficiency might have already entered Friday's password into the computer system.

A man like Harris, however, wouldn't just pluck a word out of thin air. He'd doodle around with it first, searching for a word difficult and exotic enough to impress the troops. Would he have doodled on the computer? Possibly. But then it would have been erased, and Jack hadn't brought along a program with which to retrieve it.

Sitting at Harris's desk, Jack felt somehow more uneasy about taking the man's chair than he had about sleeping with his wife. Before he could dwell on that puzzlement, however, he spotted the neatly stacked note pads. From the desk of S.J.H. A brandy snifter etched with the same initials held a dozen soft-lead pencils.

Taking a pad, Jack held it horizontally against the lights, searching for an impression left from whatever might have been marked on the top sheet. Nothing. The guy was fastidious or suspicious enough to tear off each page before writing on it. In which case he would use the blotter as a pad.

Opening the magnifying glass from his knife, Jack began minutely scrutinizing the blotter. No words. Columns of figures. All large.

Maybe he was wrong, Jack thought, disconsolate. Maybe the man did pluck his passwords from air. Rocking back and forth in the padded chair, Jack began to feel that something about Harris's well-ordered desk was odd. His eye took in the multiphone system, the desk blotter, the packet of paper clips, the pen holder, the paperweight. . . .

Where was the framed photograph of Jenny? Jack wheeled about to check the table next to the computer screen. Not there either. Jack tugged at the desk's drawers. All empty—except for the middle drawer, which was locked. Opening the awl on his knife, he inserted it into the keyhole.

The lock turned, easy as that. Shoved into the middle drawer was the frame. The glass was cracked. And the photo gone.

Before Jack could even begin to guess whether the frame had been dropped through carelessness or thrown in anger, he heard a throat being cleared behind him.

SEVENTEEN

Jack's heart and mind momentarily stopped. When he nerved himself to wheel around, he found to his enormous relief that he was being stared at by a stocky black man in coveralls and soggy work shoes holding a mop and bucket.

"Didn't mean to startle you."

"No problem. I was so engrossed in what I was doing . . ."

"Those locks hardly worth making keys for, looks like."

"You're right about that." Jack's laugh was frail. "I misplaced mine."

"If you're busy I can skip your office."

"Come back later? It has to be cleaned before you leave tonight."

"Sure thing. I'll take the trash basket now if you want."

"Thanks, no. I need to look through it first. I've lost an important document. As well as my keys."

The black man stared at Jack a moment longer before walking out. Jack leaned back in the chair to get his wind. Then pulling the wastebasket from beneath the desk, he began going through it an item at a time, careful not to cut himself on the glass from the shattered picture frame.

Most of the discard was mail, nothing important—solicitations from bond salesmen and charities, copies to Harris of instructions and memos and FYIs whose originals had been sent to other section heads. Nothing from Harris to anyone else.

He probably sent his memos by electronic mail, Jack thought. If he doodled, there was no sign of it here.

Frustrated, Jack was about to sweep the papers back when, for no reason he was conscious of, he gingerly reached into the basket and lifted out a large section of glass. What was that smear across it?

Blood? Had Harris, in a fit of temper, smashed his fist against the picture frame?

Careful not to cut himself, Jack lay the section into the frame, and picking out those smaller shards easiest to handle, tried to fit them into the frame as well. It was like working a jigsaw puzzle.

Other pieces were also smudged. But with enough of them in place, Jack saw that the stain wasn't blood. Someone had written on the glass with a red marking pen, then smeared the ink with a blow.

Holding the frame at an angle to the light, Jack was able to make out several of the letters.

ar ot.

Carrot? Jack thought. Car lot? He began going through the alphabet. At the letter *H* he stopped.

Harlot?!

Not a word you'd expect Harris to use, especially in the heat of temper. A strangely archaic word, puritanical, almost biblical, used by fundamentalist preachers or crossword puzzle addicts and scrabble fanatics, not . . .

Suddenly inspired, Jack walked the chair he was sitting in over to Harris's computer terminal.

Booting the computer up, he asked for Account Records. P a s s - w o r d ?, as expected, appeared on-screen. Crossing index under third fingers, Jack punched in H - a - r - l - o - t.

The wait seemed interminable. The screen remained blank. Then, like magic, like an Utterance from the Highest and Most Powerful Being in the Mysterious Beyond, the word E n t e r appeared, shimmering before him.

Taking a moment to thank God or the Holy Ghost for his luck, Jack called up Rollover Accounts. Working swiftly, he tagged those six-month Certificate of Deposits over one hundred thousand dollars that had been automatically renewed, but with interest not yet transferred. Placing the accounts tagged in a separate "holding" file, Jack went on a search for New Accounts, narrowing them down to those opened the day before.

He took a moment to think. It went against the grain to simply pull money out and just hand it over to Al. There must be a better way. There was!

Jack inserted the name A l b e r t B l a c k, and returned to the holding file.

Taking deep breaths to keep himself steady, and using a technique learned just last year at a computer hacker gathering, Jack backed the computer clock up to show the time of entry as just before closing yesterday. Finally he typed in T r a n s f e r I n t e r e s t N o w.

S p e c i f y A c c o u n t, the computer asked.

Albert Black, Jack typed, repressing a triumphant shout, then pressed the activating key.

Verifying Interest Transfer, the computer announced a split-second later. Congratulating himself, Jack checked the total that had been transferred. Twenty-one thousand. Clocked in at 3:55 P.M. yesterday. In the name of Albert Black. Who'd have to sign his name to get the money.

No matter that it was four thousand short of what he'd told Jenny he could probably get. And only half of what Al had demanded. It was still a sum that couldn't, wouldn't, *shouldn't*, be sneezed at. Al would jump at the opportunity, not realizing he was being entrapped. His greed would overcome caution.

Imagining Jenny's gratitude, Jack felt as if he were being slowly immersed in a warm bath.

Remain calm, Jack cautioned himself, and went back over what he'd done, making sure he'd covered his tracks. On a sheet of notepaper, he listed the accounts and the interest amounts he'd borrowed. If there was an unlooked-for hitch, he could shift the money back from someplace else.

Slipping the paper into his shoe, Jack untagged the files, and carefully resetting the computer clock to current time, instructed the computer to Abandon File.

Only then did Jack, almost giddy with relief, convinced he'd made it impossible for anyone to discover that an intruder had been prowling the system, exit the files.

Of course he still had to exit the building. That lobby ledger had a space left blank for his time out.

Dumping the shattered glass of the frame back into the wastebasket, Jack took a last inventory of Harris's desk. When he was certain everything was exactly as he'd found it, he headed out the door.

At the far end of the room the janitor looked up from his mopping. Jack hesitated. He'd stupidly forgotten something. Going back into Harris's office he brought the wastebasket out. Jack made a show of putting it on a desk where the janitor could not miss it, then, mouthing his thanks, at last headed for the stairway door.

The elevator he'd ridden up was still waiting. Riding it to the lobby for its obligatory stop, Jack rehearsed what he would say to the guard. But when the doors opened he saw the guard sound asleep.

For a moment Jack was tempted to keep going. But that might lead someone to wonder why Jonas/Joiner hadn't signed out. Jack tiptoed across the polished floor. Reaching carefully over the counter, he pulled the in/out ledger toward him. Gently, he tugged a pen from the guard's shirt pocket. Signing left-handed, he entered his departure time as fifteen minutes before that of Harris and his group.

When he attempted to return the pen, the guard, teeth grinding, shifted in his chair. Jack sucked in his breath. But the guard remained asleep. Leaving the pen open on the page, the sweating Jack tiptoed back to the elevator.

A moment later the doors closed and he was descending to garage level, elated, but mouth as dry as if he'd just finished a long-distance run. He was in need of drink, and companionship, he thought, slipping behind the wheel of his truck and soothing the grumbling Roger by ruffling his fur.

If only he could call Jenny and boast about what he'd done. They could have come up with some code, one ring for yes, two for no. Then, lying sleepless in the middle of the night, when the phone fell silent after the single ring, she could sink back into her pillows reassured that with Al out of her life forever, she wouldn't have to put up with the brutelike Harris much longer.

Thinking about what she did have to put up would make sleep difficult for himself, Jack knew. To give himself time to unwind, he decided to drive surface streets back to his lot.

Traveling up Sunset from downtown, he switched around the radio dial, hoping to find music that would slow his pulse, not match it. At Cahuenga he went north past the Hollywood Bowl, then traversed the canyons west along Mulholland, a winding road hacked out of the cliffside, deserted at this hour except for occasional lovers parked to moon over the necklace of lights glittering from the sprawling valley below, like some tawdry whore decorated with fake jewelry.

The velveteen night hid an architectural hodgepodge zoned by corruption and greed. He'd hated the valley since his dad had moved them to Van Nuys after his mother's departure. Rents were cheap, the psychic damage high. Not that the West side was any bargain. Zoning in residential areas was strict, but variances in commercial districts had been given for the asking, resulting in the traffic clog destroying Westwood and points south.

It was pointless to berate himself for not following rules, Jack told himself, when those in charge of enforcing them let everything slide.

This rationalization hadn't made him feel any better, he realized, finally arriving at his lot. If anything, he felt worse. Thick clouds had drifted in from the sea, shrouding the mountains in funereal wreaths. He opened the door for Roger, who opened one eye, grunted, and stayed where he was.

Jack stripped to his shorts and lay in the narrow bunk, hoping for sleep, anxious for morning. But he tossed from side to side, worrying over any clues he may have left behind, unable to suppress obscene images of the Harrises in bed.

Getting up, Jack made himself cocoa, treating himself to a double marshmallow. It had been a good night's work deserving of celebration, he told himself, watching the gummy sweet melt in the foaming chocolate. What was the point in feeling so glum?

Pulling out the art museum's recorder, he tried listening to the tape, remembering Jenny's face as she'd studied the painting, wondering again what there was about her melancholy, whether based on current situation or childhood memory, that could lead her to attempt suicide.

His heart, full of his own loss, went out to Jenny. He tried to imagine how she'd look when he told her about his plan for trapping Al. Awed, no doubt. Possibly adoring. Certainly grateful.

And then, to Jack's disgust, Sister Theresa, in her penguinlike robes, pushed her way to the forefront of his mind, more pitying than angry, which increased his feelings of impending doom.

Opening his computer, Jack booted up his football betting system. Maybe if he concentrated on readjusting his calculations, he could calm himself down. Gather, Sort, Compare, Evaluate. Maybe he hadn't gathered enough random factors. What would happen if he figured in an additional percentage for star-quality players, and deducted a percentage for conservative coaching?

Suddenly stimulated, Jack dug out his research on games of seasons past and began excitedly factoring in new data. He became so engrossed that it took the chatter of birds and squirrels, a growing irritation on the peripheries of his consciousness, to alert him to the light that had begun spilling down the mountainside, illuminating the pine and scrub oak.

Jack felt enormously better. His dark mood seemed to have dissipated with the rising sun.

Mornings promised fresh starts and new beginnings. This morning, in particular, had taken on an auspicious outlook. Within the hour he'd be presenting his beloved a hope of release from her terrible bondage.

Jack yawned and stretched, then, stripping down, walked barefoot to the hose at the sprinkler connection. He couldn't help smiling while he sponged himself head to foot, though his flesh goosepimpled in the morning chill, picturing himself a knight errant riding to the rescue of his lady fair, an image from childhood stories read to him by his dad. Forgotten was the fact that he'd always imagined those entranced, castle-kept, and bewitched maidens in the person of his absent young mother.

By seven-fifteen, Jack, freshly charged, dressed in stone-colored pants and a pale-green cotton shirt from the Gap, a store favored by the upwardly yearning who couldn't afford the hip stores on Melrose or Rodeo, was chewing on a cinnamon bun and dialing the rest home from the gas station phone at the bottom of the canyon road.

"Mr. Noble's unavailable," said the woman answering.

"How do you know that?" Jack was suddenly anxious. The woman hadn't even bothered to check.

"No personal calls until after eight. Gives the residents time to enjoy breakfast."

"What they need for that, ma'am, is a good cook, not time." How the old man must hate this newest attempt at regimentation. "Tell him his son called. And that I'll try again when I get a chance."

"You the son supposed to be paying the maintenance fee?"

"I am paying the maintenance fee."

"Computer shows you've ignored several overdue notices."

"I never got any notices."

"The computer sent 'em."

"To Mountaintop Road?"

"Nothing here about Mountaintop Road."

"I'll send you another change of address. This time make sure it's entered into the computer. When it mails me a notice I can look at, then the fee'll be taken care of."

Jack hung up. He was trembling. Sugar rush, he told himself, ignoring the possibility that fending off creditors was taking its toll. Returning to his truck, he fed the remnants of the bun to Roger.

It wouldn't do to be shaky when he told Jenny what he had in mind for Al. He had to convince her that it was worth the risk. And, more importantly, that he was capable of taking over the negotiations.

EIGHTEEN

Like clockwork, Harris's sleek Cadillac came booming up out of the underground garage at a quarter to eight, braking only momentarily at the street before shooting off in the direction of Los Feliz Boulevard, where the chainsaw-grind of commuter traffic was getting louder.

Jack, shielded from view behind a tree on the opposite side of the street, whistled for Roger. He enticed the lethargic dog back into the van, waiting impatiently until the parking attendant brought a blue Acura sedan out. When the doorman opened the door for a matching blue-haired woman dressed for elegant shopping, he hastened down the ramp, concrete already cracking, into the garage.

The back elevator was in use. Ducking behind a nearby pillar, stucco scraped by a careless bumper, Jack waited, looking anxiously over his shoulder for the garage attendant's return.

The elevator arrived. Its doors opened. An unkempt couple losing the fight against age, in baggy knee-length shorts and pink high-top tennis shoes, each carrying an overflowing basket of clothes, remained slumped against the padded walls.

"I don't see any laundry room," whined the woman, in a voice hoarsened by cigarette abuse, tossing dirty-blond, tangled hair out of bloodshot eyes.

Behind him, Jack heard the attendant whistling "La Bamba." "'Scuse me." He pushed between the couple, who stank of booze and pot. "I think the laundry room's out there somewhere. He'll know."

Jack pushed the penthouse floor button. The couple lurched hastily outside. As the doors closed Jack caught a glimpse of the attendant arriving.

He jabbed his finger into the Close Doors button. Sure enough, the doors bucked, the attendant trying to open them. Jack leaned on the button until finally the elevator rose.

Trotting over the penthouse floor's already scuff-marked corridor carpet, noticing wallpaper peeling at the edges, Jack rang the lighted bell. He waited. Lifting the lion's paw knocker, he rapped the rhythm of a tap dancer's finale. Why wasn't she answering?

He was about to rap again when the door opened the length of the security chain.

"Whosit?"

"Yo."

"Are you crazy?" Jenny, rubbing sleep from her eyes, allowed him to push through before quickly relocking the door. "What if someone saw you?"

"Not to worry." She was in the flimsy nightgown, hair in disarray. She smelled of sleep, and . . . Shaking away images he was unwilling to identify, he took her right hand, avoiding even the possibility of touching her wedding ring, and brought it to his lips. He wanted her so much he ached, in spite of the fact—or possibly because, though such a thought had never before occurred to Jack— she'd spent the night with someone else.

Don't push, he warned himself. It wasn't as if he could take her for granted. That magical interlude had receded so far into memory it seemed more imagined than real. "Sorry if I woke you. But I couldn't wait to tell you the good news."

"You got the money?"

"Didn't you think I would?"

"All of it?'

"Almost all."

"You planning on teasing me to death?"

"Twenty-one thousand."

Her face, which had been surprised, then curious, became hard. She pulled her hand away. "Al wants fifty."

"You agreed we might be able to buy time with twenty-five."

"Well, you didn't get twenty-five, did you."

Jack's fantasy of how he would deal with her gratitude had not prepared him for this. She was more than disappointed, she was furious.

"It's still a lot of money."

"It's *bubkes.*"

"Translate?"

"Bird shit, the league we're playing in."

"Al doesn't look like a major player to me."

"I wouldn't say you were the best judge of character in the world."

"Based on what—my admiration for you?"

She stared at him. A reluctant smile tugged at her mouth corners. "You do have a temper, don't you?"

"I don't think so, no. I'm considered very easygoing."

"I'll have to be more careful what I say to you. Coffee?"

"No need for caffeine when you're around." It had slipped out. He began to worry whether she might find him juvenile.

"Sweet. But mornings are not my best time. And I've got to think what to do about Al. Pour me a cup, there's a dear, while I put on my face." She squeezed his arm, then walked, barefoot and sinuous, regal as a favored harem maiden, toward the bedroom. Hesitating at the window, she turned.

Could that be deliberate? he wondered. She was standing so that he got the full benefit of her body, her familiar, pleasuring, sensual body, outlined against the morning light. "You will wait for me?"

He berated himself for his sudden suspicion. "For as long as it takes."

But in the kitchen, finding a five-cup thermos with coffee grounds still dripping through the filter, he became upset again. Apparently their protocol was for Harris to make the morning coffee. Maybe a jealous husband, but a devoted one. He'll be difficult to get away from, Jack thought.

When Jenny returned she was wearing a low-waisted, short-skirted, bone-white pleated dress of a material that clung to her thighs. A curl of hair, tied with a rose-colored silk bow at the nape of her swanny neck, was still damp from a quick shower. And she smelled of the perfume that suddenly caused him to flash back, every sensory detail intact, to the afternoon they'd filled with sounds and smells of love.

"Something the matter?" Still barefoot, she was carryng rose-colored leather flats that looked soft as dancing shoes.

"Nothing." But he was short of breath. "I was hoping we could stay in for a while. Or go somewhere together."

"Al's expecting me at nine-thirty. A.M."

Jack felt an inner glow. "You made the date before you knew whether I'd have the money?" She had trusted him to deliver after all.

"Either way, I'd have to talk to him."

"I'm coming with."

"Not a good idea." She was shoveling heaped teaspoons of sugar into her coffee. Strange he hadn't noticed that before.

"I've opened an account at the bank in his name." Could meeting him have caused old bad habits to return? "That's where the twenty-one thousand dollars is. Since I'm the one who can get him more, I'm the one should be explaining how it's going to work."

She eyed him over her cup. "You've got something cute going."

"He has to sign the new account cards in order to get the money out. The money came into the account illegally. The minute he signs, it's a criminal act. We can demand your pictures back or threaten him with jail."

"He'll never buy it."

"I think he will. I think twenty-one thousand will mean a lot to him. Anyway, time he knew you've got a friend as mean as he is."

She finished her coffee, got up, and rinsed her cup in the sink. "You're not as mean as he is. But I suppose it's worth a try."

They rode in her Jaguar. Jack, frustrated by her remoteness, willing to endure whatever it took to prove that her affection and trust had not been misplaced, scrunched up underneath the dash again. When she'd driven well away from the Regent Tower, he pulled himself up into the passenger seat, brushing at his clothes, attempting to speak with a confidence he was a long way from feeling.

"Where we meeting?"

"A place called Duke's in West Hollywood."

"Supposed to have great breakfasts."

"Al picked it."

"He stayed at Duke's Motel?

"I wouldn't know. It's of no interest to me."

Jack frowned. Hard to believe she wouldn't want to know where her enemy was holed up. This lie, if lie it was, made no sense. His uneasiness increased.

She'd been quick to learn her way about town, too. She showed no hesitation about which streets to take, rolling at a good clip along Santa Monica Boulevard. Commuter traffic had thinned, though pool cleaners and plumbing and gardener trucks were picking up the slack. She sped past the barnlike recording and video transfer studios, producers of the commercial din that polluted the airwaves, not even shrinking, as he did, from the sight of proliferating minimalls, which had sprung up like diseased spores at every intersection.

As they neared San Vincente, the structures gradually segued into small office buildings and trendy boutiques, and then the blue whale of the Design Center dominated the horizon.

Duke's Motel was at the edge of Gay Alley. Shops with names like Ah Men stocked clothing that startled even Jack. He had, for a time not so far past, dressed like a dedicated member of the counterculture: bleached jeans carefully ripped at knees and crotch, a bejeweled cross dangling from his ear.

He'd hoped to shock the nuns and catch the eye of his father. But the nuns had confused him by complimenting him on his religious fervor, while his father seemed to be steadily losing interest in everything, including changes in his normally dutiful son.

The parking lot was unattended. She parked in an empty slot between a steel gray BMW and a fire engine red Porsche, out of sight of the street. She looked at her watch, which he'd noticed before was not as expensive as an executive in Harris's exalted position should be able to afford.

"We're early." She made no move to get out.

"We'll have the advantage."

"There's no advantage with Al. I keep telling you."

"I'd feel better if we could get settled in first."

Opening her purse, she pulled out a small automatic, offering it to him. Jack felt his heart skip a beat.

"Why would I need that?"

"He's unstable. It's not loaded. It might calm him down."

"I'll take my chances."

She shrugged, putting the gun back, and got out of the car without another word.

Duke's was fifties coffee shop *moderne,* all chrome and streaked mirrors with black-and-white photographs of forgotten celebrities mounted above the long counter. Booths of patterned red vinyl ran along the windows, most of them filled. Blocking access to the room was a saggy and worn velvet rope. A gay couple who had walked to the last empty booth with hands intertwined were being seated by a graying hostess in an embroidered toreador pants suit. Handing the couple menus, she returned to the rope.

"Two for breakfast?" Her teeth had been poorly capped.

"Three."

"Rest of your party here?"

"We'd like to sit now, if you don't mind. I've been dancing all night and if I don't take a load off I may collapse on the spot."

Both Jenny and the hostess squinted at Jack. Then the hostess, with a sidelong glance at Jenny, picked up three menus and led the way to a table in the middle of the back room.

"How about that table, against the wall?"

The hostess, forcing a smile that spoke of long suffering the peculiarities of Duke's clientele, threaded her way through the sparsely occupied tables to the one Jack had indicated.

"Party we're expecting is not someone we'd ordinarily want to be seen with." Jack spoke softly, taking her into his confidence. "Man's got a rotten complexion, and I'm not sure how often he bathes. But he may be willing to bankroll our movie, so treat him like he's somebody, whatya say?"

The hostess perked up. "A part for me, I'd like to read for it."

"We'll mention it to Mr. Moneybags."

"*Ole.*" The hostess wet her lips, kissed air, and left.

"Think that's smart, calling attention to ourselves?"

"He goes off the deep end, we might need a witness."

"We're never going public with this. You hear me? Never!" Her face was pale.

"I wasn't thinking."

"Get it in gear, sonny. Don't make me sorry I brung you."

Jack wondered how stress brought out a coarseness that, given the way she dressed and her station in life, was otherwise not evident. Before he had time to dwell on that, however, he spotted Al, looking as if his teeth hurt, being led to their table.

"Sit right here, Mr. Moneybags," the hostess said, holding a chair. "Gives you a view of the room."

Al stared. The hostess, who was fluttering her eyelashes, seemed suddenly transfixed. Her smile ghosted away, and she quickly followed suit.

Al, who had remained standing, now gave Jenny a similar stare. "What kind of asshole would tell her that was my name?"

"I didn't think she'd take it seriously." Jack was trying not to laugh.

Al continued speaking to Jenny. "You know I don't like dealing with middlemen."

"I'm her banker. I need to make sure she's getting good value for the loan."

Al finally acknowledged him. The coldness of his eyes sent a shiver through Jack. "How would a chump like you squirrel enough together to loan anybody anything?"

"I got twenty-one thousand acorns says otherwise."

Al abruptly sat and leaned very close to Jenny. "You playing with me? I told you the entire amount or I'll see you back in the pits sure as shit!"

Jack started to rise, blood surging. At a warning glance from Jenny, he reluctantly settled back. "What's the rush?" Jack hated that his voice suddenly fluted. "You satisfy her about the negatives you'll have the rest in a week."

Al thought about it. "You got that much money, show it to me."

Pulling the MetroBank pouch out from under his jacket, Jack slid it across the table. Al squeezed the pouch. Unzipping it, he turned it upside down. The bank book, signature card attached, fluttered out. Al studied the material.

"I'm supposed to sign the card, that it?"

"Money's there for the taking."

Al grinned. His teeth were yellow as urine. "Cute." He looked at Jenny. "You think of this?" Jenny, who appeared remarkably calm except for a paleness about her nose and mouth, shook her head. "The kid's cute, I'll give him that." Al lost his smile. "I told you cash in hand!"

Jack tried to keep his voice reasonable. "It is cash. It'll be in hand soon as you withdraw it!"

Fastidiously, Al tucked the bank book and the card back into the pouch and pulled the zipper closed. Without warning then, he threw it at Jack.

Jack raised his hand, almost too late. Deflected, the pouch fell against Jack's glass. Water spilled over the table and began dripping into his lap.

"Don't play games with me, you downy-cheeked dickhead. You want to be involved, you sign the cards, you withdraw the money, and you bring it to me. At a time and place of my choosing. Am I going too fast for you?"

Jack, nerves strung so tight he felt himself tremble, mopped up the table and his lap, prevented from going across the table at Al by Jenny, no doubt panicked that his temper might have wrecked whatever chance they'd had of buying time. But after folding the soggy napkin and congratulating himself on his self-control, he found himself throwing the napkin into Al's face.

Al skidded back in his chair, stopped from toppling by the wall. Jack leaped to his feet, cursing himself for a fool, certain that he had disgraced himself before Jenny.

Righting his chair, Al borrowed Jenny's napkin to wipe his face. Then sudden and slick as a magician performing a trick, he produced from inside his jacket a gun equipped with a silencer.

Jack, dry-mouthed, reached for Jenny's purse. Pale and distraught, she pulled it out of his reach.

"Sit down, hero." Al was shielding the gun behind the napkin. "This makes a bigger hole going out than going in. That'd make you a double asshole."

Jack, stunned and humiliated, sat, unable to believe that Al would actually shoot, but not eager to put him to the test. He also saw an opportunity to redeem himself in front of Jenny.

"What do we get in exchange for the money?"

"Twenty-one thousand cash? Buys you a week."

"We need two."

"*Solamente una semana, Senor* wiseass."

Jack cleared his throat. "What about the negatives?"

"They'll be turned over at the final payment."

"We're giving you twenty percent down. We expect twenty percent of the negatives in return."

Al laughed, slipping the gun and napkin into his lap as a waitress approached with a pot of coffee. "You're some kind of a bookkeeper, huh?"

"And we want your signature agreeing to a marriage annulment. Backdated. Before any money changes hands."

Al gave Jenny an unreadable glance, then turned to Jack again. "You're not a student of human nature, are you, kid? I look like someone'd toss in my hole card?"

"Everyone ready to order?"

"Denver omelette, extra ham and burnt potatoes."

Jack, noting with part of his mind that the two of them shared a similar taste in breakfasts, stood and walked to Jenny's chair. He was hoping she'd follow his lead, but would not blame her if she'd lost faith. "Nothing for us, thanks."

Jenny, perhaps too kind to humiliate him further, got to her feet. What she said then surprised him. "You agreeing to our terms?"

"What's this *our* shit *kemosabe*?"

"We're an item. Didn't I tell you?"

Jack, not sure whether to be pleased, wondered if she might be using him to taunt Al. Al had already shown he had an emotional stake in her that went beyond bleeding her for cash.

But Al didn't think twice. "I'll give you a week. And twenty percent of the negs. Not a damn thing more. And I'll let you know where and when to make delivery." Then Al shook his head. "You keep coming up with losers, babe. I give this snotnose a month, tops."

"That'd still give me twenty-nine days more than you."

Al's face twisted. "You forgetting, Lancelot, others got there first? You're playing with a wet deck."

Jenny grabbed Jack. Surprisingly strong, she managed to turn him before he could move, and, tucking her arm in his, urged him toward the exit.

"Be cool. You handled him perfectly. Don't blow our chances now."

NINETEEN

"Why didn't you l-let me have your gun? We'd s-see how mouthy he'd be with a gun j-jammed in his teeth!" Jack was stuttering with humiliation and rage, convinced she'd lost confidence in him.

"Don't be ridiculous." She was concentrating on her driving, unwilling, for reasons he could guess at, to look at him. "Al would never back off."

"Everyone backs off for someone."

"Not for someone he reads as not having the guts to pull the trigger."

"He made the wrong kind of move I would have. I w-would have!"

"You're kidding yourself."

"If he ever pushes me to the brink again . . . What're you doing?"

She was pulling over to the curb, behind taxis lined along the rear driveway of the Beverly Hilton Hotel. "I'd like to be alone for a while. You can catch a cab back."

Jack pressed the palms of his hands against his suddenly aching eyesockets. "I thought you said we were . . . you're disappointed in me."

"Not in the slightest. It worked out better than I expected."

"You can't be serious."

"Al thinks he's got me on the run. Now he won't be as careful as he ought to be."

Jack stared. What was it she'd said when she'd pulled him away from Al? He couldn't remember. "Now it's you got something cute going."

"You're better off not knowing."

"Hey. Remember me, your friendly neighborhood loan shark? I have to protect my investment."

"I promised you'd get it all back, didn't I?"

"You think it's the money I'm worried about?"

She leaned across him to grab the latch on his door. "Remember me telling you I'm bad news? Split while you still can."

Jack leaned forward to bury his face in her lemon-rinsed hair. Her body trembled. He guessed that she was fighting back tears. "It's you who doesn't understand. I'm crazy-glue stuck on you."

"This isn't fun and games. It could turn out badly for both of us."

"I'll take my chances."

The cab line moved. Behind them someone honked. Straightening, she brushed her lips across his. Before he could respond, she suddenly twisted the wheel, and flooring the accelerator, made a screeching U-turn into traffic, driving west along Santa Monica Boulevard.

"We going for another swim?"

If he'd hoped to catch her off guard it was a failure. She barely glanced at him. "Some other time."

"Have something better in mind?"

She didn't respond. Nearer the ocean the temperature got appreciably cooler. An offshore breeze whipped the flags on the used-car lots, stirring the litter in front of the small bars on every corner, cleansing the mote-laden air of its persistent odor.

At Ocean Avenue she turned north along Palisades Park, where the retired played cards at tables on the grass, while joggers, males stripped to the waist, females with unfettered breasts leaping with every stride, dodged through towering palms, past men with burned, dirt black faces rooting through trash barrels. Jack, man of property and technical skills, shuddered, thinking that only his salary, scant even when intact, separated him from them. At least prison, if it came to that, meant he'd receive his bread fresh daily.

"You find this amusing?" She was staring at him.

"I was just counting my blessings. . . ."

But she'd stopped listening, taking Wilshire down the incline to Pacific Coast Highway, where she continued north.

"You've borrowed someone's beach house in Malibu."

"Malibu? You mean the lousy swimming beach with shacks worth three million dollars in spite of the hour commute along a highway closed at least twenty days of the year because of brush fires or rock slides. . . ."

"Yeah. That Malibu."

"I don't know anyone in Malibu."

They were speeding alongside a rocky stretch of beach open to an ocean blue as the steel on Al's gun, the memory of which cramped Jack's stomach. "But you know where you're going."

She slowed. "The store gave me directions."

"A beachfront swim shop that hand fits string bikinis."

Without warning she pulled off the road, braking in front of a driftwood cafe advertising clam chowder and abalone steak.

"What I want to buy is dynamite."

"You'd be dynamite whatever you wear."

"You're not paying attention. I'm talking about the stuff you blow things up with."

He met her gaze, remarkably serene considering the subject matter. "What kind of things?"

"Al's just aching to break the news to Sam that our marriage isn't valid."

"I read him as more greedy than vindictive."

"You read him wrong. I could never pay him enough to buy myself peace of mind."

"You can't be talking about . . ." He couldn't bring himself to say it.

"Look, go in and get yourself a bowl of chowder and a beer. By the time your wonderfully flat little gut is full I'll be back."

"Stop treating me like some kid."

"You can't hide the fact that you're too sensitive for rough stuff. One of your many charms. But I can't risk my future because you're queasy!"

"There's got to be another way."

"Tell me one."

Jack's mind had been racing desperately, considering and rejecting one option after another, none making enough sense to propose. "We scare the shit out of him!"

Everything had suddenly clicked into place, giving him the same sense of overwhelming relief and excitement as when a computer program he'd been experimenting with suddenly produced results. "We get the dynamite, booby-trap the money — we wrap a few bills around dynamite, see, so he can tell if we'd actually set the stuff to go off he'd've been blown to kingdom come!"

Jack was grinning fiercely, though inside he was shuddering at the picture he'd formed of Al exploding. "While he's still in shock we tell him all we care about is him fulfilling his end of the bargain — turning over the negs and back dating a marriage annulment."

"And if it only pisses him off, and he says screw the money and sends Sam a copy of our marriage certificate?"

"He does that, he loses everything. You have him arrested for extortion, sue him for damages . . . ten'll get you twenty he'll go for the money. For Christ sake, it's worth a try!"

After a wait that seemed interminable, she eased the car into traffic again.

"I guess we'll still need the dynamite to make it look convincing." He managed to sound casual, though he was disconcerted by her volatility, and uncertain of what, besides delay, he'd accomplished.

"Place in Topanga Canyon stocks it. They sell to landscapers for clearing tree stumps. . . ."

"You're not actually going to buy the stuff? They probably keep records of all purchases. . . ."

"Damn!" She hit the steering wheel with her fist. "I'm not thinking clearly, am I?"

"I'll say not." It was an effort to laugh.

"But how else can we get it?"

There was phlegm in his throat. "Steal it."

"You don't mean B and E?"

"Say again?"

"Breaking and entering."

"No need to. All those signs the way out here—'Watch Out For Falling Rock'? They blow up boulders on hillsides hanging over the roads. They probably have the stuff lying around." He hesitated, then, hoping to get his mind at least temporarily off the ungodly situation he'd found himself in, "They say all California's sliding into the sea."

"Good riddance, I'd say."

He felt a pang. He'd been watching the city sink into decadence and decay, beginning to choke on its own excrescences, but he still loved the place with the loyalty that came with the memory of landmark moments: his moonlit graduation trip to Catalina with the other nerds too shy to ask for dates; bodysurfing off Playa del Rey under the airport flight pattern, the roar of waves drowning the whine of jets; a rock concert at the Forum of *Led Zeppelin's* final tour that gave him a momentary identification with his ecstatic generation that both depressed and elated him. This indication that she could not share his nostalgia distressed him.

"What is it?"

"*Nada.*"

"You're staring."

"Can't help myself—you turn me on."

"That supposed to flatter me?"

"Isn't there any way I can compliment you?"

[114]

She put her hand, her strong, skillful hand, on the inner side of his thigh. "Don't let my cynicism rub off on you. Okay? Stay as sweet as you are."

"Sweet's not one of my all-time favorite words." But at her touch a wave of pleasure washed over him, and he put his hand over hers, hoping to keep her from noticing his immediate response, wanting her to believe that lust wasn't all there was to his feeling for her.

"Is it much further?"

He came back to reality with a start. "A few miles. Hear that?" In the distance, thunder.

Then they were slowing as four lanes of traffic, encountering a huge flashing yellow arrow on the flatbed of a Cal-Trans truck, funneled into two. A workman in an orange jacket flagged them to a stop.

A hillside off to their right suddenly exploded. A cloud of rocks obscured the sun. A moment later they felt the impact; a moment after that, heard the delayed boom.

Earth-moving equipment, undulating like giant slugs, began to chew into the open hillside. As grit-filled dust drifted across the road, traffic began moving again. Jenny stopped the car alongside the flagman.

"Where would I find the construction foreman?"

"Up about half a mile cut over to the access road, then take the dirt road on your right. You'll see a fenced-in field with trucks and stacks of supplies." He was appreciating her.

Jenny smiled thanks. She bumped over the divider gravel to reach the access road running beside the freeway. Less than a mile later they found a rutted road running toward the hills. As soon as they spotted the construction headquarters area she leaned forward, reached up under the back of her blouse, and, with a practiced wriggle, produced her bra. She tossed it to the startled Jack.

Pulling into the fenced-in enclosure marked with a Cal-Trans sign, Jenny drove past several outdoor privies and cement trucks loading up with gravel, parking in front of a portable shack marked OFFICE. Both had seen the small shed marked DANGER! EXPLOSIVES!

Jenny tucked in her blouse and tightened her belt, which outlined her breasts until the nipples showed. Then, careless of how much thigh was revealed, she swung out of her seat and walked, hips swinging, to the office.

Workmen paused in their conversations, as mesmerized as Jack.

"I'm looking for my brother—Bud Whilhoite—told me he'd be working on a road crew in this area . . . any of you know him?

Jack, reminded of the business at hand, slipped out, heading for the farthest privy. A workman came out adjusting his pants, stopping to stare as a crowd slowly gathered around Jenny.

"Mind if I use your can?"

The workman, barely glancing at Jack, jerked a thumb over his shoulder, then moved on to join the gathering. Jack shoved the door shut, then quickly slipped around the privy and headed for the explosives shed.

The door was padlocked. Jack picked up a rock. He hesitated. Someone might hear. A small stack of material had been discarded nearby. Tossing the rock aside, Jack found a strip of lumber that seemed the right size and inserted it under the hasp. Leaning his weight on it he had the satisfaction of watching the screws slowly pull out of the wood.

Inside, Jack waited for his eyes to become accustomed to the semidark. It didn't take long. Light sifted through gaps in the poorly constructed wooden shed, and he made out boxes stacked against the walls. Moving cautiously, Jack suddenly stumbled.

Heart in his throat, he rubbed his shin and stooped to look. It was a box like the others, but partially open. Blood red paper-wrapped sticks, looking much like road flares, were arranged in orderly rows. A dozen were missing.

If those were what had been used to demolish the hillside, Jack told himself, then four should be plenty to demolish Al. Or scare the shit out of him, he hastily amended, aghast that he'd even inadvertently accepted the alternative as a possibility. He took six, preferring to err on the side of too much rather than not enough, unwilling to risk her contempt.

Opening his shirt, Jack tucked the lethal sticks into his waistband underneath. He tried not to think of what they might do to his internal organs should he trip and fall.

Outside, the workmen were still engrossed with Jenny. The entire operation had taken less than four minutes. Quickly pushing the hasp's screws as deep into place as he could, Jack then ducked around the shed. Keeping the stacks of material between himself and the men, he reached the privy without being seen.

Pretending to be emerging, Jack self-consciously adjusted his pants, then headed for the circle of men.

Jenny was drinking from a can of beer.

"Everything come out all right?"

Jack blushed as the men roared, barely managing to catch the can Jenny tossed to him.

"Wrong site. Bud's probably at Kanan Dune Road." She turned back to the men. "Sure thank you all for your help."

[116]

They assured her it was their pleasure, and escorted her to the car. The men watched as she started the car and circled the headquarters shack. She waved as she floored the accelerator. Then, swearing, she had to brake and swerve as a dump truck came barreling through the gate.

Jack, holding the beer in one hand and trying to buckle his seat belt with the other, came slamming up against the dash, grunting as the sticks jammed into his belly.

"You okay?"

Jack closed his eyes, waiting to be blown into smithereens. Settling back, he felt around his waist.

"No thanks to that crazy sucker."

She drove through the gate, and they didn't speak again until they were almost to the freeway.

"Let's see them."

Jack lifted his shirt.

"Omigod!" Jenny braked the car, skidding onto the road's shoulder.

She carefully removed the dynamite from Jack's waistband a stick at a time. Before placing them into the litter bag hanging from the dash, she gently lifted a small lid off each.

"I do something wrong?"

"The damn things are armed—these are blasting caps! Don't you know anything about dynamite?"

"Nothing." Though the blood had drained from his face, Jack managed a grin. "I didn't think it was worth mentioning."

TWENTY

At the mouth of the canyon leading to Jack's lot, where Jenny followed after he picked up his van, they stopped at the True Value hardware store in the minimall across from the gas station. She sent him in to buy a mechanical windup alarm clock, some electrical wire, and flashlight batteries.

"Batteries? But if it's only a dry run . . ."

"He has to realize we're serious."

He was nervous under the clerk's gaze, sure that anyone alert to the bombings that seemed the current violence of choice would know exactly what the components he was buying were for. But then he reassured himself that the clerk was looking through, not at him, trying to overhear what the redhead in the ripped denim shorts was saying to another clerk attempting to peer down her inadequate halter top.

At the lot, he waved Jenny past his van, so her car would remain in the trees out of sight of the road. Though they were in the shadow of the hills behind, the distant city gleamed in the afternoon sun, its heat, traffic, and smog creating a shimmering mist that made it seem insubstantial as a mirage.

She sat for a moment, worrying Jack by what seemed a sudden descent into melancholy. While he was debating how, or whether, to bring her out of it, again remembering the brooding demeanor that had proceeded her solitary swim, she suddenly removed her shoes and sliding out of the car, walked past the partially framed house to the outer edge of the berm, staring over the purple-hazed canyons toward a sea that gleamed like the hammered copper on the giant funeral urns he'd seen at the museum.

"Want a tour of the house?"

She brought her gaze around. Realizing he'd made the same offer to Nancy, he suddenly blushed.

Jenny hadn't seemed to notice; the shadows had covered his emotion. He wasn't fickle, Jack told himself. He hadn't knowingly sought out someone like Jenny, who had, because of missteps in her youth, confronted him with impossible choices. But if he managed things right, he didn't see why he couldn't get her life, then his, back on track.

"I'm situating the house at an angle, and building it on levels, so that every room, except the one for my computers, will have a view. Any ideas more than welcome."

"You're actually building a house yourself?"

"I'll subcontract the skilled jobs—but if I do the scut work personally, I can save a lot."

He walked her through the rooms, keeping for last the area that might show him, once and for all, whether she considered him more than a transitory distraction.

"You haven't shown me everything."

The flicker of interest encouraged him. "That's an apartment for my dad—part of the house, but separate. I told you my dad's going to live here too?"

"I don't recall your mentioning it."

"He's easy to live with. A stickler for privacy. That's why the retirement home's such a bummer for him."

"I can see that."

"You'll like each other."

"I don't think this is a good time for us to meet."

"And if you've got a parent needs a place we could probably work something out there, too."

She stared at him as if he were some kind of freak. He touched her arm. "You're not going to cry?"

"Laughing's more like it." But her eyes glistened.

"I don't see why."

"I'm sitting on a powder keg and you're fantasizing about family life?"

"I want you to understand I'm in it for the long haul."

She stepped into him as if she meant to hurt him. But as he grabbed her raised fists, she collapsed, burying her face in his neck, her sobbing breath shivering his skin. "Damn you. *Damn you!*"

"I say something wrong?"

"You're dear. A dear boy."

He stiffened, and she clutched him tight to keep him from moving away. "Don't be offended. I adore you. The way you stood up to Al—wanting me in spite of—even though. . . .make love to me!"

Her knee parted his thighs, her hands running down his back to his hips, pulling him in against her so close he could feel the ridge of her pelvic bone. . . .The cloth of his pants where she straddled him dampened and his nostrils suddenly cleared with the now-familiar scent of overripe fruit, instantly triggering his own excitement.

His mouth felt so bruised he had difficulty finding the words. "S-Shouldn't we go inside the van?"

"Here. Do me here!"

He came out of his hypnotic state and struggled to match her aggressiveness. As she fumbled with his belt and yanked down his pants he put his hands under her dress and lifted. She came up with her legs spread. They coupled with such speed he half expected to hear the crash of freight cars colliding, and the rip of her panties. But she was wearing none. Mouth to mouth, greedy for breath, Jack staggered in a half circle under her weight, coming to rest against the car's fender. He could feel the afternoon breeze, cool against the fever of his exposed skin.

"Someone might see us."

"Who cares?"

Neither had spoken aloud. He had thought it, imagining her response. Her legs clamped so tight around his waist he was unable to move, frantic as he was to. She startled him by reaching her hand underneath, fondling his sac as if the stones they contained were precious. Electrified, he responded to her lead, tracing her earlobe with one hand and her arched vertebrae down to the line between her cheeks with the other, suddenly transfixed to feel his tongue sucked deep into her mouth and her position shift so that he was at once, mouth, tongue, and fingertips, penetrating and being penetrating at every orifice.

He quivered from head to toe, nerve ends flaming, lungs collapsed, stars kaleidoscoping behind his fluttering eyelids, struggling to move before he exploded. He felt as if the two of them were wheeling in space, all sense of gravity or balance lost. An insistent pounding, hammer against muffled anvil, he mistakenly attributed to his runaway heart.

"Listen! Hear that? That's us. Dear Jack. Hold me!" The scream was so deep in her throat he thought it was a cat lost in the surrounding canyon. His answering moan, unbidden, seemed from a species of creature whose existence he had never suspected.

Locked, they slid down the car's side until they fell on their sides in the dust. They were unwilling to separate, but unable to prevent a gradual slipping apart. She mewed with disappointment; he murmured in affectionate apology.

[120]

Holding each other, they listened to the first tentative sounds of wildlife, momentarily hushed by their encounter, beginning to stir. Then they were galvanized by the sound of a car straining to make the hill. He helped her to her feet, slapping ineffectually at her dirt-streaked skirt. The car, a battered Volkswagen, went by, its lone occupant seemingly so anxious about his car's capability that he barely glanced at the trailer.

"Better do something about that skirt."

"I have a spare in the car."

She opened her trunk and pulled out her attaché case, then followed him into the van, leaving the door open.

"You mind? I get claustrophobic."

"Oh."

"Oh?"

"That's why you wanted to make love outside."

"No." But she didn't explain. Going to the sink, she removed her clothes, then, as casually as if she were alone in her own bathroom, began sponging herself off.

Unwilling to stare, but uncertain what else to do, Jack picked up another cloth, stepped out of his clothes, and began cleaning himself, though he couldn't help half turning from her out of shyness. Jenny walked up behind him and, to his immense chagrin, took his cloth. Putting her arm around his chest, she began cleaning him with a skill that made him wonder whether she'd been a nurse.

"Let mamma help you with that, sailor."

In spite of his new concern about whether it was hospitals where she'd received her training, he became stimulated. Turning, he reached for her. She accepted him for a moment, then gently pushed him away. "Towel off. We've got work to do."

She took panties out of her handbag, a fresh skirt and blouse out of her attaché case, and put them on.

"Leave the other clothes here. I'll get them cleaned."

"You're a dear. But I couldn't impose." She opened the attaché case on the table, then pulled the clock, wire, and batteries out of the hardware store sack.

"Hand me the dynamite?"

He hastened to comply, watching, fascinated, as she taped the sticks together, replaced the blasting caps, then attached the electrical wire to the caps with the facility of long practice.

"Where'd you learn about dynamite?"

"Coal mines. Pennsylvania."

"Thought you were from Phoenix."

[121]

"Raised in Pennsylvania. Everyone in the town knew about the mines. I went below once in a while as a lark."

"Thought you were claustrophobic."

"Happened to me later. Guys I knew used to show off for me. One guy . . ."

"What?"

"Blew himself up."

She took a Kleenex from her purse and blew her nose.

"You cared about him."

"He was clumsy. And a blowhard."

Picking up the clock, she used the screwdriver to take off the top shielding the alarm bell. With the clapper exposed, she twisted the wires running from the blasting caps together, then wrapped the intertwined strands around the clapper.

"I thought we weren't going to arm those!"

"Make him sweat a little before he realizes the clock's not running."

Like me, Jack thought. Somewhat clumsy. And maybe a blowhard, too.

A beeper made them both jump. She reached into her purse and pulled out an electronic page. She showed him the digitally displayed number. "Sam."

She went to the car for her phone, then surprised him by bringing it back inside to return the call. Jack attributed his sudden discomfort to those vestiges of his Roman Catholic upbringing he hadn't yet got rid of. He dismissed as unfounded a suspicion that she might get a perverse enjoyment out of his unease. If anything, it was an indication of how close to him she felt. They were now fellow conspirators, he reminded himself. Why didn't that make him feel better?

"This is Mrs. Harris." She did have the grace to turn aside while she waited for Harris to get on the phone. "How long?" Whatever her husband had said had disconcerted her. "Not possible. I carry the pager with me. Well . . . I did leave the pager in the car while I took a little walk . . . I wanted the time out! You think I enjoy sitting around all day waiting for you to call? I'm not being snotty — you're being unreasonable. Being married doesn't mean we're joined at the hip. . . . Yes . . . you've been very good to me, I know that. . . . Of course I'm grateful. . . . Tonight? Well if you work as late as you usually do I'll probably be asleep. You don't need my permission to wake me — but I don't see what's the point, when you come home so exhausted. . . . Yes. I said yes. If you want. Your every wish is my command."

She hung up and remained still. He went to embrace her and she slipped away. "Please don't — I'd rather not be touched just now!" She looked at him, her eyes luminous. "I want to be rid of him so bad I can taste it. You can't imagine what it's like to be at the beck and call of a man I despise. It's Jenny do this and Jenny do that . . . come to bed, Jenny . . . I don't know how much longer I can stand him putting his hands on me!"

"Is he . . . kinky?"

"If I loved him it wouldn't matter."

"Wouldn't it."

"I'd do anything for the man I love as long as it wasn't under duress."

"Would you."

"This business with Al has got to work. It's got to! Otherwise . . ."

"It will." Jack put all the confidence he could muster into his voice, uncertain of what he might agree to should she suddenly change her mind about merely scaring Al.

But after taking counsel with herself for a few unbearably tense moments, she nodded and walked to him. "Okay, sailor. We'll see if we can't get his attention. Now give me all of yours."

He wouldn't have believed it possible that with all they had on their minds they could even think about making love. But when she gripped him he responded, and within moments, elbowing the loaded attaché case aside, they were testing the weight-bearing strength of the fold-down table, as well, he was to think later, as the stability of the wired dynamite.

TWENTY-ONE

Jack awoke feeling something was wrong. He tried to tell himself that it was similar to the anxiety he usually felt at the start of games on which he'd bet too much. God knew these stakes were high enough. Considering the dynamite-laden attaché case under his bunk, it was a wonder he wasn't climbing the walls.

But when an activity that never failed to soothe him failed — taking Roger outside to pee, and relieving himself over the berm into the brush below, looking in vain for a rainbow in the arc of the droplets glistening in the rising sun — and his nerves continued to butterfly, he guessed it was Jenny's behavior that was troubling him.

Last night, after they'd made love, she'd been uncharacteristically silent, unresponsive to his murmurs of affection, pulling away when he'd tried to stroke the tenseness out of her body. She was probably bracing herself, he'd glumly thought, to endure the coming night's mattress tumble her husband had threatened her lay in store.

When she'd picked up her attaché case on her way home, he'd swung up out of the bunk, deciding it was time to assert himself.

"Why cart it back and forth? It'll be safe here."

Roger, who'd been leashed at the back, stood and sniffed at her crotch. She finger-snapped his nose. "It doesn't take two of us to make delivery." Stooping, she hugged the sulking dog, talking at Jack past Roger's flattened ear. "I suppose there won't be any better time to tell you . . . it's over, Jack. Try to understand. We're basically incompatible."

For the first time in his life Jack had understood what it must feel like to be turned into the biblical pillar of salt. He'd watched helplessly, unable to move or utter a sound, as she continued to ruffle Roger's fur. Only when she pushed the dog aside and stood to leave did he manage to come back to life.

"You're not fooling me. You want to renege on our deal. You

think by blowing Al away you'll get rid of all your problems. But you couldn't be more wrong! The consequences will be dire. You'll spend the rest of your life eating yourself alive because you killed someone!"

She studied him. "You left the church but not the faith."

"You can have a conscience without being religious."

"Why can't you admit you're running scared?"

Hurt, he'd retreated into what he hoped was a dignified silence. When she had trouble opening the door panel, he watched for a time, then, gently moving her aside, kicked at the rusty latch to free it. She began to weep.

No wonder he was subject to premonitions of disaster. Her sudden mood shifts, which had been limited to intermittent, unexplained, but mercifully brief outbursts, had suddenly rocketed into overdrive, sending out signals so mixed it seemed to confuse her as much as himself.

Gently, taking advantage of her momentary helplessness, Jack had wrested the attaché case from her.

"Insult me all you want. I'm not letting you act against your own best interests."

Now, every muscle aching as he filled Roger's bowl with dried kibble, remembering with awe the love stretches that would have tested the flexibility of professional gymnasts, he mourned his inability to make sense of Jenny's behavior. Was she manipulating him? Or had her paranoia triggered his?

If only his mind operated as efficiently as his computer. Of course the mind, like the computer, depended on the accuracy of the information fed into it. In order to understand Jenny, he needed to know more than he'd been able to find out so far. Intuition was no substitute for facts.

But the frequency with which her personality seemed to contradict her background—was that really so unusual? His own persona wasn't much better: an outward wiseass masking someone inherently shy, a cautious personality perversely compelled to take terminal risks.

What if his growing unease had more to do with his leaky courage than Jenny's contradictory behavior? He examined his morning stubble in the mirror he'd polished out of a scrap of tin. The thought of once more confronting Al, a thoroughly pissed-off Al once he saw the macabre joke they intended to play, could be causing him to lose his nerve.

What if Jenny's intuition was better than his? What if this were an exercise in futility? But the alternative, he reminded himself, was unthinkable. Picking up a many-times flattened tube of shaving cream, Jack pressed the back of his razor along it, squeezing out the last of the cream, rubbing the little left into his skin, deciding that a sign of deteriorating confidence would be neglecting to keep up appearances.

A sudden ringing startled him enough to slice a zit that had appeared overnight, probably a result of stress. What was that? None of the equipment he stored in the panel truck rang. All his electronics beeped, buzzed, or hummed. His digital operated in godlike silence. Unless—but why would Jenny wind the alarm clock when he wasn't looking? What if, in the tussle over the attaché case, he asked himself, short hairs rising, the wires had somehow crossed?

But as the ringing continued with no explosion, Jack, shuddering with relief, realized that Jenny had left her cellular phone behind when she'd left last night. And now he couldn't locate the damn thing. Its ring was muffled. It must have slipped under the bunk bed or behind a shelf. What must she be thinking—that for all his protestations his courage had finally gone south?

Roger snarled. Jack found the dog under the bunk, worrying the phone. He'd been sleeping on it. Jack lifted the receiver, slippery as bone.

The phone line crackled with static. "Hello?"

"We have to cancel."

"Jenny? What's wrong with your voice?"

"I woke up with the flu."

Jack's first reaction was relief, followed immediately by dismay. After all the elaborate preparation, what a letdown. But Al wasn't going to go away just because Jenny called in sick.

"Al's expecting the package. He won't believe this. You said yourself he's just looking for an excuse to sink your ship."

The phone hummed.

"You stay home. I'll make the delivery."

"No way. I'm not having you do my dirty work. Don't you dare do anything till I get there." And the phone went dead.

Suddenly hungry, Jack ate the slice of stale toast and the packet of marmalade he'd copped from the restaurant. Then, unable to sit still, he began rearranging the play money she'd left in the attaché case, making sure the dynamite was covered.

Jenny had hoped to layer the top with real currency, wanting Al to feel a flush of triumph. Then, when Al discovered the packets underneath were phony, he'd go into a near-uncontrollable rage—which Jenny believed would intensify his fear when he uncovered the dynamite. That, she'd said with disconcerting glee, would cause him to take bowel-emptying moments longer before it dawned on him the sticks weren't armed.

Though Jack believed there was every reason not to goad Al unnecessarily, he'd decided not to argue the point, unwilling to have her confirm him timid.

He'd just finished making sure the exposed wires were far enough apart to prevent even the remotest possibility of a connection when he heard a car coming up the road. Pulling aside the sheet that curtained the driver's seat, Jack peered out the bird-dropping-streaked windshield. His heart stopped. Harris's black Cadillac was turning into the lot.

A moment later, wearing a warmup suit, scarf over nose and mouth, Jenny got out. Needing a moment to steady himself, Jack hastened to greet her.

"Don't come close. You'll catch your death. . . ." Coughing painfully, she hawked and spat.

"Watch your tongue."

"Sorry."

"Not that I'm superstitious. Why the Cadillac?"

"Sam took the Jag to be serviced at the company garage." She coughed again, so deeply his own lungs hurt.

"You get home. Get your tail into bed. I'll manage the delivery."

"Not without me."

"What's the big deal? Al's expecting the money at his motel, right? I'll leave it at the desk, make sure he doesn't see me." Jack put his hand on her forehead. "Your skin's clammy. Maybe you ought to see a doctor."

"I don't feel well, that's a fact." She coughed fiercely, putting a shaky hand on his arm for support. "Maybe if I could lay down for a bit?"

He helped her inside, shooing Roger off the bed. She collapsed into the bunk. He covered her with a blanket.

"Where's my phone?"

"You calling a doctor?"

"Al."

Gently, he kept the phone from her. "I'll drive the Caddy, be back before you know it." He walked to the table and started to close the attaché case.

"Wait!" Jenny was sitting up, cheeks flushed. "That play money won't fool him. We need to cover it with the real stuff."

"Why waste it?"

"He'll eventually figure out it's what I offered as a good-faith deposit."

[127]

"I wasn't able to get any more." Jack hated having to say it.

Coughing, she rolled off the bunk, stood for a moment swaying, then, reaching into her jacket, pulled out a handful of what looked like hundred-dollar bills.

"How'd you manage that?"

"Sam rewarded me. For being a good girl."

Jack felt his face grow hot. He turned away from her shame, which had somehow become his. Grabbing Roger, who was attempting to nuzzle her behind, he dragged the amorous dog to the door. "I'll take Roger with me. You rest."

"No!" Her vehemence surprised him. "I need company." She smiled piteously. "But if you could take him out to do his do, so I won't have to get up again?"

Jack took Roger out as she put the money in the case. He waited impatiently as the dog tracked his spoor around the lot, finally lifting his leg over a new sapling. "No!" Too late. Jack snapped Roger's nose, and was rewarded with a muted snarl.

Jack followed the dog into the truck. Jenny was back in the bunk, covered by the blanket, which Roger attempted, unsuccessfully, to crawl under. The attaché case was still open. She'd done a neat job. At first glance, all the money seemed real. Jack closed the lid, spinning the combination numbers. "In case you were worried about me slipping any into my own pocket."

"You mean you've forgotten the combination?"

"You mean you didn't change it?"

She stared. "When'd you start not trusting me?"

"You've got that backward, haven't you?" He picked up the keys and blew her a kiss. "Back within the hour. Love you."

Her lips formed words, and then she began to cough. When the coughing, deep and hacking, continued, he worried that her lungs might deflate. Returning, he began gently pounding her back.

"Please go!"

Her tears were probably the result of stress, Jack thought, carrying the image of her wet-eyed stare with him all the way to the freeway, pushing away the unsettling idea that it may have been something other than her coughing that prevented her admitting that she loved him too.

At the freeway on-ramp, traffic suddenly slowed. Jack stamped on the brakes, grabbing the attaché case before it could rocket toward the dash. What kind of impact did it take to detonate dynamite? Sweating, he put the case under his legs and, as he finally moved into freeway traffic, reminded himself to concentrate on keeping his distance from cars ahead.

He didn't like driving the Cadillac. Power steering presupposed an extra intelligence. Not unlike Jenny, he thought, who seemed to respond to some other consciousness before she made any move. Except, he reluctantly conceded, in making love.

Finding himself drawing up on a fume-spewing old truck loaded with debris from some demolition site, Jack eased up on the gas pedal. The truck's splintered back gate had several rails missing. Those remaining bowed outward from the pressure of the shifting load. A stained tarpaulin meant to keep pieces from sliding off flapped like a sail in a gale, one of its frayed ropes whipping air. Carelessly knotted around a plank was a faded rag meant to serve as a warning flag.

Where were cops when you needed them? The truck's cab, from a glimpse Jack caught through its cracked side-view mirror, was crammed with three sweaty, torn-shirted workers, probably undocumented aliens who didn't know, or were ignoring, the law.

Jack, anxious to get out from behind that hazardous rattletrap, glanced impatiently at the adjoining lane. But the vehicles zipping by were hard on each other's bumpers. Frustrated, Jack edged a fender into the lane, trying to force his way in. An angrily honking horn drove him back.

As Jack considered another attempt, the flapping tarpaulin ripped loose from the truck bed and sailed, like a giant prehistoric bat, out over the freeway. The truck's cracked taillights flashed. Jack stamped on his brakes.

The flagged plank slid off the truck, followed by tangles of wire, wood, and concrete block. Jack tried desperately to swerve away from the falling debris.

Too late. The Cadillac slammed into what felt like a stone wall. A tire bounced over a concrete block. The wheel twisted in his hands.

A report, loud as a thunderclap, brought sweat to his brow. Blowout, Jack thought, momentarily relieved, when he saw the attaché case still intact. He had pictured himself, like the tarp, sailing over the freeway.

The car, however, brakes locked, suspension rocking like a boat in rough water, was skidding sideways toward the shoulder. Jack fought to keep the car from whipping into a turn that would take him plunging over the embankment. He was bracing himself for the crash when the car bounced to a stop at the shoulder's edge.

Slowly, the car listed to one side. Miraculously, Jack, and the attaché case, were still intact.

Behind him, brakes were squealing and horns honking as following traffic tried to avoid the mess scattered across three lanes. Sliding out on the passenger side, Jack, hands shaking, mouth dry, examined the damage. The right-front tire was shredded flat.

Reaching inside to pull the keys from the ignition, Jack walked, somewhat unsteadily, to the trunk. With any luck, Sam Harris would prove as meticulous here as he was at the office, and he'd find an inflated spare tire, with tools for changing it, ready to hand.

Unlocking the trunk, Jack lifted the lid.

It took a moment for his mind to register what he was looking at. Though her eyes, her mannikin-like, electric blue eyes, were open, it didn't take an expert to know that the woman was real. And that the woman was dead.

TWENTY-TWO

Jack had no idea how long he stood looking into the trunk. Certainly long enough to laser every detail into his memory for the rest of his changed-forever life: glassy, unblinking eyes, peculiarly frosted lashes, thick-penciled brows, a slack, unlipsticked mouth, flowing chestnut hair streaked from brow to freckled shoulder in a color like . . . ice.

Jack turned and ran. He sprinted all out, up on his toes, knees high, arms pumping, breath whistling in his nose, lungs screaming for air, in an approximation of the form that had won him second place in the all-Catholic city high school finals.

Frost and ice. A subliminal reminder of he didn't know what telling him to get out of there fast. Better safe than sorry. His mind, with a speed to equal the fastest microprocessors, computed dreadful possibilities. What if it had been planned for this secret passenger to accompany whoever was going to deliver the attaché case, the case loaded with dynamite, supposedly unarmed?

The force of the blast blew Jack off his feet. Only a few pieces of shattered glass, a wheel cover, and some hot shreds of metal raining down from the smog-banded sky hit his sprawled figure. He'd gotten just far enough away.

Face in the gravel, deafened by the explosion, Jack wondered if he were still alive. As pain began throbbing from his various hurts, he sobbed with relief. But he'd no sooner struggled to one knee than he found himself flattened again by a jet-engine-strong burst of wind, followed moments later by the sonic-boomed second explosion.

When Jack found the nerve to lift his head again, he craned back over his shoulder. The gas tank had blow up. Bits and pieces of the car, and he shuddered to think what else, lay scattered along the freeway. All that was left of the Cadillac was a burning shell.

Painfully, Jack got to his feet. Vehicles, trying to avoid collisions, were skidding in all directions. Radiators crumpled. Rear ends accordioned. Drivers, tires squealing, forced to make impossible choices, became unwilling participants in a deafening steel-drum chorus.

All traffic, except for the fast lane, finally ground to a halt.

Jack took several halting steps toward the smoking debris, then stopped. A few passengers, hanging onto cellular phones, were venturing out of their cars. After a melancholy appraisal of their own damage, some began to advance, arms shielding faces against the heat, toward the burning Cadillac. Wide-eyed survivors, bleeding from mouths, foreheads, and noses, huddled in cars. A few glanced curiously his way.

Jack started toward a nearby telephone call box. As he reached for the receiver, however, he hesitated. If he identified himself as the Cadillac's driver, there would be questions. What kind of answers did he have?

"You all right?" A woman was getting out of a nearby ranch wagon.

"Fine."

In the distance hyena-like howls echoed off the surrounding hills. Jack shivered. Sirens.

"Stay right there, I've got a first-aid kit in the boot."

Jack looked down at himself. His left knee, bloodied, could be seen through his pants. His hands, used to cushion his fall, were spotted with blood from gravel embedded in his palms. His side, knee, and hands burned.

The sirens drew closer. The woman found what she wanted in the ranch wagon. Carrying a tin blue box with a white cross, she hastened toward him.

Jack, aware that the edge of the embankment was just behind, forced a smile of thanks before stepping backward, into thin air.

The woman disappeared. The thick ice plant cushioned his fall, and then, slippery as its namesake, released him. Before he could grab on he was tobogganing down the steep incline toward the retaining wall below.

Jack's feet shot over the wall, then his legs, thighs, and waist. His belt buckle caught, slowing his momentum. Arching, he was able to lift his chin just enough to avoid striking the concrete, managing, at the very last moment, to clutch the top with his hands.

Looking up, Jack saw the woman's startled face peering over the embankment. Though the street was more than ten feet below, Jack released his grip and simultaneously kicked away from the wall. Tucking chin into chest, Jack hit the ground with his knees bent to absorb the impact, as he'd been taught in phys ed, and somersaulted. He went head over heels twice before crashing into the wall.

Staggering to his feet, Jack tried to run. But wind and sense had been knocked out of him. He slowed, chest heaving. He became aware that now his thigh was hurting. Something bruised his flesh. Keys. When he'd opened the Cadillac's trunk, he'd instinctively pocketed the metal ring.

They were no use to anyone now. Jack was about to toss them when he noticed there were extras. One probably for the condo, the other long and thin, the size used to lock filing cabinets—or safety deposit boxes. Jack returned them to his other pocket.

Now what? A phone, to warn Jenny. If the Cadillac had been rigged to explode, separate from and coincidental to the dynamite, she was probably in danger. But he was in a neighborhood of stuccoed apartment houses. He couldn't knock on any doors, not disheveled and bloody as he looked.

A nearby alley seemed deserted. Jack spotted a hose connection next to an empty carport. He cleaned himself as best he could, wincing as the water burned his raw skin. There was nothing he could do about his ripped pants.

Limping along interminably long blocks, Jack finally came to a street wide enough to make him think it would lead to a commerical district. Heading east, in the general direction of his canyon, with the comforting idea of shortening the distance Jenny would have to drive to pick him up, Jack, after a dozen more blocks and no stores in sight, began to curse his luck.

When he spotted the convenience store around the next corner, he reminded himself that his luck was fine, considering how narrowly he'd missed being blown into a thousand bloody bits and pieces.

Who was the dead woman? What was she doing in Harris's Cadillac? Had Harris, guessing that Jenny was having an affair, started up with someone himself, triggering another man's lust for revenge? Jack's brain whirled. He had to call Jenny. Sick or not, Jenny always kept a cool head. She'd help him sort this out.

Two graffiti-scrawled phone booths stood outside the store, both occupied. Jack searched his pockets for change: empty. He went inside, forcing himself to be patient as he waited in the line of dusty construction workers and shirt-sleeved salesmen picking up candy and sodas.

When Jack reached the counter and pulled out his last twenty, the Asian clerk, barely visible between the racks of lighters, throw-away razors, and stomach pills, stared at the bill as if he'd never seen one before.

"I need change for the phone."

The Asian pointed to a sign: WANT CHANGE FOR PHONE, ASK AT9T.

"It's an emergency!"

"Next."

Jack turned to those behind him. "Anyone got change for a twenty?"

A few shook their heads; most ignored him. Jack went outside, blinking in the afternoon sun. Cars were pulling into and out of the lot.

"Spare change?"

"Get a job, wino."

A black-haired young woman with a tear tattooed below her eye came out. Jack forced a smile. She opened her patent-leather purse, pulled out a handful of coins, and dropped then into Jack's outstretched hands.

"Pennies from heaven. Thanks, angel."

A Latin male who'd emerged from the store behind her frowned, and Jack, though his face hurt, managed a wink before going back inside.

Impatiently waiting his turn again, Jack spread the coins on the counter. "Dimes." When the Asian hesitated, Jack leaned across the narrow space. "You denying an American citizen his rights? Let's see your green card."

Glaring, the Asian counted the nickels and pennies, then angrily pulled five dimes out of the register and slammed them down.

Outside, both phones were still busy. Sick with a growing apprehension that he was somehow missing a significant point, Jack leaned his forehead against the glass. The occupant, a young black wearing gold chains, becoming aware of him, immediately hung up and fled.

Inside the booth, redolent of expensive after-shave, Jack reflexively hit the coin release, then watched in disbelief as coins clattered into the tray. Steady, he warned himself, resisting laughter that he guessed would be hysterical, and dialed the number of Jenny's cellular phone.

No answer. Where was she? Probably fallen into a feverish sleep. Taken his advice and gone to a doctor. Or. . . ? Jack felt a sudden anguish so keen it was all he could do to keep from bawling. He hung up.

He'd been in shock. He hadn't been able to consider even the possibility that he'd been the target. It may have been planned all along for him to be blown up, along with his unknown passenger.

But that meant Jenny was involved, meant he'd been the focus of some diabolical plot ever since Harris had asked him to deliver that attaché case full of money to Jenny. The money wasn't the bait. Jenny was.

Pull yourself together, he berated himself. He was too ego-centered. The world didn't revolve around him. More likely Harris had been the intended victim. Those "auditors" he'd overheard talking tough to Harris probably had outside connections who resolved problems with violence.

Steady, Jack cautioned himself. His imagination was running amok. Probably the bouncing about of the Cadillac had caused the blasting-cap wires to cross. Even though he'd taken elaborate care to prevent it, he'd put the Cadillac through so many contortions the near-impossible must have happened.

Jack suddenly felt as if he were going to be sick. From the swirling fog in his mind a suppressed memory had emerged: Jenny rearranging money in the attaché case while he was taking Roger for a walk.

Jack came hurtling out of the booth. A motorcycle stood directly in front of him, motor idling. God was good. Jack was about to jump at the miraculous opportunity when a red-bearded giant in a sleeveless sweatshirt, a snake entwined in a skull tattooed on each muscle-crawling shoulder, emerged from the store with two candy bars, both of which he was cramming into his tin-fillinged mouth. God had been teasing him, Jack thought bitterly.

Jack held out his twenty. "This for a ride home."

Crumbs of chocolate and peanut bits flecked the beard as the giant tried to talk. "Call a cab."

"It's an emergency."

"Call nine-one-one."

"Please?"

The giant tossed the crumpled candy-bar wrappers aside. "Outta my way."

"It's against the law to litter." Jack stooped to pick up the wrappers, noticing that the other was standing awkwardly in cowboy boots next to raised brick defining a planted area.

Rising, Jack launched himself at the other's substantial belly. With an enormous grunt, the giant tripped backward over the raised brick and, unable to cushion his fall, hit the ground so hard the earth shook.

Whirling, Jack straddled the motorcycle. Twisting the throttle

[135]

while pushing the cycle off its stand, he roared away, barely keeping his seat, just as the giant scrambled to his feet.

"I'll remember you to your dying day, motherfucker!"

Jack leaned over so far in taking the first street left and then an alley right that the metal footrests raised sparks from the paving. Each time, by kicking at the rising ground, he managed to push the powerful machine upright.

The cycle had a bad muffler. Echoes reverberated off the apartment buildings. If anyone had decided to follow they'd track him by the sound. Though not at all sure he could maintain control, Jack twisted the throttle for more speed. To his surprised delight, the cycle became more buoyant and easier to his touch.

He made it to his canyon lot in fifteen minutes. Roaring up the winding incline, he peered ahead, anxious for a glimpse of his panel truck through the trees and brush.

His truck was not there.

How was that possible? She'd been too sick to drive. He'd felt her clammy forehead, flinched from her racking cough, watched her clutching her cramping stomach.

Maybe her fever had broken, enabling her to drive the truck back to her condo, where she'd feel a lot more comfortable. But what if Harris had planned the explosion to get rid of them both, and discovered that she was still alive. . . ?

Jack kicked the cycle around, rear wheel whipping up dirt, and rocketed back down the canyon road.

The parking lot of the store at the canyon's bottom was almost empty. Skidding to a halt at the phone booth, Jack hit the ground running. With shaking hands he inserted coins, then dialed the Harris number.

He let the phone ring. Even if she were in the bathroom she should have eventually heard. Why wasn't she answering? Though the day was hot, he felt corpse cold.

Jack dialed the number of his desk at MetroBank.

"Data Processing. Nancy."

Palming the receiver, Jack cleared his throat, hoping to clear his head as well. "Don't let anyone know it's me on the phone, okay, Nance? I need to know if Harris is in his office."

"Conscience bothering you?"

"Why should it be?"

"He's been there all day, even had sandwiches brought it, running through your computer logs from day one."

"He won't find anything there."

"You forget about the mainframe backup files?"

Jack's heart stopped. "I cleaned those out when I was put on leave."

"Before or after Harris had copies made?"

Jack's heart suddenly raced. "The morning I left you in charge — you didn't save what I had on-screen?"

"Of course I did. One of your unbreakable rules, remember? But it's my initials on it. That makes me responsible, doesn't it?"

"Nothing there that can hurt you."

"You expect me to take your word for that?"

"If there was ever a time for you to trust me, Nance, it's now."

"You shit! Trust? I drove by your lot day before yesterday during my lunch hour. You two sure had that truck rocking!"

Heart sinking, Jack remembered the beat-up Volkswagen that had strained to make the grade on the afternoon Jenny had visited. Even in the midst of his anxiety, he felt shamed for himself, embarrassed for her. "Please, Nancy, when I get a chance to explain you'll understa —"

She'd hung up. Jack started to redial, but put the receiver back. Was it coincidence that Harris was tracking his personal computations now? His life was coming unraveled, pulled apart by forces beyond his control.

Another thought riveted him. He was suddenly chillingly certain that the dead woman, though for the life of him he couldn't think why, had been meant all along to point an accusing finger, for crimes of passion, crimes of plunder, directly at him. Worst of all, he'd helped them do it.

TWENTY-THREE

Jack ditched the noisy motorcycle a few blocks south of Los Feliz. Hastening toward the Regent Tower, trying to disregard his painful limp and the sickening feeling that whatever he might discover was only going to make a bad situation worse, he was surprised to find his truck parked just around the corner from the limp-flagged entrance. Why hadn't she driven it into the garage? Had she reason to be afraid her husband was coming home early?

The truck was unlocked. Roger was not inside. Two dynamite sticks armed with blasting caps were. Jack felt the marrow in his bones dissolving. Hadn't he packed all the sticks into the attaché case? If two had been overlooked, why were they now in view, begging whoever found them to assume they belonged to him?

It was not in his best interests to leave them. Carefully removing the blasting caps, Jack slid the sticks into an inside jacket pocket, and the blasting caps into another, before heading toward the garage.

Under the front awning, already fading in the summer sun, the parking attendant and the doorman were, as usual, exchanging jokes. Ducking behind the poisonous, blood purple oleanders lining the ramp, Jack slipped around them to enter the underground garage.

He half expected to see her Jaguar, which would mean Harris was home. The empty slot was only partially reassuring. At least that part of her story had been accurate. That still didn't explain why she hadn't left him some sort of message at the lot.

The elevator gate was locked. On a hunch, Jack tried the condo door key—and the lock clicked open. Hearing a car approaching, Jack quickly stepped into the cage, slammed the gate shut, and leaned on the button for the penthouse floor. The elevator delayed for a moment, causing sweat to gather at his armpits and brow, then lurched upward.

He'd no sooner stepped into the corridor than the doors banged shut behind him. With a jerk, the elevator started back down. Who had recalled it? Had someone seen him come up?

Hastening to the Harris condo, Jack put his ear up against their door. Not a sound. Inserting the key, he had a pulse-quickening moment as the door stuck, imagining it as having been locked by her. Probably she was inside, he told himself happily, and in a moment her explanation, like off-shore wind sweeping pollution before it, would make everything refreshingly clear.

But a stronger push that sent pain through his shoulder popped the door open, dashing his expectations.

Throwing the dead bolt shut against surprises, Jack made a beeline for the bedroom. The bed was unmade. Trying to avoid looking at those disorderly sheets, or identifying the all-too-familiar scent, which caused him a brief, unexpected, and shameful quickening of sexual excitement, Jack, becoming more depressed by the moment, went into the bathroom.

He was certain he'd find her toiletries gone. But the row of creams, unguents, bath oils, and perfumes was glitteringly intact, with nothing, so far as he could see, missing. Not even her diaphragm, drying on a pink, monogrammed washcloth.

Heartsick, Jack opened her closet.

That part of his mind dealing with the unacceptable had also expected her clothes to be gone. But the closet was full.

Why was he so convinced that Jenny would flee? It made no sense. If she were part of a conspiracy against him, she'd believe him dead, with nothing to fear.

And then he spotted the warm-up suit she'd worn that morning. It was hanging on a hook to the side of the closet, her jogging shoes placed neatly underneath. For a moment, he felt relieved. Someone on the run wouldn't take time to be so orderly.

He was about to turn away when something about the shoes brought him back. They were well-worn, dusty-pink, a matching color to the sweat suit. But Jenny's shoes had been new, he reminded himself. And red. The color of oleanders; the color of poisoned blood.

Anxiety levels soaring, Jack explored every inch of the stuffy closet, paying particular attention to the rack of French- and Italian-made shoes, none of which he remembered her wearing. Not finding the pair he was looking for, he went back into the bedroom, and, distasteful though it was, looked even under that unmade bed.

No red shoes anywhere. She'd come back here, changed out of

her warm-up suit, but not her shoes, and left. What would she be wearing? Where would she have gone?

Clinging to the faint hope that the explanation, when it came, would be so obviously simple it would give them one of those wonderful memories long-loving couples delighted in, Jack, sore of muscle as well as of heart, limped into the living room.

Nothing out of the ordinary. Bottles on the breakfront bar glistening in the afternoon sun, magazines neatly displayed on the etched-glass coffee table, the piano closed to protect the keys from dust, two gold-framed photos on the ebony top . . .

Where had those come from? He hadn't noticed photos the last time he was here. Suddenly uneasy, Jack walked to the piano for a closer look. He stopped, unable to breathe, feeling as if his veins had opened and all his blood was draining from his body.

There were two photos. One a wedding portrait of a younger Harris in morning coat and striped pants alongside a young woman in a satin bridal gown and jeweled veil. The companion portrait was of the same couple years older: Harris in an English-cut dark suit alongside his wife, who was wearing a strand of pearls over an elegant black dress. Her long hair, tied back with a velvet ribbon, showed off pearl earrings, secured to each delicate lobe by a small, beautifully cut diamond.

She also wore a bejeweled watch and a diamond pin.

She was the woman in the Cadillac's trunk.

Jack, fighting against a primal urge to scream, managed to stand his ground, despair turning to growing fury.

Jenny had worn those earrings. Jenny had bought a watch and diamond pin. Jenny had claimed to be Mrs. Samuel J period Harris. Jenny had taken the place of the woman in the photograph. Jenny had played him like the worst kind of sap.

Jack became painfully aware that the keys he'd been clutching had cut his palm to the bone. What did that long, thin, and now bloody key fit? Not a filing cabinet, or a closet safe, as he'd earlier thought. Something more prosaic. A padlock.

Frost and ice. A sudden insight, the same intuition that had warned him to run from the Cadillac before the explosion, now pushed him, a sinner dreading but unable to avoid the ultimate confrontation, through the kitchen to the service porch.

The freezer. Stocked with a slaughtered deer, Jenny had said. Sam a hunter who enjoyed making a kill. And the padlock, installed, according to Jenny, to discourage theft during the move from Phoenix, was open.

Jack lifted the lid. The freezer badly needed defrosting. Ice crystals an inch thick lined the spacious, and now empty, interior.

Something had been caught in the door hinge. Reluctantly, Jack tugged it free. A wisp of hair. Chestnut hair. Like Jenny's. Like the woman's in the Cadillac's trunk. Only her hair had been natural, Jack remembered with a shudder. Jenny's was not, he'd discovered, with some surprise, during the first of their passionate encounters.

What if Jenny had dyed her hair to match that of the woman in the trunk? What if she'd penciled her eyebrows to match the arch of the other's as well, what if her eyes had been changed to china blue by colored contact lenses?

Skin crawling, Jack shook the sticky hair loose from his fingertips and ran back into the living room. Pouring himself half a glassful of Napoleon brandy, he took a large gulp, eyes watering as the alcohol heated his throat and stomach. His heart speeded, bringing needed oxygen to his suffocating brain.

A radio on the kitchen counter. Jack plugged it in, twisting the dial to find an all-news station. He drank again, listening to an interminable commercial about pest control, and then a woman's voice with:

"Sigalert update. Four lanes westbound on the Santa Monica Freeway from Sepulveda Boulevard east still blocked by a multicar accident. Alternate routes are advised for at least the next few hours."

A man's voice: "Stacey, we've got reporter Bill Goland on the scene. You have a report for us, Bill?"

"Yes, I do, Chuck. It's a gory one. We've got half a dozen ambulances taking away the injured and fire trucks using foam to try and smother the fire from spilled gasoline. According to fire captain Leo Schmidt, there's a suspected car bombing involved here, with at least one victim, a woman, not yet identified. Police on the scene have sent out an alert for the driver of a Cadillac Coupe de Ville with Arizona license plates who was seen fleeing the scene on foot. I'm told that police bomb squad experts believe, because of the unnecessarily huge amount of explosives used, enough to blow up a train, that it was the work of an amateur whose plan went awry. More details as they come in."

Another commerical, an airline pushing travel to Alaska and Hawaii. Jack went cold, and then hot, and then cold again. Could he hide in Alaska? He began to shake. The aftermath of shock. Quickly, he took another drink, hoping to calm himself. He went over what had been said. A car bombing. A murder victim who would be identified as his boss's wife, blown up, so it would appear, by alleged carelessness on the part of the driver . . . who happened, accidentally or not, to be himself. He was the number-one suspect.

He was in danger. Word was out that he was still alive. Whoever had planned the bombing—Al and Jenny? Harris and his "auditors"?—wanted him, as well as Harris's real wife, dead, for reasons probably having to do with the bank. If Harris had somehow discovered Jack had been switching accounts, he'd be the ideal candidate for scapegoating for the massive leak in funds.

Jack resisted pouring another drink. What he needed now was a clear head. If he was going to make sense to the police, he needed to keep what was left of his wits about him. Calling information, he got the police number.

"Please hold, an officer will be with you shortly. This message will not be repeated. Don't hang up. Your call will be answered in the order in which it was received."

Jack slammed the receiver down. Where were all the cops? Arresting traffic violators? Moonlighting for movie companies? Bouncing at rock concerts? He was about to dial 911, and hesitated. They'd know where he was.

How long would it take him to work his way up the police hierarchy to someone who would understand what he was telling them, and could do something about it? While he sat around answering interminable questions, Jenny would be getting farther and farther away.

He remembered being given the business card. Finding it in his wallet, he dialed the number.

"Law offices."

"Harry Burgess please."

"Mr. Burgess is out. Take a message?"

"This is Jack . . . Harry's brother." Jack pulled the receiver away from his ear. Was that someone at the door? "I'm not where I can be reached. When he gets back tell him to stay put until I can talk to him. It's an emergency."

Jack hung up. Someone was banging on the door. What was that buzzing? The intercom. Probably the doorman. Had he inadvertently triggered a security alarm?

Jack limped/ran to the service porch. There had to be a rear exit. As elastic as the building codes were, with variances given for the asking to the politically connected, surely the fire department would have insisted that each apartment have more than one way out.

The fire escape was a ladder of narrow width and thin iron imbedded in the stucco just below a balcony so small it looked like an afterthought. Before easing himself over the edge, certain that the concrete poured for this building had the consistency of cheese, Jack dropped the dynamite sticks into the freezer and closed the padlock. He swung carefully onto the first rung, then watched, transfixed, as the stucco plaster around the top joints of the ladder cracked and bubbled.

The ladder pulled an inch out of the wall—and held. Sweating, leaning into the wall in the wistful hope that his weight would push the ladder's brackets back into the plaster, Jack carefully slithered down the rungs, imagining that he could hear someone breaking open the front door of the condominium. How long before someone thought of the fire escape?

The ladder ended twelve feet above the ground. A six-foot extension was attached by an S-hook. Jack worked to release the extension, skinning his fingers as he finally twisted the hook free.

But the ladder didn't budge. Paint was binding the ladders along the channels where they joined.

He was running out of time. But one look convinced him he couldn't risk dropping that far; he was too beat-up.

Tentatively at first, then harder, Jack began jumping on the rungs of the extension, praying that the ladders would separate before his weight pulled the cheap structure out of the wall. With a jerk that almost threw him off, the extension broke free and dropped with a clang that echoed along the alley.

Jack clung desperately to the swaying tin. Reminding himself that he had no choice, he spidered his way down to the last rung, gratefully jumping the remaining three feet to the ground.

Running as best he could, Jack headed for the nearest corner. Above him, from the rear balcony, someone was yelling. Grabbing his bruised thigh for support, Jack managed to break into an awkward gallop.

The truck was hemmed in front and back by almost identical gray BMWs. Sliding into the driver's seat, Jack reached for his keys, then remembered that he'd given them to Jenny. It took precious moments to hot-wire the ignition, and a long moment after that before the protesting starter turned the motor over.

Gears clashing, transmission shuddering, Jack made a half-dozen moves forward and back, banging off the bumpers of the BMWs bracketing him. Finally, just as the doorman and the parking attendant came hollering down the block, he forced the truck out of the cramped space, flinching as his side-view mirror bent and shattered against the side of the front BMW.

In the shard of mirror that remained intact, Jack glimpsed a young man in a Zachary All three-piece suit and mirror-polished wing tips come sprinting out of the corner apartment building, only to skid on his slippery, metal-capped leather soles and fall.

Too bad, pal, Jack couldn't help commiserating as he floored the accelerator.

Not that he felt the least bit guilty. Anyone willing or able to spend what a Beamer cost ought to have sense enough not to hem in a truck as beat up as this one. In a city as crowded and hostile as El Lay, foresight was necessary to survive.

If anyone could testify to that, who better than he?

TWENTY-FOUR

Back at Harry's office door, Jack scribbled on a lined yellow legal pad balanced on his good knee, breaking one soft-lead point after another in his haste to get everything down before it was lost in the gathering haze of panic, rage, and memory. From time to time he glanced up at the little black-and-white TV set on the bookshelf between two encyclopedic tomes containing the criminal codes of Los Angeles County and the State of California, watching for a newsbreak while trying to remember whether California practiced the death penalty.

After a harrowing trip downtown, he'd parked the truck in a slot in Harry's office building garage reserved for delivery and maintenance trucks, ignoring the questioning glance given him by the overweight security guard. Then, though H. BURGESS ESQ. ATTY-AT-LAW was listed on the directory, he'd had difficulty locating the office, finally discovering it around the corner of an L-shaped corridor next to a maintenance supply closet.

He'd given Harry's fright-wigged receptionist, a moon-complexioned young woman engrossed in a copy of *Playgirl*, quite a start when he'd limped in.

"You should see the other guy."

"I don't think I'd want to."

"I'm Harry's brother . . . we talked on the phone?"

"He's not back yet." She managed a nervous smile. "Can I get you coffee, or a soft drink, or . . . a Band-Aid?"

"Got a radio?"

"There's a TV set in Mr. Burgess's office."

"That'll do fine." Jack started for the connecting door.

"Wait. I don't think—"

"Harry won't mind. We've never known the meaning of sibling rivalry."

Once inside the windowless office, Jack paced up and down, his mind a whirlwind of furious recollections. Afraid that he might forget something important, some random fact that, if overlooked, would seal his doom, he'd picked up a pad from Harry's desk and begun writing down everything he could recall from the moment he'd first met his arrogant, manipulative new boss. Forget pride, accept humiliation, that way lies absolution, he tried to tell himself, pencil flying over the paper.

Behind him, Jack heard the door bang open. He swiveled to face Harry, who, unfortunately, looked hot, disheveled, cranky, and out of sorts.

"Might have guessed it'd be you. Have you forgotten I'm an only child — and I prefer it that way?"

"I'm in deep shit, Harry. Don't give me a hard time. I didn't want to wait where anyone walking in could see me, so I told a little white lie to your receptionist."

"You look terrible."

"Not half as bad as I feel."

"Mind if I sit in my own chair?"

Jack stifled a groan at the effort it took to get up, gingerly settling into the chair facing the desk. Harry slapped his briefcase down and reached for the TV set control. "Game's on channel eight."

"Fuck the game. I'm waiting to see if I'm on the five o'clock news."

"No kidding. I hope they caught you trying to bribe the Bear quarterback. You remember I've got the office rent riding on this game?"

"I sent you a message not to bet!"

"Too late." The disgruntled Harry pulled one of the criminal code encyclopedias from the shelf. Opening it, he removed the bottle and two glasses nestled inside.

Jack pushed the legal pad across the desk, accepting a drink in return. "Promise not to laugh."

Harry let his eyes slide down the pad, blinked, took a drink, then read the page again more carefully, going on to the next and the next while forgetting his drink. Finally looking up, he pursed his lips and whistled soundlessly.

"What a beautiful scam — course they needed someone with his brain in his dick to pull it off."

"Never mind the compliments. Tell me what to do, Harry."

"Sue the dynamite manufacturer for defective fuses?"

"Get serious. I need advice, bad."

"You've come to the wrong place. Personal injury cases are my forte—what I don't know about criminal law would fill these shelves."

They stared at each other. On the TV screen behind Harry, the logo for the Action News Team came on, with still photos of the toothy anchors followed by the news events they were going to cover, finishing with an aerial view of the massive pileup on the freeway.

"Christ, looks like a war zone." Jack stood as the female anchor, whose facelift had twisted her mouth into a crooked smile, fluttered her gummy eyelashes into the camera. "Turn up the sound."

". . . one of the most massive traffic pileups in the history of Los Angeles when a bomb exploded on the Santa Monica Freeway shortly after two-thirty this afternoon. At least one person known dead, half a dozen injured. Mrs. Jennifer Harris, wife of a vice president of MetroBank Corporation, as well as the daughter of a principal shareholder, has been identified as the bombing victim. Reporter Tony Sanchez, at the county morgue, has more. What have you got for us, Tony? Tony? Can you hear me?"

A huge screen behind the TV anchor showed a mustached reporter, finger pressed against the plug in his hair-covered ear, standing next to a disheveled Harris. "Chris, I'm with Samuel J. Harris, who just identified the bombing victim as his wife. Can you tell us how you feel, Mr. Harris?"

"How would anyone feel when you see there's almost nothing left of the woman you've been in love with for every single minute of a twelve-year marriage? Angry, grief-stricken, deprived, and . . . and . . . ashamed, yes ashamed, because she took the hit intended for me." Harris shook his head, blinking furiously.

"You believe you were the intended target?"

"I'm certain the bomb was intended for me. Jenny—Mrs. Harris—didn't have an enemy in the world. She hardly knew anyone here—we'd just moved from Phoenix. . . ."

"Why would someone want to harm you?"

"I was investigating discrepancies in the bank's accounts. Apparently I was getting too close for somebody's comfort. . . ."

"Is it true that yesterday your wife complained to the police that someone was harassing her?"

"Harassing her to intimidate me! I should have known better than to let her borrow my car." Harris turned away from the camera, a perfectly folded handkerchief pressed to his eyes.

"Just a minute, Chris, I see Brad Wilcox, detective in charge of the investigation. Oh, Detective Wilcox . . ." A large man in a rumpled suit turned. "Is it true you have a warrant out for the arrest of a principal suspect?"

"It's premature to call him a suspect. We do want to speak to Jack Noble, former manager of MetroBank's data processing division, who may be a material witness. Mr. Noble may also have suffered injuries in the explosion, which could have left him somewhat unstable, both mentally and physically. We have his photo, and a license number of a panel truck he was seen driving in the vicinity of the victim's apartment. We'd appreciate hearing from any citizen who may have knowledge of Mr. Noble's whereabouts."

The camera moved in on a card Detective Wilcox was holding. On the screen appeared Jack's MetroBank photo ID, followed by the license number of his truck.

"Back to you, Chris."

"Thanks, Tony. Good report. In a just-breaking development MetroBank has announced a fifty-thousand dollar reward for information leading to the arrest and conviction of this freeway bomber—"

"Turn it off!"

Harry turned off the set and concentrated on his drink. Jack waited until Harry met his eyes. "You going to help me?"

"Maybe you ought to turn yourself in. Doesn't sound like they're putting it all at your door yet. And if you're worried they're out to kill you, at least you'll be in protective custody."

"That's like asking me to climb into my coffin. They've got a motive, and witnesses who saw me driving the car, and other witnesses who saw me running from the Harris condo . . . if I tell my side of things to the boys in blue, they'll laugh me all the way to the death house!"

"I don't think they'd be laughing."

"Thanks. That's very consoling."

"Unless you can produce this babe you say rattled your balls."

Jack stood so suddenly he became dizzied and had to grab the desk for support.

"Maybe you ought to see a doctor."

"I'm going to show those guys that I can play hurt." He handed Harry his parking ticket. "I assume you validate?"

"You forgetting they got an all-points on your license plates?"

Jack hated it that he had forgotten. He'd need to be a lot sharper to go up against Harris and his cohorts. "Loan me twenty?"

Harry stood and went to the connecting door. "Sylvia, before you go—got a twenty? Add it to your paycheck." He returned with the bill in his hand. "What I think you ought to do is head for a country that doesn't extradite to the U.S. . . ."

"That's twenty I owe you—plus how much for the advice?"

"On the house."

Jack paused at the door. "What I forgot to tell you is she took my dog. She shouldn't have done that. That really pisses me off."

"You know what they say. No use crying over spilt milk."

"You know what else they say? He who laughs last, laughs best."

"First you have to find her."

"That's just what I'm planning to do."

"Rotsa ruck."

Hobbling through the empty receptionist's office, Jack fought a growing sense of panic, wondering whether his bravado in front of Harry was anything more than whistling in a world growing darker by the moment. He suddenly stopped and stared at the phone.

Something else he'd forgotten. And no wonder. From the moment he'd realized all his plans for a shining future had blown up with the bomb, he'd dreaded having to make this call.

Reluctantly, Jack dialed the retirement home number and asked to speak to his father.

"He's busy at the moment."

"Can he hurry up whatever it is? This is his brother. His long-lost brother. The one in the merchant marine. Calling from San Pedro. My ship's about to sail, and God only knows when I'll get another chance. . . ."

"I'll see if the police are finished talking to him. . . ."

Jack felt as if his bones were shrinking. He could picture his father trying to absorb the shameful story the police were telling, struggling against the understanding that his eternally optimistic, risk-taking, rattle-brained son had destroyed any hope of his ever getting out of the Lysol-saturated place they had their nerve calling a home.

"It's the brother in the merchant marine! Got that? And the minute I finish this cruise I'm coming to get him!"

"Mr. Noble?" A voice that came all the way up from heavy *cojones.*

"Depends on who's asking."

"Sergeant Wilcox. Homicide. I suggest you tell us where you are and allow us to come pick you up. The longer you delay the worse things are going to go for you."

Jack held the receiver under his arm. Cupping his hands around his mouth he moaned in his best imitation of a foghorn. He grabbed the receiver again. "Sorry, you've got the wrong Noble. Gotta run. Gangplank's going up. Tell my brother I'll send him a postcard from the next port."

"Your dad says—"

Banging down the phone, Jack limped out the door, footing as unsteady as if he were indeed on a pitching ship's deck. For a moment he deluded himself that the imp inside his head who spoke without thinking had hit on the right solution: he'd head for Long Beach, stow away on a foreign-flag freighter sailing for some exotic clime, and end his days on a jungle beach sucking up fermented coconut milk while scantily clad, brown-skinned maidens cooled his sweated brow with palm fronds.

Then a humiliation so great that he had to lean against the wall for support swept over him. The shame was unbearable. He'd always known he had as many faults as the next guy, but never had he considered himself the kind of simpleminded fool who could be taken advantage of so easily. What he hated most was that he'd been so predictable. We'll hook him, Harris had said. Not a fish. Pavlov's dog. Show him a shapely hiney and he'd go slavering after.

He considered going back inside and calling the police to come get him. It all seemed so hopeless. His only chance at survival was to find Jenny. But since she'd lied from first moment to last, he couldn't take anything she'd let drop about her background as even close to the truth, let alone a lead to tracking her down.

The moment passed. And the anger returned, but this time it was controllable. He'd be damned before he gave it up so easily. Somewhere, somehow, if he bought himself enough time, he'd find a clue to her whereabouts, either in memory or when Harris and his cohorts made a move to cash in.

Right now his first priority was a hiding place. Someplace no one would ever think of looking. Someplace where he could lick his wounds, nurture his anger, gather his strength, and wait for the opportunity to strike back.

TWENTY-FIVE

Jack drifted through stifling haze. The smell of dust clogged his nostrils. A stab of pain in his back suddenly wrenched him out of his doze.

For a panicky moment he couldn't remember where he was. He was stiff and sore, lying in a cramped position. The bump under his aching body had prevented him from stretching out flat.

How had he been able to drop off? What had awakened him—a shot? Then, before he made the mistake of sitting up, he heard the sound of muffled voices and the banging of car doors. Engines started, revved up. Cars began driving away.

The parking lot of the Sports Cafe. After dark, after spotting the unmarked police car staking out the front entrance, he'd managed to slip unseen through the cars in the unattended back lot to Claire's car, an aging Honda Civic with a bumper sticker that read I (HEART) LOVE.

The flimsy catch had been easy to jimmy. He'd crawled through the hatchback trunk into the backseat. That bulge under his legs was the transmission.

Footsteps, coming closer. More than one pair. Both flat-footed. Why hadn't he considered the possibility that the cops might be checking each employee's car? Flattening himself against the floorboards, Jack heard weary voices saying good night, and then the car door opened and closed.

Jack tried not to breathe. The motor started. Why wasn't she driving off? His pulse quickened. Had she promised a ride to some kitchen illegal? Music—tape cassette violins playing "Some Day My Prince Will Come." Funny. He hadn't scoped her as having a romantic streak. Then a lurch as the automatic clutch was engaged, a bump and bounce going over the one-way steel grate, and they were rolling.

Jack waited until he could be certain they weren't being followed. Pulling himself up, he couldn't help groaning.

Claire shrieked and slammed on the brakes. The small car slid, tires squealing, against the curb. Jack came hurtling forward and caught himself against the front seat. Now his ribs hurt as well.

"Don't be frightened, Claire. It's me."

"I think my heart actually stopped."

"You all right?"

"I'm okay now."

"Then do you think we might get going?"

The motor had died. Claire fussed with her hair a moment, then adjusted the rearview mirror so she could see him. Averting her eyes, she started the Honda again and continued down the street.

"I'm really sorry to scare you like this. But I couldn't risk coming inside. . . ."

"I know. Cops were asking about you."

"That bomb was meant for me."

"That's what her husband claims."

"He's lying."

"Okay."

"Claire, I need a place to hide out, at least long enough to —"

"You can stay with me as long as you like."

Claire's place, near the golden, trumpet-playing-angel-topped dome of the Mormon Temple, was a small garage apartment just below the tracks on little Santa Monica between Overland and Westwood boulevards. Though at this hour it was unlikely any of Claire's neighbors would be up, Jack hunched into his coat collar as he followed Claire up the worn stone staircase.

Inside, Clair flicked on the light switch and watched, pleased, as Jack's eyes widened. Glitters of light, like a fall of silent hail, stormed from the enormous glass chandelier into a surreal glow provided by a half-dozen dimly lit lamp shades, beaded with glass the color of honey, scattered about the apartment. Doilies embroidered with tiny beads green as ocean foam covered the arms and headrests of overstuffed chairs. Curtains of lacquered bamboo stalks, separated by clear tubular glass and strung together with colored twine, divided front room and kitchen, hallway and bedroom.

"Beads are my hobby." Claire walked through the curtain to the kitchen, a sound like a muted marimba band trailing from the hollow bamboo stalks rattling against each other. "I'll make us some tea."

"I'd prefer something stronger."

"You need something to calm your nerves, not crank you up more."

"Please don't mother me, Claire."

She glared at him through the curtain. "I look that old to you?"

"I didn't mean it to be insulting."

"That an answer?"

"Of course you don't look old."

"Then how come you never made a pass at me?"

Jack blinked. " . . . I think of you as a friend."

Clair disappeared. A trumpet sang "I'm in the Mood for Love," the music filling the apartment. Apparently the record player was in her bedroom. She returned with two china cups of steaming tea.

"What kept you?"

"Microwave." She handed him a cup. "You never got the hots for a friend?"

"What's gotten into you?" Jack grimaced as the liquid burned his mouth.

"Nobody, for too long. Don't act so surprised. You think I load your plate with extra goodies because of my maternal instincts? If I had the bucks to shop Beverly Hills, get my hair blown and my body steam-cleaned, I could damn well attract a young stud to service me."

"That's not how it was!"

"Tell me about it. You were attracted by her sensitivity, her love of the finer things. The fact that she wore French perfumes and drove a convertible Jaguar XJ-S had nothing to do with it. If she told you her arches hurt and the starch in her uniform gave her a rash you'd still follow her around with your tongue hanging out."

"You're confusing me with my dog."

"Don't flatter yourself."

"I guess I deserve this."

"Only because you still don't understand what happened to you. You're an easy mark, Jack. You want it all, right now, like those high rollers your bank supports—this babe had you programmed from the beginning, sucker."

"I do deserve this. But it won't happen again. Believe me."

"Yeah? If she put her mind to it she could still convince you her piss runs uphill."

Jack swallowed his anger along with his tea. He wasn't in any position to argue. And stupid as it might seem, he couldn't deny that deep within himself resided a faint hope that if he could only find Jenny she'd be able to explain away everything.

"I'm too tired to argue, Claire. Shall I take the couch?"

[153]

"Bed's more comfortable."

"I couldn't deprive you of your bed."

"It's big enough for two — when they're friends."

The blood drained from Jack's face. She couldn't be serious. This was her idea of a practical joke. But there was no mistaking the amorous look on Claire's face.

Take it easy, he cautioned himself. Her aggressiveness was merely a cover for a lack of self-confidence. She was exposed and vulnerable. If he was to bring her back to her senses without hurting her irrevocably, it would take every bit of skill he possessed.

"Have you taken a good look at me, Claire? I'm beat up. I'm walking wounded, inside and out. I'm too shook to do anyone any good."

"I'll be the judge of that. All you need is a hot bath with Epsom salts and some fuel in your tank. While you're soaking I'm gonna cook you pastrami and eggs. You've been too busy to have et in a while, I'll bet."

"I'm not hungry, Claire. I doubt I could keep anything down."

"I'll draw your bath." The bamboo chattered, like the laughter of lustful monkeys.

"Claire . . ."

She poked her head back through the curtain, her moussed hair suddenly crowned, glittering like a tiara on an aging queen. "You want to stay here, you do what I say."

Jack's head whirled. This couldn't be happening. Another record had dropped on the changer. "If I'm Not Near the One I Love, I Love the One I'm Near."

Didn't women claim that sex was a man's thing, love a woman's? He couldn't believe she'd want to make love to him against his will. What pleasure could she possibly get from a reluctant lover? Surely, he consoled himself, she'd had enough experience to understand that the very idea was a turnoff.

But when he slid his aching flesh into the steaming tub and the water stung his hurts, he was horrified to discover that his member was extending. What was this? What perverse part of his nature was causing him to respond? Was that salacious imp inside himself taking over? Or did his concern for Claire's needs supersede his own? It didn't comfort Jack in the least to consider that while it may have been all of those things, it was mainly an instinct, his specifically and man's in general, to survive.

"How're you doing? Feel better? Oh, I see you do feel better." She had taken off her uniform, reapplied her makeup, and was wearing a mauve dressing gown trimmed with a feather boa. The gown had no belt, and she wasn't doing a very good job of holding it closed.

He couldn't help noticing that her breasts, though large, were firm. Her perfume was overwhelming.

"Claire . . ."

"Don't say anything. Don't spoil the moment." Her voice had gotten throaty.

She flicked off the overhead light switch, and, in the rainbow glow of a beaded lamp set on the back of the toilet, started taking off her gown. She was as large and rosy as a woman in a painting by Rubens.

"Claire! The food's burning. . . ."

She was sliding into the tub. "Food's on hold. It's me that's on fire." She straddled him and clasped his hand. "Touch me, Jackie. Please!"

To his everlasting dismay, Jack found that for reasons beyond his control he was unable to resist her heartfelt plea.

TWENTY-SIX

Jack slept the sleep of the dead, not of the just. When his body stirred at the twitter of nocturnal creatures, his mind fought against awakening, sensing the misery and discontent that would come with consciousness.

"You slept like a baby."

Reluctantly, he opened his eyes. Claire, dressed in a freshly laundered uniform, beamed at him from the doorway. She was still in an afterglow. The glass-beaded curtain continued its muted chatter.

"Bet you're hungry now."

He was. He was also unable to meet her eye. Last night, after the command performance, overflowing the tub and dampening the polyester sheets in the queen-size bed, he'd dropped into an anesthetized sleep, her cries of encouragement, at once stimulating and revolting, still echoing down the darkening corridors of his brain.

Had they traded sexual roles? For the first time he understood what women must feel when they'd been coerced into trading sex for favors. He felt diminished in some fundamental way. No more, he vowed fervently to himself. He had to get out of this situation, now.

"Want breakfast in bed?"

He flinched from her suggestive tone. "I'll come to the kitchen." He managed a melancholy smile. "If you'll give me a minute?"

"I'll give you five."

He limped to the bathroom and did his best to avoid looking at himself in the mirror. The inadvertent glimpse he got of a face that revealed very little of his inner distress only added to his resolve to get out as soon as possible.

But when he returned to the bedroom his clothes were gone. Dismayed at the thought that she might have misinterpreted his unwilled arousal as enthusiasm, he put on the faded dressing gown she'd laid out on the bed, kicking aside the deerskin slippers to preserve what was left of his self-respect.

Humming under her breath, she was sliding a great heap of scrambled eggs and pastrami from the nonstick skillet to a plate rimmed with fresh sliced tomatoes sprinkled with scallions.

"My clothes?"

"I'm dropping them off at the cleaners on my way to work." She poured him coffee that gave forth the smell of cinnamon, which she should have remembered he hated, then began buttering toast. "Those tomatoes are fresh from the garden. Eat. Keep your strength up."

That almost cost him his appetite. But his bruised body needed sustenance; he'd see about repairing his soul later.

"There a morning paper?"

"Nothing in it you don't already know."

"I'd like to see it."

The headline, though expected, gave him a jolt.

CITYWIDE HUNT FOR BOMBING SUSPECT

Embezzled Five Million Dollars, MetroBank Executive Says

The data processing manager of MetroBank's headquarters unit, suspected of accidentally triggering a bomb that killed a bank official's wife, was the subject of an intensive search by police today. All airports, bus, and railroad terminals are being watched, and car rental agencies in the greater Los Angeles area have been alerted.

It is believed that the intended target was the victim's husband, Samuel J. Harris, a MetroBank vice president supervising a system-wide audit, as part of an attempt to cover up a money laundering scheme. Bank officials asserted that the suspect, Jack B. Noble, MetroBank's data processing manager for the past two years, had been in a perfect position to manipulate the bank's accounts, and may have embezzled more than five million dollars. The bank claims to have unearthed an account that Noble had opened under a pseudonym that would have enabled him to illegally appropriate funds from other accounts.

Noble, who is thought to have injured himself in the explosion, is alleged to have a gambling problem. He is known to have been a frequent habitué of the Sports Cafe, a hangout for gamblers, whose license is currently under scrutiny by the State Beverage Control Unit for possible violations of state liquor laws.

Though Cafe owners insist that any gambling on the premises is strictly small-time, private and between individuals, they do acknowledge that Noble was working on a computerized sports betting system that they believe he may have tested by illegal wagering with bookies or Nevada sports books.

Noble's fellow employees, none of whom would speak for the record, seemed divided on the accusations against their colleague. Some expressed astonishment that such a "shy, self-effacing individual" could be capable of even contemplating such a massive theft, let alone committing murder.

Others, however, termed him "arrogant and supercilious, a person who in his official capacity may have been guilty of sexual harassment, relishing, it was said, the role of dominant male."

Noble supervised an all-female data processing pool, which he himself nicknamed the "henhouse," and some workers characterized him as a "strutting cock-of-the-walk," complaining that Noble attempted to sexually humiliate them by "crowing like a rooster at inopportune moments."

According to other co-workers, Noble continually "bragged about his ability to make a computer do tricks, and boasted about a mansion he would soon be building on his million-dollar-view lot in the Hollywood Hills."

Noble's salary, however, it was pointed out by loan officers in the bank's mortgage department, was not adequate for him to even apply for a mortgage loan large enough to build such a mansion.

In applying for a murder warrant, police asserted that they have obtained statements from fellow executives who have heard Noble make derogatory comments about his new boss, Samuel J. Harris. He is further alleged to have been furious when put on forced leave during the audit of the bank's books, which, it was pointed out, effectively removed him from blocking the discovery of his own responsibility for the massive leak in funds.

Jack's face burned. It's a put-up job, he wanted to yell. Couldn't everyone see it was all too neat, a preconceived, malevolent plan to enmesh him in an intricately plotted circumstantial web?

"Those aren't very good pictures of you."

One of the photos displayed on the front page was from his ID card, the other a snapshot of him surrounded by the chicks in the henhouse. Nancy, darling Nancy, was looking at him with trust and affection.

The food tasted bitter in Jack's mouth. He could imagine what she must be thinking now. Had she, confronted with fresh evidence of his betrayal, provided the authorities with the photo, as well as those awful quotes about his character? Even if she had, he couldn't bring himself to blame her.

On the continuing page was a portrait of the real Mrs. Harris, captioned "Bombing Victim." The story below announced "Funeral Services For Mrs. Samuel J. Harris, Socially Prominent Banker's Wife, To Be Held in Phoenix."

Of course. Harris had moved here from Phoenix. Harris must have murdered his wife on the eve of his transfer. Her friends and acquaintances would think she had moved to Los Angeles. And there was no one in Los Angeles to question the substitution of Jenny as his wife.

"Claire, I've got to get out of town."

"How? You read the paper. They're looking for you everywhere."

"If you loaned me your car and a few bucks for gas . . ."

"You mean you blew the whole five million? Just kidding.

Honey, best thing is stay put till you're no longer news. Meanwhile, I'll make sure you're well fed. And taken care of otherwise."

Jack tried not to show his dismay. "Don't think that I'm not appreciative. . . ."

"You showed me that all right. Boy." Claire leaned over and offered her lips. Jack, careful not to shrink from her or sulk, met them as chastely as he could without making it an insult.

Claire hadn't seemed to notice. "Make yourself at home. There's music, TV, and some brand-new paperback romances I just bought. Savage romances. They're make-believe, of course, but stimulating. I'll call you on my break, see how you're doing." And she was gone in a rustle of beads.

Though he'd lost his appetite, Jack forced himself to finish the platter of eggs. God knew when or how he'd get his next meal. Taking his dishes to the sink, he washed and dried them, trying to overcome the feeling that he was trapped. How could he get to Phoenix with no clothes and only a little over twenty dollars cash?

He went into the bedroom. Averting his eyes from the tangled bedcovers, he lifted the mattress. Claire had made a crack about banks; she probably distrusted them. But no stash was revealed.

He opened Claire's closet. Dresses, of a style appropriate to someone who'd wear a feather boa. Not even any pants suits. Even if he had the nerve to dress like a woman there was no way this clothing would fit.

Tomatoes, Jack thought then, as he tongued a seed from a tooth and cracked it between his front incisors. Fresh from the garden. Surely Claire didn't weed in dresses.

He found the coveralls on a hook in the garage. A little tight in the crotch, but otherwise not a bad fit. The fact that the elbows and knees were stained with earth, making him look something like a bum, was probably a good thing. In a city crowded with homeless it could prove an advantage.

Jack was in such a hurry to leave that he started out the door before reminding himself that he wasn't as well prepared as he should be. Going back to the kitchen, he used up what was left of the bread to make four and a half peanut butter sandwiches, knotting the plastic wrapper to keep them reasonably fresh. God only knew when he'd get another chance to eat.

He scoured the pantry one last time. There had to be money somewhere. On the refrigerator's back shelf he found it: a half-gallon milk carton partially filled with coins. Stuffing his pockets with quarters and half-dollars, Jack scrawled an IOU for $22.50 before replacing the carton.

He was halfway across Santa Monica Boulevard, climbing the embankment to cross over to the more heavily trafficked side, when he stopped.

Tracks. The railroad had once traveled here, from downtown to the sea. They still owned the right of way, but he hadn't seen trains here since he was a child. No money, dressed like a bum—what better way to get to Phoenix?

Jack caught a bus marked DOWNTOWN. He dropped four quarters and a dime into the receptacle.

"This go anywhere near the railroad yards?"

"You mean Amtrak station?"

"I mean freight yards."

The driver, a dour, heavyset black woman, handed him a transfer slip. "I'm not sure. Take a bus south at Alameda."

The bus was half-filled, mostly cleaning women and maids enduring the long ride to the cheaper rent sections of town. Taking a seat adjacent to the rear door, in case he had to exit hastily, Jack kept an eye on those boarding, though he doubted that these low-income, non-English-speaking riders would have paid much attention to the news about bank embezzlement.

The trip seemed interminable. The bus stopped twice in every block. The driver seemed oblivious of anyone's need to make time, braking at every signal, whether red or not. It was near midafternoon by the time they passed through the battered brick buildings of a deteriorating commercial area, coming down the hill above a downtown whose buildings were being built higher and higher, trying to get away, Jack thought, from the litter and bedlam on the mean streets below.

The bus groaned its way alongside crowds swarming through curbside flea markets and stores, most of whose merchandise seemed displayed on outside racks. Spanish-language movie theaters announced double and triple features, and from buildings once occupied by posh department stores, signs in Spanish identified discount jewelry and immigration lawyers. The streets swarmed with the colorfully clothed, multiracial humanity of a third-world city. Only an occasional sign in English served as a reminder of a once-dominant culture being submerged by this tidal wave sweeping west from the Los Angeles River.

Jack coughed. He couldn't seem to clear his throat. Fumes from bumper-to-bumper traffic, mostly trucks and buses, spewed from diesel-engine standpipes, spotting the brown air with particles of soot. Jack's eyes and nose began watering.

It seemed hours before the streets widened into an industrial district. Then, when the bus stopped at what seemed the middle of the street, Jack saw the tracks. This must be Alameda. Spirits lifting, he pressed the signal for the next stop.

Descending, he saw the street sign: Central Avenue. Blocks short of his goal. Before he could get back aboard, however, the bus had pulled out, its exhaust enveloping him in a cloud of soot.

Disgusted at this latest in what seemed a never-ending series of bad decisions, Jack limped to the corner. He seemed to be the only pedestrian, and no other bus in sight. He began heading east, swearing to himself, when he heard a sonorous horn, then the clanging of a crossing bell. Turning, he saw an engine pushing a string of freight cars.

Running reminded him that he was bruised and sore. Nearly out of breath, Jack finally managed to gain on the slow-moving train.

An iron ladder ran up the side of the last car. Reaching for it, Jack became aware that, slow-moving or not, a misstep could propel him under those grating iron wheels. It was awkward maneuvering with his left hand. But he was reluctant to drop the sandwiches, which he'd need for his trip. No more trusting the Lord to provide, he told himself, as he concentrated on grabbing the ladder and jumping for the bottom rung.

He slammed into the side of the car with more force than he'd intended. But his feet were securely on the bottom rung. And he'd kept his grip on the sandwich bag.

Jack decided against climbing to the top. The train was probably heading for the central yards, which shouldn't be too far away.

He didn't notice that down the tracks ahead of the train a brakeman was unlocking a siding switch. But the brakeman, looking up, had noticed him.

TWENTY-SEVEN

The brakeman, a burly man with a face leathered by sun, unsheathed a club that looked as long and lethal as a sawed-off pool cue. Trotting forward, he bounced his club off the sides of the passing freight cars.

"Okay, asshole, off the train!"

Jack, startled, clung to the ladder. He didn't want to get off. Not sure what else to do he pulled the punched slip out of his pocket. "I've got a transfer."

"This ain't a streetcar, wiseass." Reaching him, the brakeman turned and trotted alongside, pounding the stick into his palm with a sickening slap.

"I've got peanut butter sandwiches I'm willing to share. Made them myself. Fresh-baked bread."

The brakeman stared. "How old're you?"

"Practically thirty."

"A bum at thirty? Shame on you. Drugs or booze?"

Jack hesitated. He didn't want to disappoint the man. But before he could choose an answer the truth slipped out. "Women."

"The worst addiction of all. But there's no ailment that chanting can't remedy." Reaching into his coverall pocket, the brakeman pulled out a pamphlet and thrust it at Jack.

Nichiren Shoshu, the cover title read. Jack looked the question.

"It's a branch of Buddhism," answered the brakeman.

"I already have a religion."

"They chant?"

"The monks do. Sometimes the priests. Nuns merely hum."

The brakeman wasn't amused. "You start chanting it'll get you through anything. Even woman sickness."

"I suppose it's worth a try."

"You ain't rode the rails before, have you, son?"

Jack hoped that what he sensed was compassion, and not some malicious tease. "I've been offered a job in Phoenix."

"The railroad dicks spot you in the yard, they'll break your ass."

"How far is it?"

"Maybe a mile."

"I'll get off before we get there."

The brakeman stopped at the siding switch. Jack hoped he'd seen the last of him. But after waiting for the last car to grind past and locking the switch back to its original position, the brakeman trotted to catch up.

"Keep a cautious eye out. Railroad men ain't the only ones you got to worry over." He quickened his step toward the engine before Jack could ask what he meant.

Sighing, Jack pressed his forehead against the ladder rungs. Life was becoming troublingly unpredictable. How much longer could he continue to improvise and luck out? He'd imagined being yanked off the train, beaten, and arrested. Instead he'd been proselytized. And not Mormonism or Christian born-agains either, but some Far Eastern sect he'd thought confined themselves to airports and Hollywood Boulevard.

By the time the slow-moving train approached the yard's outskirts, Jack had pretty much forgotten the brakeman's warning. He rode well into the yard before jumping down. Tenting his hands, in the manner of talk show hosts and the head-wrapped Hindus he'd seen in movies, he bowed to the brakeman, who, leaning out the engine window, began frantically jerking his thumb.

Jack hastily examined his surroundings. A maze of tracks looped into and around maintenance sheds and loading platforms. Two husky crewmen were approaching from a siding. On a track directly ahead freight cars coupled, iron clashing and air hoses gasping as cosmically loud as if the devil himself were being shackled.

Jack hastened purposefully across the tracks toward the other train, hoping the crewmen would mistake him for one of their own.

But what was this train's destination? The names stenciled on the cars were from all over the country. CHESAPEAKE 9 OHIO. ATCHESON 9 TOPEKA. NEW YORK CENTRAL. SOUTHERN PACIFIC. GEORGIA PACIFIC. GREAT WESTERN. SANTA FE.

If the train were headed east, wasn't it likely it would go through Phoenix? he asked himself. With night coming on, he didn't want to find himself traveling hours in the wrong direction.

A cardboard manifest had been stapled to the side of the car marked SANTA FE. Coffee destined for Chicago. Maybe he should just go to Chicago and start life over.

[163]

"Hey, bud—lookin' for samples?" An unshaven man in a filthy knit cap and a vomit-stained, buttonless jacket tied with twine was squinting at him from behind a partially opened door.

"Just a ride. This train go to Phoenix?"

"Bingo. Hop aboard." His grin, front teeth missing, was not reassuring.

"I'm waiting for a friend."

"You're friend's SOL. Dicks come through and kicked everybody's ass off."

"How'd they miss you?"

"I got ways. Better hop on 'fore they spot you."

None of the other freight cars in the gathering dusk seemed open. Telling himself that his concerns were unfounded, Jack reluctantly grasped the hobo's offered, yellow-nailed hand and jumped up. He sprawled inside the car, and sneezed.

The metal floor was covered with a layer of what looked like coal dust. In the darkened interior a large, indistinct figure leaned against bags stacked to the roof. Getting quickly to his feet, Jack almost fell as his foot skidded.

"Coffee beans. One of the bags split." The other's lips were not stained with tobacco, as Jack had thought, but with the residue of chewed coffee beans. "Whatcha got in the sack?"

"Sandwiches. Want one?"

The train lurched forward, and Jack grabbed at the door to catch himself.

"How many you got?"

"Enough to give you one. If you like crunchy peanut butter?"

"What about Gus?"

Jack peered into the dark. Gus, a bulky man, remained silent. "Guess I can spare one for Gus."

"You're a generous soul. God bless you."

The train was picking up speed. Jack leaned against the trembling aluminum wall to balance himself while he unknotted the bread sack. Pulling out two sandwiches, he handed them to the hobo.

"Why ain't you eating?"

"I'll be hungrier later."

The other considered this, then, walking over by the shadowy Gus, he placed a sandwich on the coffee sack Gus was leaning against. Returning, he crammed as much of the sandwich as he could get into his mouth.

Jack, mesmerized by the trouble the hobo was having masticating the sticky bread, finally looked away, concentrating on the passing scenery. They'd left the yards behind, and were crossing the dry bed of the concrete-lined Los Angeles River. In the distance, through the saffron-tinted smog that lined the sinking sun, he could see the frame houses of old developments hanging off the rolling hills, built there for a view that had long since disappeared into the eye-stinging haze.

"That was good. Wasn't it, Gus? Sticks to your ribs. But damned if I ain't still hungry."

Jack decided it was prudent to ignore this.

"How many sanniches you got left?"

"Enough for me."

"Maybe you ain't the generous soul I thought you was."

Jack examined the scenery flashing by, trying to calculate how fast the train was moving. The rapidly clacketing wheels told him a bailout would be disadvantageous. He wouldn't be able to get his legs moving fast enough to prevent serious damage to himself.

The other was reaching for the bread sack. Jack pushed his hand away. "Fuck off."

"You hear that, Gus? This selfish sumbich gonna deny two starvin' human beans sustenance!" The hobo reached for the sack again. "Gimme the sanniches you sumbich or I'm gonna let Gus there, who is a rump ranger, fuck you in the ass!"

Jack, feeling moisture gather in his armpits, held the sack at arm's length out the door. The other, smelling of dried sweat, urine, coffee, and sour wine, leaned against him, tugging at his arm.

Jack felt his stomach turn. Retching, worried about Gus at his back, he braced himself against the door and raised his knee to keep the unwashed hobo off.

The bread sack was whipping in the wind created by the train's speed. Reaching, the hobo stretched himself across Jack. Jack felt himself being slowly pushed through the opening. But giving up the sandwiches would only delay the inevitable, he knew.

Jack panicked. What was Gus doing? Jack grabbed a handful of the hobo's stained jacket with his free hand. "If I go you come with me!"

"Leggo the sack!"

Jack wasn't clear about what happened next. One moment, he was struggling to keep from being pushed through the door. The next the stretched-out hobo's feet, splayed over the spilled coffee beans, moved in a scarecrow's dance. The material of the jacket Jack was clutching ripped.

Jack grabbed for another hold, too late. The hobo, mouth open in a scream sucked away by the wind, was sailing headfirst through

[165]

the door. He bounced, then disappeared. Which way had he fallen, down the embankment, or under the wheels?

Jack, imagining he heard the rhythm of the train's wheels momentarily interrupted, recoiled in horror. And then, in spite of his shock, he remembered Gus.

Whirling around, he braced himself for an attack. But the imperturbable Gus still leaned, casual as an unconcerned bystander, against the coffee sacks. It was somehow disconcerting that Gus's sandwich remained untouched.

"I didn't push him. You could see that, couldn't you? I tried to grab him and he fell!" Jack risked a glance out the door. The night was dark and thick as tar. He felt sick as death. "He brought it on himself."

Gus said nothing. Jack eased himself away from the open door, feeling exposed and vulnerable. He didn't like it that Gus remained so ominously silent. He might be a mute, unable to express rage except through violence.

Moving around a stack of coffee sacks to put a barrier between them, Jack remained alert for the other's slightest movement. Some big men could be quick.

The moon, almost full, came up, flooding the freight car's interior with milky light. Jack blinked, wondering if his eyes were playing him tricks. Gus didn't seem to have any face. And then, with a start, he realized that his fellow passenger was a bundle of clothes.

A coffee sack, half on end, had been tricked up with a jacket and a crumpled hat. Gus had been created either to give any vagabonds with hostile intent pause, or simply to provide the hobo companionship on his long, solitary rides.

Jack felt his eyes tear as he tried to resolve contradictory feelings of anger and compassion. That poor, uncoordinated, lonely wretch had created so realistic a threat it had resulted in his own death.

Going to the open door, Jack threw up. Immediately after he felt hungry. But then he discovered the sack was no longer in his hand. He'd apparently dropped it when grabbing for the falling hobo.

Gus's sandwich, of course, remained uneaten. Jack picked it up, and, munching vigorously to remove the sour taste in his mouth, settled in for the night.

He didn't think he'd be able to rest. But the rhythmic, alternating soprano/bass thrum of the wheels soothed his troubled spirit. Adjusting a sack of beans to pillow his head, he soon dropped off into blessed sleep.

TWENTY-EIGHT

The air was heavy with menace and still as a tomb. Jack's eyelids became transparent. The train had stopped. Had the iron wheels' vibration caused the door, which he'd shut before sleeping, to slide open? Or had it been pulled open by a railroad cop, who was now training a flashlight on his face?

Trying not to panic, Jack opened his eyes — and flinched. He was staring into light. But it was morning light, spilling through gaps where the car's sides did not quite meet the roof. Relieved, Jack got shakily to his feet.

The scent of coffee made him aware of his hunger. Jack threw a handful of beans into his mouth, cracking them between his teeth. He opened the door a hair and peered out.

The train was standing in an area of deserted warehouses. On a multiwindowed building a sign stenciled along those opaque panes not broken identified the P OE IX   MA H N   TO L   C RP   A I N.

They were on the outskirts of Phoenix! Pushing the door open just far enough to stick his head out, Jack looked up and down the length of the train. In the distance, through an early-morning haze that glowed like warm ashes, he made out skyscrapers shimmering in the blast-furnace sun.

A sudden jolt almost threw him out the door. The train was starting up again. Should he get off here? Jack prepared to jump, then hesitated. Except for the abandoned factory, and, next to a wooden water tower, a few sun-bleached, old, one-story frame houses built in the days when railroad workers lived on company property, there was no sign of any bus stop, country store, or phone booth from which he might call a taxi.

The dirt road on the other side of the houses, only one of which had a car in the drive, appeared so little used that hitchhiking didn't seem an option either.

He remained in the door, indecisive. The train had picked up so much speed that jumping would be hazardous. But every minute he delayed was taking him further from his destination.

Reaching back inside the car, Jack dragged a sack of coffee beans toward the door. Crouching, he embraced the sack. Taking a breath, Jack straightened his legs and murmuring a prayer, jumped.

They hit alongside the tracks. The sack burst open. Jack bounced, losing his grip, and felt himself sliding along a pile of cascading beans. The breath screamed out of his lungs. He lost consciousness.

Coming to, face in the weed-grown dirt of an embankment, Jack slowly pushed himself to his knees, praying that none of his bones had been broken, or muscles ruptured.

Coffee beans had spilled everywhere. Jack struggled to his feet. Vision refocused, he saw that he was no more than thirty yards from the house with a car, a very old, faded-green Chevrolet, in the drive. The car must be in running condition, he told himself. Otherwise why keep it around?

Halfway down the embankment, he stopped and retraced his steps. Gathering up that portion of the sack still intact, he pushed as many beans as would fit back inside, tying the torn burlap into a makeshift knot. Swinging the sack over his shoulder, he strode unsteadily toward the house again.

A gate hung askew from rusting hinges in a gaping fence enclosing a backyard patchy with weeds and dirt. A bicycle lay twisted on its side, front tire flat, a faded saddlebag spilling weather-warped schoolbooks. A partially deflated basketball sat under a hoop whose net hung in shreds.

Was the house abandoned? The window blinds were drawn, screen doors torn and rusting. He walked to the car. Its doors were locked, a hopeful sign. He peered inside. Vinyl seats were cracked. A visored cap lay on the dashboard, and cigarette butts filled the open ashtray.

From inside the house then, Jack heard a dog bark. Hastening to the door, he rapped sharply, causing the barking to intensify. Stepping back from under the overhang, Jack used the sack for a seat, elbows on knees, chin in hands, helping whoever was inside to decide that, in spite of his disheveled appearance, he was harmless.

A window blind parted. Jack put what he trusted was an ingratating smile on his face. A moment later a hoarse, dispirited voice cried, "Quit yapping, dammit!" and the door behind the torn screen squealed open.

A woman in a soiled bathrobe, stringy brown hair unkempt, cigarette dangling from her unlipsticked mouth, stared at him.

Feeling that she might be ill, Jack stood, trying not to show his dismay. "Sorry to bother you. I've had a little accident, and I was hoping you might phone a taxi for me."

"They toss you off the train?"

"I realize I'm not exactly dressed for company. But I'm not a bum, just temporarily short of funds. Though I think I've got money enough for a taxi."

"No taxis come here."

"I'll trade you this sack of imported coffee beans if you drive me to the nearest place they will come."

"That's stolen property."

"It was already ripped. Shame to waste it."

"Where you headed?"

"Serenity Acres Funeral Park. Is it anywhere near?"

"Not far." She opened the screen only far enough to flip her cigarette away, then closed it again. "Who died?"

"My mother." It had slipped out. And why not? For what good she'd done him, she might as well be dead. "We haven't been in touch for twenty years. But I want to pay my last respects."

"Wait there." She shut the door.

Jack had barely got himself settled again when she reappeared, carrying a fresh pack of cigarettes and car keys. She unlocked the driver's side first, then the passenger door from inside. She opened the pack, tossing the cellophane aside.

"Cigarette?"

"No thanks."

She lit one for herself before turning the ignition on. The motor turned over so slowly Jack began to worry the car might not start. But it coughed, backfired, and she kept it going by pumping the accelerator.

She leaned partway out the door to back out the narrow driveway. The motor died. She swore, but this time it turned over again immediately.

They headed down the dirt road in second gear, rolling through several intersections without pausing for stop signs. Arriving at a two-lane blacktop highway, she pushed the gear into drive, flooring the gas pedal until the car vibrated from wheels that needed balancing.

The cigarette never came out of her mouth. He rolled his window down for ventilation. She glanced at him, then, taking a deep drag, crushed the cigarette in the overflowing ashtray.

He heard the freeway before they came up on it, rising out of the flatlands.

"Cemetery's seventeen miles down the road. You know what section she's buried in?"

"Funeral's today."

She glanced at him. "You planning to attend your mother's funeral dressed like that?"

"I'm going to stay more or less out of sight."

"Not gonna say hello to your kin?"

"Some got weak hearts. Like my mother."

She drove at a speed that encouraged Jack to believe he might get there in time—if they didn't broadside another vehicle en route. But other drivers stayed out of their way, intimidated by the old Chevy.

"Twenty years. Your ma split on your dad, did she?"

"On me. I was a difficult kid."

"Your dad convince you of that?"

"He told me the opposite. But I know better."

She lit another cigarette. A few minutes later she pointed off to the right. A series of undulating hills was carpeted by a green so intense he didn't want to think about what fertilizer may have encouraged this luxuriant growth. In a moment he saw granite stones imbedded in the hillside lawn spelling out SERENITY ACRES.

She took the next exit, following an access road to the entrance, a paved road lined with mournful Italian cypress. She slowed at a gate marked INFORMATION.

"The Harris funeral?"

The uniformed guard hesitated a moment, disconcerted by the Chevy and its disheveled passengers. "Chapel's top of the hill to your left." In the side-view mirror Jack saw the guard watching them drive off, which made him edgy.

"You don't mind, let me off down here."

She pulled over to the curb. Sniffing deep, she hawked, chewed, leaned out her window, and spat. "For someone claims to be obnoxious, you got a soft side."

Jack wasn't pleased to hear this. To accomplish what he intended, he had to be tougher than those he was after. "People who know me would disagree with you."

"Care to tell me why?"

Jack shook his head, disconcerted by, and fighting back, a sudden urge to confide in her.

"Isn't there anyone who'd welcome back the prodigal son?"

"Actually, I lied." The words burst out. "It's not my mother's funeral. It's the wife of my ex-boss. It's the only chance I've got to talk to him."

She stared. "You played on my sympathy!"

"Not exactly." Jack swore at himself for letting go.

"Maybe you are a hard one. Like you say."

"It's a hard world."

"You make light of things you ought to take serious."

"Told you I was obnoxious."

"I'd of give you a ride anyways."

Jack sighed, and opening the car door, couldn't stop himself from reaching out to her. "I'm sorry about your kid."

"How you figure that out?"

"You're not the kind would leave her kid alone in the house."

She gripped the wheel so tight her cracked and reddened knuckles whitened. "I did once. To drag my husband home from a bar. The electricity was cut off. My boy Billy lit a candle to read—his life was reading—and fell asleep. Before I could get the drunk sonofabitch I'm married to home the candle had fell to the carpet and the fumes had smothered Billy." She began to cry.

Jack was appalled. "You're not blaming yourself?"

"We make our own beds, don't we?"

"You're not still living with him?"

"He's got nobody but me."

Shaken by this example of a loyalty he hadn't thought existed, Jack slid hastily out of the car before he might tell her his own troubles in a wrong-headed attempt to alleviate her grief. It would be once again perverse, putting his well-being in the hands of a stranger.

Why did he keep putting himself at risk? The sisters had suggested the uncontrollable part of himself was devil-inspired. What he was coming to believe was that part of him was trying to avoid the confrontation that would put him to the ultimate test.

He leaned to the open window. "I appreciate this."

"Don't do anything foolish."

Abandoning the road, Jack hastened across the manicured grounds, trying to put all doubts out of his mind. There was no reason to believe the woman would alert anyone to his presence, even under the misguided notion that it would be for his own good. Most people, he assured himself, his own behavior to the contrary notwithstanding, tended to mind their own business.

TWENTY-NINE

The motor whined loud as a buzz saw, shattering the encased-in-aspic-like serenity of the landscape. Amongst the flower-bedecked grave sites visitors looked up, startled, from their harrowing contemplations of eternity.

What day was this? Sunday? Would anyone find it odd that a dirt-caked, unshaven gardener was furiously trimming already manicured lawns while funerals were in progress?

Jack shifted on the narrow seat, having difficulty steering the mower. He'd found the unwieldy vehicle standing unattended below a water-soaked hillside just up from the road, apparently forgotten. A perfect camouflage, Jack thought, for zigzagging nearer the hilltop chapel without causing undue attention.

But he hadn't counted on the noise. He started to shut the teeth-grinding motor off, then spotted activity under a giant pine near the crest of a hill. A prime site. Men were shoveling dirt under the supervision of a black-suited man, no doubt a mortician.

The Harris plot? Was there to be a graveside ceremony? Jack's hopes rose. He could get a better look at the mourners outside than by trying to peer through the chapel's stained-glass windows, and without worrying over being spotted himself.

Was anyone watching him now? Jack twisted the vibrating wheel to take a path away from the new grave site. Putting behind him first one and then another rolling hillock, like the humps of a deformed camel, he then circled to come at them from the opposite direction. Between the two humps he stopped, turning the raucous motor off.

In the blessed silence, keeping his head low, Jack scrambled toward a cluster of trees nearby. Once among the trees, however, he could not get a grave-site view that was unobstructed.

Jack began climbing a large tree with branches low to the

ground. Wincing as his skinned and sore knees gripped the warted, sap-sticky trunk, he paused to regain both breath and nerve, then continued muscling up, snaillike, until he got one foot planted on a branch he thought strong enough to support his weight.

The limb bent, causing him a momentary panic, then held. The climb became easier, a matter of moving, monkey-quick, from sticky branch to branch, until he found a reasonably comfortable perch hidden within a cluster of full-needled limbs.

By pushing one or another limb aside, he could see everything. The distant chapel, built in a medieval style, was surrounded by parked cars, most of them luxurious, but discreet in color and design, as befitted friends of the socially prominent. The mournful strains of an organ drifted along the sun-baked, rose-scented air. "Nearer My God to Thee." Protestants, Jack thought, lip curling out of Catholic schoolboy habit.

The organ stopped. The chapel's double doors opened. Two functionaries in black suits, walking sideways, semaphored directions to the middle-aged, sweating, button-straining pallbearers, struggling under the weight of a lacquered mahogany casket. They stumbled down stone steps toward the gleaming hearse. As the mourners straggled after, Jack leaned forward, anxiously scanning the sorrowful faces for Harris.

And there his boss was, the hypocrite, wiping his eyes with a newly starched handkerchief, dressed in an Italian-cut silk gabardine suit of a chocolate so brown it was near black, being ushered to the black limousine parked behind the hearse by a burly, black-suited figure with slicked-down hair and carnationed buttonhole.

Why should that mortician, clearly in charge of the proceedings, seem familiar? Before Jack could think who the man reminded him of, his heart leaped. Another figure seemed familiar.

A leggy woman in impractical thin spike heels, a finely meshed veil covering her face, seemed unsure which direction to take. Moving awkwardly, she tripped on the last step. As she grabbed the burly man's arm to right herself, her hat twisted awry.

Jenny, Jack thought, heart racing, nervy enough to attend her double's burial. And then, as the woman readjusted her veil over tear-ravaged makeup, Jack saw that, leggy or not, she was very old.

Probably Mrs. Harris's mother, he thought, disappointed, yet somehow relieved. He watched the mortician handing the old woman over to Harris, who reached out impatiently from the limousine's backseat.

He should have known Jenny couldn't be that tasteless or cold-blooded. And for a wonderful moment, forgetting all that had gone before, Jack loved her again.

Then, remembering how she'd been used to hook him, Jack cursed himself for an idiot, and worse. Had he been hoping that when he found her she'd explain how she'd been forced to become the instrument of his humiliation? This wasn't a good sign, he told himself. He still had a propensity for foolishness.

Greatly agitated, he watched the hearse pull away from the curb, followed by the family limousine. The mourners, climbing into their cars, inched along after them. The procession, more than a quarter-mile long, slowly wound along the curving road toward the newly opened grave. As they drew nearer, Jack saw the discreet lettering, in gold leaf, on the hearse's tinted rear glass: PEER 9 MASON MORTUARY.

Opposite the grave site, the hearse pulled off the road. The funeral director, who'd been sitting next to the driver, got out. Walking to the hearse's rear, he opened the tailgate and pulled the casket, on rollers, out far enough for the gathering pallbearers to take hold of the ornate handles.

A waste of an expensive casket, Jack thought with a shudder as the pallbearers reluctantly shouldered their burden again. After that explosion, they might as well have put the few mangled parts left into a bag. The funeral director, turning to lead the pallbearers toward the grave, unexpectedly gave Jack a full, unobstructed view of his face.

A rage so immense that the tree shook swept over Jack. For a giddying moment, as the blood left his brain, Jack thought he might fall. Fighting to regain control he shrank back, an endangered species, into the branches.

Al. The funeral director was the blackmailer, Al. Of course. He'd been in on the scheme from the beginning. Harris had brought him in to preserve the body until it was time to ship it to Los Angeles. And the supposed blackmail scheme was probably nothing more than a further device to ensnare Jack B. Noble, horny boy wonder susceptible to melodrama, whom Harris had sorted out of the personnel files.

If only, for his own select-a-winner football program, he'd had use of whatever criteria Harris had devised to identify him as a sucker. He'd have made so much money he wouldn't have had a need to "borrow." Preventing Harris from zeroing in on him in the first place. If. If *ifs* were bananas, he'd be one fat, contented monkey.

The pallbearers, marching now like a team of ill-rehearsed skaters, were clumsily placing the casket on the material-draped rig covering the grave. Just beyond the pile of dirt, discreetly covered with a carpet luxuriant enough to walk on, a few chairs had been set up.

Harris and the veiled old woman took seats. A half-dozen elderly men and women joined them. Behind them the mourners shuffled forward, looking toward the robed minister, who stood patiently on the other side of the casket, ringed finger holding his place in the Bible.

Al, the funeral director, nodded to the minister. The moment the minister opened his Bible, Jack left his perch and began climbing down the tree, trying not, in his haste, to shake the limbs so much it would catch anyone's attention. It was pointless to remain here, pointless, even, to confront Harris, which had been his first thoughtless, enraged reaction.

Al was the person he needed to face up to. Not here, but somewhere private, where the two of them could have it out without fear of interruption. Al was as likely to know where Jenny was as Harris — and would be a damn-sight easier to wring information from. Al was the weak link, his toughness show, the plan no doubt having been to so deliberately infuriate the hapless Jack he wouldn't have time to think.

And if Al's toughness wasn't a put-on? Jack shrugged the troubling thought away. He had to put himself to the test sometime. Whatever happened was better than waiting, like a rabbit stunned by fear and indecision, to be taken.

Reaching the ground, trying to keep trees between himself and the ceremony, Jack hastened back toward the place where he'd abandoned the mower. Though he was in a very big hurry, some innate caution caused him to drop to his hands and knees before peering over the top of the second hill.

He sucked in a breath. The mower was there. But gathered around it were a gardener and two security guards. Had that bereaved woman conveyed her suspicions to the gate guard? Or an angry Claire found the newspaper clipping and sent it, signed *A Concerned Citizen*, to Harris?

Jack swallowed bile from his churning stomach. He had to shake off this paranoia. It was bad enough being absolutely alone in the world without compounding his difficulties by creating terrors that didn't exist. Those were security guards, not police. They weren't looking for Jack Noble, but for some homeless bum the gate guard had watched the woman drop off on the road near the chapel.

Somewhat comforted, but keeping his head down, Jack headed at a businesslike half-trot in the general direction of the mortuary. From a grave he plucked up a newly placed bouquet.

With the flowers he felt less conspicuous. Anyone might think him part of the landscape. He hustled across the road. The farther off it he stayed the less likely he would be noticed at all.

But the winding road doubled back on itself like an uncoiling snake, and he found himself crossing it frequently. He kept his distance from the occasional parked car, occupants probably visiting graves nearby. And then a quick glance inside a glass-bowl-like BMW tempted him. A creamy linen jacket had been casually tossed on the backseat.

Of course the BMW was unlocked. Who expected thieves to hang around cemeteries? Jack whipped the jacket from the car, eased the door shut, and in a moment was off the road and hastening down the rolling hills again.

The mortuary was designed like a Norman castle. Turrets overlooked a moat on which swans floated amongst lily pads. It could be reached only by crossing a simulated drawbridge.

The parking lot leading to the bridge was empty except for an iridescent-blue 1980 Ford. Another hearse was parked at the building's rear, next to a black-cherry-red Cadillac Coupe de Ville, no doubt belonging to Al.

Slipping into the jacket, which hung loosely in what was still a current style despite the demise of the television series that had spawned it, Jack turned up the sleeves and buttoned his shirt. Lamenting the absence of a tie, he did what he could to comb his unruly hair with spit and fingers.

Walking across the bridge to the building's entrance, he managed to overcome his inclination to break and run when the doors swung soundlessly open. Instead, trying to slow his racing heart, he squared his shoulders, and like a knight who had no recourse but to enter the cave of the dragon, he walked boldly inside.

THIRTY

The inside of the mortuary building—"All Services On The Premises At One Convenient Location"—was as cool and dry and hushed as Jack had anticipated, considering the business transacted there. Suppressing a shiver, he walked directly past the unattended reception desk, surrounded by flowers he was not surprised to discover were artificial, and opened the first door he came to. Inside, displayed against midnight blue, velvet-covered walls under lighting that would be the envy of museums, were coffins, ranging from sanded pine to lacquered mahogany.

Hastily, Jack yanked the door shut and returned to the main corridor, where sepulchral music seemed to surround him. At the end of the marble-floored hall he turned right, almost colliding with a security guard. The guard, a stocky, pale-eyed man with an incongruously dainty mustache, recovered and stood in his way.

"Excuse me, sir—we're closed."

"I have an appointment with Mr. Mason."

"Mr. Mason's dead."

"Of course he is. I meant Peers. With all on my mind since my wife died I can't keep them straight. Peers's office this way?"

"You sure Mr. Peers said meet him today?"

"Positive. We've got to get my wife in the ground before noon tomorrow. Been in mourning for two days, can't eat, take a bath, change clothes, or shave . . . it's our religion."

The guard pursed his lips. "Your wife in our cold box now?"

Jack hesitated. Why did he imagine it a trick question? "They picked her up this morning."

"Guess he forgot to let me know. This way."

Jack followed him through a door into a small reception area. A facing door had ALFRED PEERS inscribed on the opaque glass. "Never occurred to me you'd need a guard inside a mortuary."

"Turns out some folks specialize in robbing corpses." The guard smiled in a way that made Jack uncomfortable. "Or worse."

Jack tried not to think what worse could be. "Embalming done on the premises?"

"Right here in this building."

"Peers rolls up his sleeves and gets into it himself?"

"The difficult ones." The guard indicated a chair. "Might as well get comfortable. Probably a while before Mr. Peers gets back. He's driving a family home personally."

Jack settled into a chair and picked up a full-color illustrated brochure of the mortuary's services. "I hope he gives my wife the same kind of attention."

The guard considered him for a moment, again causing Jack a momentary disquiet, then left without another word. Relieved, Jack went immediately to the door and slipped it open, watching the guard turn and enter the adjoining corridor. Listening to the sound of diminishing footsteps, he closed the door, then, putting the brochure down, hastened to the one leading to Peers's office. To his surprise, it wasn't locked.

The walnut-paneled office was small, containing only straight-backed Danish-style chairs on either side of an oak table. This Spartan place hardly looked like an office a man like Al would be comfortable in. No drawers, files, or decorations, except for a Plexiglas certificate of award on the wall from the National Funeral Director's Association. Jack looked about, disappointed. No wonder the room hadn't been locked. No secrets here.

Where then? Jack continued to examine the room, checking, out of habit, for signs of poor workmanship. A seam in the paneling seemed to have a gap wider than the others.

Jack ran his hand along the gap, pausing at a ripple in the wood. He thumbed the bulge. It did not give. He pressed again, harder. Something clicked, and part of the wall swung open.

Delighted with himself, Jack stepped through into an unfinished concrete-block corridor. Closing the panel behind him, he followed the corridor to an unmarked door. It too was unlocked. On the other side was a large, windowless, fluorescent-lit room with drains in its concrete floor.

A sickly sweet odor, like decaying greens, permeated the air. For a moment Jack could not identify it. Then he looked at the plastic-topped tables the size of hospital gurneys, and realized, with a shiver, what had been lying there. Next to the tables were steel carts with multiple shelves and drawers for storing surgical tools. Those white plastic jugs, he realized with a shudder, contained embalming fluid. He didn't want to think what had stained the concrete drains.

Here Al practiced his arcane art. But where were the newly dead? At one end of the room were double-glassed doors to what looked like a walk-in cold box. Reluctantly, Jack approached the glass and peered inside.

It was the size of a meat locker. Arranged neatly on dimly lit pullout shelves were five bodies, naked except for large tags hanging from big toes, one of them blood scarlet with nail polish. Jack, feeling somehow witness to a profound humiliation, was about to turn away when he heard footsteps in the outside corridor.

Opening the double-glassed door, Jack stepped inside. Immediately, the cold seemed to freeze the end of his nose. His eyeballs ached. It was an effort to blink. His blood felt as if it were congealing.

For a moment he stood indecisive. But when he saw the room door open and the daintily mustached security guard come in, he shrank away from the glass and retreated to the furthest wall.

The guard's muffled footsteps couldn't be coming in this direction? Hastily, Jack pulled out an empty top drawer and pulled himself up on it. Placing his palms against the cold ceiling, he managed to tug the drawer back into place. But would he be indistinguishable from the others in the dimness?

Yanking off his shoes, socks, pants, and shorts, Jack placed the clothing under his head. Keeping his body from the waist up as much in the shadows as he could, Jack stretched his legs, goosepimpling in the freezing cold, out into view. He warned himself to lie absolutely still.

But part of him was moving of its own volition! At first his genitals shrank. Then, to his dismay, he became aware that his penis was slowly stiffening. Surely in this dimness it wouldn't be noticed?

He hadn't thought about the guard having a flashlight. The beam, distorted by the glass, swept past his blueing, untagged feet and focused for a long moment, unsteadily, on the privates of a fishpale female corpse with wiry black hair.

Jack held his breath. The door opened, then closed. Why was the guard coming in? With mounting horror, Jack wondered what the man could be up to. Could he be trying to confirm Jack's story by looking on the tags for date of arrival?

The guard put down his flashlight. He used his fingers to brush his mustache. Then Jack did not want to believe what he was witnessing. No one could be that depraved. But the guard had spread the female corpse's legs, and gone down on one knee between them.

Jack closed his eyes. But he couldn't shut his ears. And unwilling to reexperience an agony he'd thought long forgotten, when, as a child hidden in the bedroom closet, he'd listened to sounds that seemed more animal than human coming from his parents' bed, Jack launched himself, feet first, off the shelf, taking the guard, and the dead woman, crashing to the floor.

The guard's scream matched Jack's own. A moment later the guard went limp. Picking himself up, Jack wondered if he'd broken the other's neck. Trying not to look at the awkwardly sprawled female, he put his ear to the guard's mouth.

Jack was relieved to feel a shallow breath. The guard had been knocked cold, or fainted in the belief he was being attacked by someone supposedly dead.

Gently, Jack lifted the female back to her shelf. Then, though the idea of having to touch the man was repellent, he dragged the guard outside the cold box. Undoing the guard's shoelaces, he bound the other's hands behind him. He used a dirty handkerchief found in one of his captive's pockets for a gag. Then carrying the guard to a table, he removed the man's belt, and taking off his nightstick and beeper, he tied his legs down.

The beeper sounded. Jack froze. Silence. So far as he could tell, no one else was in the building.

Quickly, thinking that he hadn't much time, he put on his clothes, looking about for the private corner he was certain must exist. There had to be a place where Al kept his personal records. What was his connection to Harris? To Jenny? Could you store a body and not make some accounting for it?

Then Jack spotted the rolltop desk, tucked behind shelving. The laminated top, warped and peeling, was locked. Hurrying to it, Jack grabbed the sides. He put all his weight into trying to twist it around. The wood splintered. He had the satisfaction of hearing the lock spring open.

Jack raised the broken lid and blinked. This was not what he'd expected. Al was a pack rat. The inside looked like a catchall. There was hardly any desk space. Wherever he had traveled, Al had collected souvenirs.

Most of the clutter was paraphernalia from bars. Matchbooks, ashtrays, swizzle sticks, and engraved shot glasses were strewn haphazardly over poker chips and oversized dice marked with the names of casinos.

Why should it surprise him that Al gambled? In a profession so morbid, he'd need some way to release pent-up emotion. Where better than in the full-throated, near-hysterical, anonymous atmosphere of crowded gaming rooms?

He began pawing through Al's desk drawers. Maybe he'd get lucky and find a personal ledger. Find some indication of when, and where, Al had married Jenny. He needed something to show the authorities that there had been two Mrs. Harrisses, but only one grave.

But the drawers were empty except for small change, ballpoint pens, and souvenir pencils. Jack slammed the drawers shut — and the pile on the desk top shifted, articles tumbling in every direction. When the movement stopped, a previously hidden deck of cards stood revealed.

A decal pasted over both sides of the packet read "Compliments of The Taj Mahal, Reno's Biggest and Best Hotel/Casino."

Jack didn't know why he bothered to open it. Slitting the seal with his thumbnail, he palmed the cards. Making space on the desk top, he fanned them out, face up. There was a full deck, including two jokers. Nothing there. Disappointed, Jack fanned the cards the opposite way, face down.

Fifty-four reproductions of a tall woman, wearing nothing besides spike-heeled sandals and a golden G-string, hands barely covering her breasts, smiled up at him provocatively.

Fifty-four Jennys.

Mesmerized, Jack pushed the cards into a loosely held deck and riffled them. Jenny squeezed her breasts and moved her pelvis suggestively. Enthralled, Jack was about to riffle the cards again when he felt something round and cold and hard pressing into his ear.

"I knew you were dumb. But I didn't think dumb enough to come here." Al. At the other end of a gun.

Jack found his breath again. "Not so dumb I couldn't find you."

"Lot of good it'll do you."

"I called my lawyer to let him know who you are and what you did."

Al snickered. "Switchboard's closed. No open lines."

"Friends know I was coming here."

"Then they won't be surprised to hear you were shot breaking in."

Jack felt sick. It was true then. They wanted him dead. His mind raced. "It'll look odd, your shooting me in the ear." The pistol was withdrawn slightly. "In fact, if I'm shot in the back instead of straight on, so you can claim I'd been threatening you, there's going to be a lot of questions about why you felt you needed to shoot me at all."

Al laughed out loud. "You think if I let you look at me I won't have the heart to kill you?"

"Jenny said you were a shit. But I figure nobody's all bad."

Al slugged him in the ear. "Are you ever in for a surprise. Sit up. Turn around. Look at me."

Jack, ear ringing and wet with blood, swiveled in the chair, not sure what he could do. He gathered himself to make a last-ditch, desperate move—and found himself disconcerted by the intensity of the hatred in Al's face.

"What'd I ever do to you?"

"I've never liked smart-asses."

"You're jealous because I got it on with your ex-wife."

Al stared, then laughed. "Jealous of my own daughter?"

Jack felt as if his head were going to explode. But the malevolent imp inside him provided an unexpected, last-chance resource. "You're a very sick man. Why should you draw the line at your daughter? At least she's alive. You fucked the original Mrs. Harris when her husband brought her into your deep freeze, didn't you?"

Al's jaw dropped.

Jack looked past Al's shoulder toward the bound and gagged guard. "Don't bother to play dumb—your security guard told me everything! Right, Adolph?"

Al turned to check out the guard, who in fact remained unconscious. Bending the deck of cards, Jack spun them outward into Al's face.

The gun boomed loud as a cannon in the concrete-block room.

The first bullet crashed into the rolltop desk. The second pounded into the acoustic-tiled ceiling. Jack, who had kicked his chair sideways to avoid the first shot, bounced off the shelving and came rolling back head-up into Al's armpit before the second, causing it to miss as well.

Somehow Jack got his thumb between the hammer and the firing pin as Al tried to squeeze off shot three. Bellowing with the pain in his pierced thumb, Jack smashed a roundhouse forearm into Al's throat and, as the other gagged, took him down. He pounded Al's gun hand against the floor. Al's bloody-knuckled hand finally opened.

In a rage, thumb still flaming, Jack stood and, kicking the gun aside, grabbed Al's coat. He lifted Al into the chair, then roughly swiveled him to face the desk. He shoved Al's elbows forward, then slammed the rolltop down on his extended arms. Al screamed.

"That's it, yell you bastard, involving your own daughter in murder!"

"She came to me."

"I don't believe you."

"Fine. It's no skin off my ass."

Jack lifted the rolltop and slammed it down again. Al yelped and, eyes streaming, sagged against the splintered wood. Jack kept his full weight on the top.

"I'll skin more than your ass unless you tell me something I can believe."

"It's God's truth! She said it'd be worth big bucks if I'd deep-freeze Harris's wife until he could make her death look like an accident—"

"How'd he kill her?"

"He said it was suicide. Carbon monoxide poisoning. She ran her car in a closed garage."

With a shiver, Jack remembered the death of his former boss, Holmes.

"He wouldn't go to all this trouble over a suicide."

"Her insurance wouldn't pay off for suicide."

"Why should he worry about insurance when he stands to inherit a hundred times more?"

"He wasn't in her will. Her family saw to that. Whatever she owned went back into the family trust. He's lucky he gets to keep his monthly allowance."

"Where'd he find Jenny?"

"Evelyn. Her real name's Evelyn."

"How did the good, sweet Evelyn get involved?"

"I learned a long time ago never to ask Evie questions about things she didn't want me to know."

Jack felt excruciating pain in his heart as well as his thumb. He was lifting the rolltop to slam it down again when an alarm went off.

"You set that off, you sonofabitch!"

"No! I swear! The trip wire's sensitive! Someone's trying to get in through a locked door. . . ."

Just as suddenly, the alarm shut off. In the resonating quiet, both men listened. Somewhere a door opened and closed. And then they heard footsteps. A measured tread was approaching down the hidden corridor.

THIRTY-ONE

Lifting the rolltop desk lid off Al's forearms, Jack, finger to lips, motioned for Al to stand. As Al got unsteadily to his feet, Jack quickly grabbed the other's right elbow and wrist. Twisting Al's arm up behind his back, Jack walked him to the door.

On the other side someone knuckled the wood. "Mr. Peers?" A muffled, nasal mumble. "You all right in there?"

Jack increased the pressure. Al went up on his toes. "Yes. Why shouldn't I be?"

Whatever was said next was indistinguishable.

Jack twisted harder. Al's voice rose. "I'm very busy. Talk to me later."

". . . better talk to you now."

Jack grimaced. He reached around Al and undid the lock, allowing the door to open a half-inch. The pressure on his arm momentarily eased, Al suddenly kicked backward, connecting with Jack's shin.

Jack bent reflexively to the blinding pain. Using the door to slam Jack back against the wall, Al then scrambled into the corridor.

"Help, I'm—"

A thunderous blast. Al seemed to have run into an invisible wall. Another blast, and Al, lurching backward like a disjointed puppet, collapsed in a torn and bloody heap.

From behind the door, Jack watched, stunned and disbelieving, as someone in a midnight blue satin warm-up suit, holding a still smoking sawed-off, double-barreled shotgun in one cotton-gloved hand, a simulated-leather computer-kit bag in the other, strode into the room. Barely glancing at the mutilated Al, the intruder began scooping up the scattered playing cards.

Ears ringing, Jack stumbled forward, hoping to catch the intruder off guard. The other looked up. Jack froze. Harris! Before Jack could recover, Harris savagely jammed the still-smoking shotgun barrels into his solar plexus.

Jack dropped to his knees, retching. By the time he regained his equilibrium Harris had gone, leaving the shotgun and computer-kit bag behind.

Still dazed, Jack examined the kit. It was his own, he realized with growing dismay, one he'd kept in his camper van. Inside, in addition to the football program diskettes, were some loose shotgun shells.

Pocketing one of the playing cards, Jack forced himself to pick up the shotgun. Then he noticed the guard staring at him with a look of abject terror.

"You saw what happened, didn't you?"

The guard, cheeks twitching, trying to make himself small on the table, shook his head. Jack undid the gag.

"This is Harris's shotgun — you must have seen him shoot Peers?"

The guard cringed. "I just this minute come to. I ain't seen or heard nothin' since you coldcocked me!"

The alarm went off again. Jack shook his head, trying to clear it. Though he'd thought his difficulties couldn't get worse, they'd suddenly increased a hundred fold. He was standing over a dead man, holding a murder weapon with his fingerprints all over it. He didn't dare leave it behind, he thought in some panic, though now he'd be considered armed and dangerous, the police likely to shoot him on sight.

Bolting for the door, Jack ran back down the hidden corridor — to find Peers's outer office door locked. Using the shotgun to break the glass, he reached through to open it. It'd been locked with a key! Banging frantically at the glass shards, Jack crawled through and dropped to the floor. Bleeding from unnoticed cuts, he ran full speed down the marbled corridor back the way he had come.

At the entrance, he became aware of sirens. Wheeling, Jack ran wildly all the way back to the mortuary preparation room. Gasping for breath, he made a show of putting a shell into each chamber of the shotgun, then released the guard from his bindings. "Show me the delivery entrance."

The guard, raising a trembling hand, pointed.

Jack shoved him with the shotgun. "Take me there!"

The guard, walking like someone with artificial legs, led Jack to a side door at the other end of the room.

"Open it!"

The guard fumbled out a key from those on this ring. After several false starts he managed to insert it into the lock.

Jack motioned with the shotgun. "You first."

Cautiously opening the door, the guard edged outside. Jack followed so close they could have been mistaken for a comedy dance team. The sirens sounded near, coming from the access road leading to the mortuary. To make matters worse, the gatehouse security guard came trotting around the corner of the building.

Jack had to do something, and quick.

Parked at the top of a ramp was a hearse. Grabbing his captive around the waist, nostrils pinching against the odor of fear and cheap cologne, Jack rested the shotgun barrels on the other's flinching shoulder, aiming at the approaching guard.

"One step more and you're a dead man!"

The other guard stopped and crouched. Agile as a kangaroo, he jumped back, disappearing around the building corner.

"Get into the hearse! Driver's side! Fast!"

The terrified guard did as Jack ordered. Jack opened the passenger door, but remained outside, forcing himself to wait until the other got the hearse's motor running. Then he opened the passenger door wide and slammed it shut again, the double slam to make the gate guard believe both had gotten into the hearse. "Take off. Now, or you won't live long enough to regret it!"

Wheels spinning, the hearse jerked backward, then, gears clashing, lurched toward the front of the building.

Staying close to the wall, Jack ran in the same direction. He reached the building's front just as shots were fired. Peering around the corner, he saw the gate guard firing at the hearse, which was racing toward the entry road.

Approaching from the opposite direction, sirens screaming, were the spinning red and blue lights of two police cars. The oncoming cars split off, each entering a different side of the concrete island on which the gatehouse stood. The speeding hearse braked, skidding into a 180-degree turn. Righting itself, it started back the opposite way.

One of the racing police cars drew even with the fleeing hearse, got far enough ahead to cut in and brake. The hearse, unable to stop in time, smashed full speed into the police car's side.

The other police car's wheels locked as it skidded to a stop, inches short of a collision. From either side a cop jumped out, gun drawn. Each ran, crouching, toward the entangled vehicles, joined a moment later by the gate guard.

"Careful, he's got a sawed-off shotgun!"

"Costac's hurt!"

"So's Alvarez!"

Jack, bent low, using the hedges for cover, began scuttling crab-like toward the gate. As he heard the continuing shouts of the cops trying to render first aid while warning each other about possible danger from the hearse, he suddenly saw his opportunity.

Abruptly changing direction, Jack sprinted all out for the undamaged police car, praying that in the excitement of the moment the cops wouldn't notice him. They didn't. Sprawling headfirst into the front seat, he prayed then that they had forgotten to lock the ignition. They had.

Sending up a heartfelt thanks, vowing to make penance for past sins in the future, should he have one, Jack started the motor. Without delaying to close the doors, he jammed the gear into drive and kicked off the brake, then, flooring the accelerator, muscled the wheel over as far as it would go.

The car shot forward. Both doors slammed shut with the turn's momentum. Fighting the wheel, Jack aimed for the exit, sliding low in his seat just as the cops began firing. The back window shattered.

The careening car bounced off the concrete island and scraped the side of the hut. Moments later Jack was racing down the access road out of range of the cops' guns, sounding like wet-corked pop-guns behind him.

Jack wheeled into the freeway on-ramp at high speed, the patrol car's spinning lights causing cars, like fish desperately avoiding a shark in a feeding frenzy, to dart out of his way.

The radio suddenly crackled. "Dispatch, dispatch – this is car three-six-three – two police officers down. Need ambulance ASAP to Serenity Acres Mortuary. There's a police car stolen, repeat, police car stolen, car three-eight-five, heading east on the Scottsdale Freeway. Suspect armed and dangerous, wanted for murder. Repeat, murder suspect's stolen car three-eight-five, last seen heading east . . ."

Jack took the first ramp off so fast he barely made the abrupt and twisting left turn. Lifting his foot off the gas pedal he stood on the brake, then, racing again through skidding street traffic, turned off the main boulevard onto a tree-lined residential street.

Slowing, he looked for switches to turn those flashing lights off. If there were helicopters aloft, he'd be easy to spot.

The first switch resulted in a hair-raising howl from his siren. The second turned everything off, including the motor. But one agonizing moment later he got everything going again, and on his next try found the light switch.

Jack forced himself to slow to a leisurely pace, going parallel to, but a few residential blocks distant from, the main boulevard. The sooner he abandoned the patrol car, the better, he told himself. After he found alternate means of transportation. With his adrenaline rush subsiding, he was too exhausted to get very far on foot.

He became aware then that the radio had stopped chattering, producing only an unsettling hum. He fiddled with the controls. They'd probably gone to an emergency channel, so they could box him in without his overhearing.

As he began to berate himself for being paranoid, he found the other channel. ". . . highway patrol units will take up positions on intersecting freeways. All helicopters—make sure you stay within your grids."

A harsh female voice broke in. "Car three-eight-five, car three-eight-five, you'd be wise to give it up. Do you read? Turn yourself in. Over."

Reflexively, Jack reached for the microphone, before he realized, chagrined, that the voice was that of a dispatcher, not a nun. They were smarter than he would have imagined, trying to find out if he was listening.

He checked his surroundings. He'd reached the suburb's outskirts, and within a block he'd slide out from under the protective tree covering.

Slowing, he spotted the road sign: A-1 AUTO WRECKING YARD, 2 MILES. Shouting with relief, Jack floored the gas pedal. With luck, he'd reach cover before they spotted him.

The wrecking yard sat alongside the road, taking up several acres. Driving slowly past, he saw a half-dozen cars in various stages of disassembly. Maybe he could get one to work.

Then Jack's heart sank. Two large dogs, gaunt as wolves, were pacing him inside the chain link fence.

Maybe he could frighten them away by firing the shotgun. He immediately dismissed the idea, remembering with a shudder how lethal buckshot was, and how wide its pattern of destruction. Then, in a sunken field beyond the yard, he saw the heap of discarded automobiles. Sticking out from the pile was a bicycle.

A bicycle? Jack thought. Why not? You could cover a lot of ground, maybe enough to get beyond the range of the Phoenix police. And they wouldn't think to look for a murderer on a bike.

But how to get it? The only access to the field seemed to be through the yard itself. Unless, Jack thought, he could somehow come around to it from the other side.

Speeding to the first corner, he turned right, then right again at the following corner, slowing when he came up parallel to the field.

A fenced pasture stood between him and his goal. He could traverse the pasture on foot. Abandoning the police car on the open road, however, would give him away.

Further down, Jack saw an opening. The fence sagged, the ditch between road and pasture relatively narrow. With sufficient speed, the car might hurdle both.

Though how would he be able to maintain speed while managing the sharp turn he'd have to attempt at the last minute?

Consigning body and soul to the good offices of Francis, saint of travelers, Jack put the car in reverse. A quarter-mile back, he again crossed himself. Jamming the gear into second, he floored the gas pedal, trying to recall the techniques he'd read race car drivers used to make impossible turns.

Jack waited until the last-possible second. Then, without lifting his right foot from the gas, he stamped hard with his left on the brake, at the same moment twisting the wheel hard over.

The car rocked up on two wheels, slammed back down. Tires spinning, it shot forward into the air. It seemed to float interminably, finally crashing down on the other side of the fenced ditch with inches to spare, all its weight on the front wheels.

There were two sharp reports. The front tires had blown! Sliding back, the car's rear wheels, still spinning, hung for a moment in midair. Then, settling lower, they suddenly found traction on the sagging fence. The car was thrust forward.

In a panic, feeling as if the car were traveling through mud, Jack struggled with the wheel, keeping the gear in low, closing his mind against the nerve-wracking sound the flat tires made.

The trip seemed to take forever. When he neared the stack of cars, Jack aimed at an opening, trying to maintain speed. The car smashed into the pile. Jack kept the pedal floored, ignoring the screech and clash of metal as the car forced itself in. The engine died.

Jack shrank into his seat, waiting for the clatter and clang against the car to subside. All finally quiet, he tried to open his door. It wouldn't budge. And the window didn't respond to the electronic controls.

Stay calm, he told himself, sliding to the passenger side. For an agonizing moment that window didn't respond either. Then, with a jerk, the glass opened partway, but stopped again. Try as he might, Jack couldn't move it another inch.

He went out feetfirst, ignoring the twinges of his various hurts as he forced himself through the narrow opening, then found himself standing in a cave made of metal. Afraid if he touched anything the heap might shift and bury him, Jack maneuvered cautiously through the precariously balanced parts. At last he reached the open field.

The car seemed completely hidden.

But where was the bicycle? Circling the pile, Jack peered anxiously into its recesses. In the heart of its darkness, he finally spotted a glint of chrome.

Jack took extreme care working his way down to where the bicycle lay, removing one piece of scrap at a time. An unhinged door was keeping it pinned. Jack tried to calculate whether moving it would put him at risk of life or limb.

But neither was of much consequence now, he told himself. Gritting his teeth, he yanked the door aside. The pile shifted. Jack leaped for safety.

But the pile held. Breathing again, Jack reached into the recess and grabbed the bicycle. A few anxious tugs later he had it clear — only to discover the front wheel bent so badly it was impossible to ride.

THIRTY-TWO

The truck parked near the diesel pumps of the Mobil station was an eighteen-wheeler, its cab spacious, Jack noted, a bunk situated behind the seat. The driver, a balding, light-skinned man with sideburns the color of rust, wearing a billed *Caterpillar* cap, was bowlegging it out of the convenience store with arms full of food, a mustard-dripping hot dog disappearing into his mouth.

Rolling the bicycle along by its undamaged back wheel, an excuse, should it come to that, for his presence on dark country roads, Jack had spotted the lighted Mobil logo in the sky next to the parallel highway, and decided it was time to test his cover.

What drew him to the truck were its Nevada license plates. The ABSOLUTELY NO RIDERS decal was momentarily daunting. But there was nothing, he assured himself, that couldn't be used to his advantage.

Jack intercepted the driver before he reached the pumps, where a gum-chewing, muscular young attendant in a fluorescent-yellow tank top was muttering indecipherable rap lyrics while filling the truck's tanks.

"You from anywhere near shouting distance of Reno?"

The driver looked Jack up and down, then, whistling, glanced at the bicycle. "What happened to you?"

"Hit and run. Bastard in a Toyota pickup."

"Lucky it wasn't a Dodge."

"My friends call me that. Lucky. Except if I don't get to Reno by tomorrow my name will be shit. You give me a lift I could pay something, that makes a difference."

"See that no riders sticker? Anybody reported you company'd fire me without thinkin' twice."

Jack forced a smile in his best imitation of a man told he had a terminal disease. "Don't worry about it. I know you'd take me if you could." He started limping toward another truck, groaning just loud enough for the other to hear.

"Not so fast. Slip around the other side, wait'll the kid finishes pumpin'. Keep your head down gettin' in."

"They don't call you guys knights of the open road for nothing. What's your name, Rusty?"

"How'd you guess?"

Jack held out a handful of change. He'd realized he was hungry. But he didn't want to go inside, where they might have already heard about what had happened at the mortuary.

"Don't suppose you could buy me a dog and a candy bar, Rusty? I haven't et since morning. It's killin' me to walk."

For an anxious moment, Jack thought he'd overreached. Then, waving away the money, the trucker handed Jack a wrapped hot dog and a package of potato chips. "Be my guest. Wife's after me to lose weight."

Unwilling to abandon the bicycle, for fear he might give himself away to the trucker, Jack shoved it behind the seat, then crawled into the bunk. He ate swiftly, and was licking his fingers when the trucker climbed in. The giant rig bucked a little in the lower gears, but Rusty soon had them rolling smoothly down the highway.

"This bunk's sure comfortable. All I can do to keep from falling asleep."

The driver popped a tape cassette into the dash player. "You go right ahead. Music's all the company I need."

To the strains of "Mothers, Don't Raise Your Sons To Be Cowboys," Jack's eyes lidded. He soon fell into a surprisingly deep, if troubled sleep.

When he came to, the truck had stopped. It was daylight. He heard voices. Jack sat up, in a panic when he saw patrol cars and uniforms. "What's happening?"

"Weight check. Nevada side. Feel better?"

"I'm still wiped. How far we from Reno?"

"Hour and a half maybe. You don't mind, lay back down."

Mind? With a contented sigh, Jack stretched back out on the bunk. He drifted off again soon after the truck left the weighing station, waking only when the truck, an hour later, swerved leaving the highway, crunching oiled gravel up to a high desert-bleached gas station and coffee shop. Jack's breath caught at the sight of brooding, snowcapped mountains. Sanctuary? Or end of the line?

The trucker kept the motor running. "Gonna have to toss you out. Company's got a lot of rigs this stretch of road. One of 'em might report me carryin' a rider."

Jack raised up, rubbing his eyes. "Where are we?"

"Bus stop half-hour outside Reno."

"Hey, terrific." Jack crawled over the seat, lowering himself painfully down to the road. "You're a prince among men."

"Watch how you spell that—hey, your bicycle?"

"Gee, thanks for reminding me. Maybe somebody here'll know how to fix it."

"Hope you live up to your name."

"My name?"

"Lucky, you said."

"Right. Thanks for everything, Rusty. You're a brick."

"Watch how you spell that."

Taking the bike from the grinning trucker, Jack bowed deeply before heading for the coffee shop.

Inside, a round institutional clock on the newly painted wall read six-twenty. A counter fan was marked FOR SMOKERS ONLY. A few elderly people sat stiff-backed in the wooden-planked booths, so concentrated on food they barely looked up when screen-door bells jingled.

A Latino cook was trying not to fall asleep over a pan of eggs. An overweight, short-haired woman in a starched apron, elbows on the gleaming counter, inhaled steam from a coffee mug clasped in her two strong hands, watching impassively as he dragged his bicycle in.

Candy-colored electronic slot machines with flashing lights stood in a row next to the door. The smallest play was a quarter. Jack, resisting the urge to risk his change, parked his bike behind them. He exaggerated his limp walking to the counter, and groaned under his breath taking a stool near the waitress. He slid the kit bag under his feet.

"Just coffee. And a paper, if you have one."

She poured him coffee from a just-brewed pot. "Papers haven't come in yet."

Jack scratched his chin stubble. "You sell razor blades?"

"This look like a drugstore?"

"You got slots, but I know it isn't a casino. And I see you stock Rolaids, so it can't be much of a cafe, either."

"You gonna insult my place you can just haul ass outta here."

"Sorry. I'm always cranky after a troubled sleep."

She seemed only partially mollified. "Bad conscience?"

"Bad luck. I not only lose my wherewithal at the tables—someone wrecked me and my bicycle too. But the truth is, if I can't have my morning shave I'm never in the best of moods. But I shouldn't have taken it out on you. Some of my best friends are waitresses."

She stared at him as if she could read his mind. "I'll bet they are." Wiping her hands on a towel, she pulled a key from the chain around her neck and slid it over to him. "You walk through the kitchen to the backyard you'll find a little house. A razor's in the medicine cabinet. Blade's practically new—I only used it once. On my legs, honey, don't get worried."

"Key's warm as your heart."

She grinned. "Don't dawdle. We get a pretty good breakfast crowd. How you like your eggs?"

"I'm not sure I . . ."

"Over easy okay?"

"Perfect."

"Keep your bag here for you?"

Jack felt his face flame. He was becoming terminally stupid. How could he forget evidence that could incriminate him? Or was it a coward's wish to be rid of a weapon he was unwilling to use?

"I'll take it with me, thanks."

The kitchen was spotless. So was the tiny house. Books, paperback and hardcover, lined the handmade shelves in the front room. On a doily-covered table stood the photograph of a grinning, firm-jawed young man in an Army uniform, the frame draped with a black cloth, pinned with a medal.

Sorry, Jack murmured, then telling himself not to be maudlin, continued into the small bathroom. He found the razor in the medicine cabinet. He scrupulously avoided examining the pills, or the haggardly desperate man trying to catch his eye in the mirror.

The shower was in the tub. Undressing, Jack felt like a snake shedding skin. This snake, he reminded himself, was no longer harmless. He turned on the water full force, exulting in also shedding layers of grime. He shaved by feel, only cutting himself once.

Pushing the heap of grimy clothes aside with his foot, Jack walked into a bedroom barely large enough to contain the neatly made king-sized bed, and found, still hanging in the closet, the dead soldier's civilian clothes.

The plaid shirt and the pleated corduroy trousers hung somewhat large, but not so much that anyone would think twice about it. He bundled up his clothes, wrinkling his nose at the smell, and stuffed them into the kit bag over the disassembled shotgun.

At the refrigerator, he hesitated, then thoughtfully pried a half-dozen large, clover-shaped magnets, forlorn without messages to hold, from the door, dropping them into his shirt pocket.

On his way back through the yard he picked a few cat-faced pansies.

Partway into the coffee shop he noticed the cops. Two of them, highway patrolmen, were drinking coffee while chatting up the waitress. He was about to ease himself back out when she looked up.

She blinked, startled at the sight of his clothes. He held up the flowers. Pursing her lips, she motioned him over. Was she angry? For a moment, he considered running. But where would he go? And so he walked to the counter like a man contemptuous of a possible death sentence. Handing her the tiny bouquet, he slid onto the stool next to the cops, dropping the bag under his feet, wincing as it hit with a thud.

"Nothing makes a man feel better after a shower than fresh-laundered clothes. With you working so hard, and me down on my luck, I figure the best present I can make you is from now on take on the ironing."

It seemed an eternity until she smiled. "Well glory hallelujah, man's seen the light."

Jack turned to the cops, who were observing him closely. "You're staring."

The cop next to him shifted his eyes to the waitress. "Didn't know you had a new friend, MayBelle?"

Jack put out a hand. "Brother-in-law. Lucky used to be my name, blackjack used to be my game."

"Blackjack's a sucker's game." The second cop, wearing mirrored sunglasses, leaned back to see around his large-framed partner.

The Latino cook banged a bell. MayBelle picked up all three plates at the pass-through. Examining them, she waggled her finger at the cook, who apologetically placed a sprig of parsley on each plate before she brought them over. Jack, who'd lost his appetite, forced himself to eat heartily.

"Don't know about that." Jack swallowed coffee to wash the mouthful of buttery hash browns and runny eggs down. "Keep track of the cards dealt you can beat it."

The sunglassed cop didn't look up from his hash. "Then how come you went bust?"

"Lost my concentration."

MayBelle lit a cigarette and, moving to the counter fan, turned it on. "Wouldn't matter anyhow. Way those gals can stack a deck they'd clean you out anytime they wanted."

Jack leaned to pick up his kit bag. Hoping his sweat didn't show he placed it on his lap, and, aware that the cops were watching, unzipped it just far enough to get his hand in and pull out the playing card. "I did get myself a little souvenir." He grinned falsely at the large cop. "I'm not incriminating myself, am I? They broke out a new deck and I sort of managed to keep a card from the ones broke me."

Both cops looked at him. Inside, Jack's heart shrank. That inner devil, quiet so long he'd thought him gone, had suddenly surfaced, as if reminding him that his capacity to self-destruct remained undiminished.

As if sensing his distress, MayBelle leaned over and examined the card. "Speaking of stacked . . ."

The cops, one at a time, solemnly examined the card, which was, Jack realized with a sense of spiritual shock, the jack of hearts, the Lord maybe showing a sometime disbeliever that the concept of chance was a mistaken notion. The sunglassed cop, dislodging a morsel of bacon from his teeth with the card's edge, tossed it in Jack's general direction.

MayBelle put her cigarette out. "More coffee? You boys don't seem your usual chipper selves. They find you sleeping behind a billboard?"

"We've been staking out the border all night."

"Someone knocked off a mortician in Arizona, and they think he mighta got on a bus for Reno."

"Jam please?" Jack held up his toast apologetically.

MayBelle took the jam tray from between the cops and placed it before Jack. He was spooning up marmalade when an airhorn raised him an inch off his seat.

"Thar she blows now." The two cops, adjusting belts and hitching at their guns, swung off the stools and pounded their heels getting outside.

MayBelle was looking at Jack. "How bad's the trouble you're in?"

He removed the toast from his mouth, unbitten. "I never killed anyone." Jack wiped off the card with his napkin. "But she made it look like I did."

"I don't want to hear about it."

Jack pocketed the card. "I hope I live long enough to make it up to you."

"Listen, hon. Let me give you a piece of advice. You can't fart in one end of this county without folks at the other end holding their nose. If that showgirl at the casino's involved, your trouble could get a lot worse."

Jack slipped off the stool. "I don't see how. But thanks for the tip — and everything else. I'll send the clothes back first chance I get."

"Don't bother. Just let me know if you make it."

Jack pulled out what was left of his coins.

"It's on the house."

"I knew that. What I wanted was quarters."

"To play the slots? The way they set up those beauties, you can't win one time in fifty."

"Let's see if I can't change that."

MayBelle looked at him skeptically, then gave him all the quarters she had. Jack, placing one in each of the slots, pulled the handles in sequence, listening to the inner machinery. All whirred to a stop. No money was disgorged. MayBelle smiled.

He liked the sound of the machine at the far end. Pulling his bicycle out from behind, Jack surreptitiously placed the magnets at strategic spots on the slot's back.

He studied the whirring, comic-strip-colored fruit. The third column was definitely slower, stopping seconds later than the other two.

Jack made a minor adjustment before inserting his next-to-last quarter. This time the third column had slowed even more.

Timing his opportunity, Jack, palming the largest magnet, waited until the first two columns showed identical fruit, then slapped his magnetized palm against the machine's side. Three plums.

Quarters showered from the coin cup.

"Aren't you going to pick up your winnings?"

Seeing the cops following the bus passengers toward the coffee shop, Jack hastily collected the magnets.

He showed them to the startled MayBelle before pocketing them. Scooping up the coins he dropped them on the counter. "That enough to cover the replacement costs?"

"Those magnets can't be strong enough to affect the electronics. Can they?"

"If they aren't, then my luck's running strong."

Blowing her a kiss, Jack tipped the bicycle on its back wheel and wheeled it toward the bus, saluting the cops on his way.

THIRTY-THREE

Even in daytime, under a brilliant morning sun, every light in downtown Reno was blazing. Between the glowing signs and the pulsating marquees lit by a bragged-about million count 'em flashing light bulbs it was unlikely there was an unilluminated spot anywhere to be found. Only the Taj Mahal, with its spotlighted minarets, artificial date palms, and plaster cast, double-humped, mustard-yellow camels holding up the billowing canopy over the gold carpet leading to the casino, had seen fit to shade the sidewalks along the hotel front.

Jack retrieved his bicycle from the luggage bins beneath the bus and rolled it up the carpeted entrance, handing it to a pimply-faced, Vuarnet dark-glassed doorman shrouded in creamy Bedouin robes. "Guard it with your life. Sentimental value."

The brightly lit, refrigerated inside smelled stale as old bread. Jack wished he'd thought to bring a sweater. Was that shiver anticipation, or fear? Scheherazadian houris, dressed in see-through pantaloons, with fat zircons in distended navels and golden slippers with party-favor-curled toes, offered drinks to players who looked as if they were running on a rapidly evaporating supply of nervous energy.

There were no windows. And no clocks. Land of perpetual day, Jack thought. He wandered toward the slots, where groups of elderly women sat punching buttons with the fixed stare of production-line automatons.

The machines called for minimum dollar plays, some in electronic voices with Japanese accents. Motioning to a vacant-eyed houri with a coin changer at her waist, Jack handed her the last of his money. "Dollars."

She counted out twelve tokens. He showed her the playing card. "Hey, how cute—I never knew the casino had these."

"I'm not sure they still do. Recognize her?"

"No, but that don't mean nothing. I never see nobody except they come to the slots."

"Any suggestions who I could ask?"

"Gus. Kinda pockmarked, silver-haired guy supervising the crap tables? He's been here since they built the place."

A bulky man in a gray gabardine suit and shoelace tie sat in a spotter's chair overlooking the gaming floor.

"You mind asking him he knows her?"

She thought about it, frowning daintily. Then, taking the card, she minced over to Gus, using more hip action than was required. Quickly, Jack placed the magnets on the back of the nearest machine. Inserting a dollar token, he punched the button.

Wrong column slowing. Readjusting the magnets, Jack punched the button again. Still the wrong column. Had some dyslexic installed the electronics? Or were the magnets, as Maybelle had suggested, ineffective? Readjusting once more, he again punched the button. This time the third column slowed.

"That machine's jinxed. One at the other end's due to be hot." The houri handed him back the playing card. "Gus says you got questions ask him yourself."

"Sounds fair." Jack inserted a token into the slot. One pear, then two. Watching the third column slow, Jack, magnet palmed, stroked the slot's side. The third pear appeared, locking into place. The coin cup filled.

"Say, you got the magic touch, or what?"

Jack tipped her a handful of tokens, beginning to wonder himself. "Don't noise it around."

A woman in the next row began signaling wildly. The houri grimaced, gave Jack's elbow a tiny pinch, and minced off.

He looked over to the gaming tables. Gus was watching him. Jack, distracted, was delayed long enough he was unable to adjust the magnets in time. No win. Frustrated, he thumbed another token into the slot. This time, making a mock show for Gus's benefit of massaging the machine, he matched two bells with a third. The cup overflowed.

Dropping the tokens into an outside pocket of the kit bag, along with the playing card, a thoroughly pleased Jack, uncaring now whether it was the magnets or luck, strolled toward Gus, sidling along the inner side of the table to the rope. "You Gus?"

The other nodded, watching a lone gambler, sweating and excited, pray over the dice. "You got business with Evie?"

"A relative died. Mentioned her in the will. My job to track all the inheritors down."

"Got papers to that effect?"

Jack thought about this for a moment. Then he unzipped the kit bag, feeling around under the shotgun and its extra shells, until he found the business card he vaguely remembered placing there. Gratefully dusting it off, he handed the card to Gus.

"Harry Bur-gess—that how you pronounce it, Burr-guess?—junior attorney-at-law."

"I'm not a junior attorney, I'm Harry Burgess, Junior. And I never carry important papers on my person. But if you direct me to her I'm sure I'll be able to explain what's involved to the young lady's personal satisfaction."

"Where you staying, I'll have her get in touch with you?"

"I'm not. I try to get whatever business I have wrapped up in the daylight hours. All I need is a couple minutes to verify her relationship with the deceased—the rest can be done by mail or fax."

The player had thrown double sixes. He prayed again, then bounced the dice against the far end of the table. Two single dots. Moaning, the player flung the dealer's rake away from his chips. Scooping them up, he turned to run.

Two security guards, alerted by Gus, appeared. They led the player, now weeping, away.

Gus turned back to Jack. For a panicky moment, Jack was certain he was going to be escorted out too. Then Gus motioned to the change-making houri hovering nearby. "Take him to the game, Carline. Don't interrupt a hand till it's played, then offer everybody breakfast—that way she and the counselor here can get a few words in."

"The game?" Carline was bewildered.

"Table-stakes poker. Behind the curtains. Tell them I said okay."

"Appreciate it, Gus." Jack held out his hand. "Could I have my business card back, please?" He grinned shamefacedly. "My secretary didn't send enough with me."

Gus brooded over this. Then, thumbing the card as if wondering what kind of lawyer couldn't afford to have his card embossed, he handed it back.

"She's not so young anymore. But still a head-turner, you can bet on that."

Carline led the way through the gaming room tables toward a curtained wall. "They don't tell you nothing till they want you to do something and then they expect you to know what it is!" Pouting, she felt her way along the velvet curtains until she found a door.

It was locked. Carline knocked again. A snubnosed, pale-featured guard in a double-breasted midnight blue blazer yanked it open.

"Table's full."

Carline took a step back. "Gus said it was okay."

The man looked Jack up and down, then eyed his bag. "Have to take that."

". . . sure. Long as you keep it handy."

Reluctantly handing the bag over, Jack followed Carline into a low-ceilinged, smoke-filled room that seemed barely large enough for the round, felt-covered table. Around the table sat five male players of various ages. The dealer was in yellow-gartered shirtsleeves, matching bow tie, and green eyeshade.

The dealer was flicking cards around the table with such speedy precision that it seemed five cards remained floating in air at all times, until, the hand dealt, the last round dropped to the felt simultaneously, forming five near-perfect fans.

It took Jack a moment to realize that the dealer, who hadn't bothered to look up, was female.

"Jacks or better open." Her voice, hoarse from the smoke, produced a familiar thrill down Jack's spine.

A man Jack recognized as a hangdog, stoop-shouldered film star famous for high-stakes gambling, sweat-stained Borsalino fedora pulled low over mournful eyes, pushed chips forward. "Five K's."

A tiny fellow with a head too big for his body, whom Jack recollected was a jockey thrown out of racing for doping horses, pushed chips forward with calloused hands. "Raise you five."

A cigar-chewing, untidy man in an orange cardigan, whose stomach kept him arm's length from the table, waved at his pile of chips. "See the ten, raise ten."

Impassive, the dealer, Evie, so recently Jenny, leaned across the table to rake his chips into the pot.

An unshaven man no older than Jack, wearing a silk shirt the color of chocolate under strawberry red suspenders, slapped his cards down faceup, then ran both hands through his unruly hair. "I'm out."

Quickly, Evie flopped his cards over. "You know better than to show your cards. Misdeal, anyone wants it?"

The players looked at each other, shrugging. The young man, shrugging angrily, turned his bloodshot eyes on Carline. "Don't just stand there—get me a tequila gold."

Evie spoke as Carline sucked in a breath to answer. "When the hand's over."

[201]

"I'm out as well." Coal-eyed, and manicured, this one was possibly Arab, dressed in a British-cut, chalk-striped suit.

"Call for cards." Evie was more than annoyed, she was furious. But she kept her anger in check.

"Two." The jockey bared discolored teeth.

The fat man moved his cigar with his tongue. "One."

"Three." The actor shook his head at his foolhardiness for remaining in the game. "Since nobody's left to draw after me, no harm done, hey?"

"Bets, gentlemen."

Why hadn't Evie spotted him? Jack wondered. Unless she had, and was planning some sudden, unexpected move. He looked worriedly to the guard in a chair near the door. Where had the guard put his bag?

"Check to the three of a kind." The fat man seemed to be having difficulty speaking around his cigar.

"I'm out." The actor winked at Carline. "But not down."

"Twenty-five K." The jockey shoved two and a half stacks forward.

"See the two bits, raise four bits." The fat man waved peremptorily to Evie, who used her rake to pull that amount in chips to the table's center.

The pot was now worth one hundred thousand, counting the house ante. Even the players who'd dropped out were intent on the game. Evie ran a pink tongue along her lips. To his dismay, Jack felt his body respond.

"Trying to steal the pot?" The jockey was serious.

"Keep me honest." A challenge from the fat man.

The jockey grinned, but his hand trembled as it hovered over his chips. He looked over his shoulder at Carline, who was returning the actor's smile. "Whattya say, sweetheart? He bluffing, you think?"

"I really couldn't say. Poker's a mystery to me."

"What about you, chum? You look like you got a keen eye for human foibles. This fella tryin' to buy the pot?"

The fat man was glaring at Jack. He'd drawn to fill a straight or a flush. What were the odds against that? Enormous, Jack thought. The man didn't look the reckless type. But if he'd drawn a winning hand, why try to silently warn him against speaking?

Sensing opportunity, Jack smiled at the jockey. "He told you to keep him honest, didn't he? Personally, I take people at their word."

At the sound of his voice Evie stiffened. Before she could look at him, however, the jockey had grinned, shoving his chips forward with such force they spilled over the felt. "Show and tell."

The fat man stood, tipping his chair backward. "Misdeal! This game is for players only!"

"Misdeal my ass!" The jockey lunged across the table, grabbing wildly for the fat man's cards.

The guard left his chair on a dead run. Spotting his bag under the vacated chair, Jack sidled over to pick it up. Evie, who'd risen and backed to the wall, was heading for a nearby phone.

Jack intercepted her. Unzipping his bag, he showed Evie the shotgun. He slipped his hand around the stock inside, finger against the trigger, then shoved the bag up under his arm so that the muzzle was pointing at her.

"Don't think I won't use it!"

Behind her the fat man, intimidated by the guard, swore and flung his cards onto the table, then crushed his cigar into an ashtray. "I want to talk to a supervisor!"

The actor, smiling, turned the fat man's cards faceup. The two, three, four, and five of diamonds. Plus a seven of clubs.

"Well looka that." The jockey, beside himself with happiness, hugged his winnings, then spotted Jack and Evie heading for the door. "You're not leaving, are you, kid? Stick around. I can use someone with your perspicacity!"

"Breakfast anyone?" Carline had guessed that the hand was over. "Gus says anyone can order whatever they want, on the house!"

Jack leaned closer to Evie, trying not to become distracted by her perfume. "Tell your thug you're sending a relief dealer in. Along with a supervisor."

Her eyes glittered. But she didn't hesitate. "Chick—keep your eye on the store till my relief gets here." She turned to the fat man. "If you'll just be patient, sir, I'll send a supervisor right in."

Jack smiled and whispered in her ear: "That's good. That's even better than I could hope for. Now show me a quick way out and nobody'll get hurt."

THIRTY-FOUR

They went out a door marked EMPLOYEES ONLY that led through a small lounge with a soft-drink dispenser, coffee machine, and lockers. The few people inside were brooding over cigarettes or reading magazines, barely glancing up as Evie, with Jack holding her elbow with his left hand, kit bag containing the shotgun under his right arm, led him out an exit that brought them inside a parking structure.

"Where you parked?"

"Roof's for employees."

They started up the concrete stairs, climbing as if joined at the hip.

"What're you driving?"

"An old Mercedes."

"Sam investing your share?"

"You're wrong if you think I'm getting anything out of this. I—"

"Save your breath." Her car was under a canvas cover in a roped-off section. She took the cover off, revealing a restored silver Gull Wing classic Mercedes.

"Old, huh? Next you're going to tell me you paid for this out of tips." He followed her to the trunk, watching closely as she stowed the cover. But the trunk had nothing in it except a spare and a packet of tools.

He motioned her behind the wheel from the passenger side, then slid in beside her. Taking her key, he opened the glove box. It held only the car's manual and warranty papers for battery and tires.

"If you're looking for my gun I left it in the Jag."

"What you've got is just as dangerous. Let's go."

"The airport?"

"And get picked up by local cops? We're driving to L.A."

"This car can't handle the desert—"

"Didn't you know—these engines were built for Rommel's desert tanks?"

"Jack—"

"You remembered my name !"

"—what do you think you're going to accomplish dragging me back?"

"You're my guarantee that I come out of this with my reputation, if not my body parts or my trust in women, intact. When a court hears how you set me up—"

"I'll be dead long before it gets to court."

"Start the car."

"And you will be too."

"Look on it as a lovers' suicide pact."

"Jack—"

"Quit stalling and start the car!"

"—I need to make arrangements for my mother. She—"

"Here we go. You're a real piece of work, you know that?"

"—'s unable to care for herself. By the time anyone found her it might be too late!"

Jack studied her: the wide eyes, the trembling pout, the pulsating energy that had drawn him to her as surely as a blooming flower attracts a honeybee. But how this bee could sting. "Fool me once, shame on you. Fool me twice, same on m—"

"Not that I give a shit. She's a vicious old woman who's already lived more years than she deserves. But I know you. You couldn't handle having her on your conscience. Not someone crippled and helpless. She suffered a stroke and can't even talk."

Jack sighed. "You try anything, so help me, I'll hurt you."

To avoid traffic, she drove them around the glitter of downtown, over the river, through tree-shaded residential areas to where the desert began, turning into an evergreen-lined driveway under a sign reading TRANQUIL ACRES LUXURY MOBILE HOME PARK.

Most of the mobile homes were wheelless, parked next to cement slabs bordered with succulents, geraniums, and glistening white picket fences. Cars parked adjacent to the homes were old but beautifully maintained Cadillac, Chrysler, Buick, Oldsmobile, and Lincoln sedans.

Evie pulled up alongside a mobile home shabbier than the others. Its plantings looked wan, the fence's paint flaking.

"Not much of a homebody, are you?"

"Not my idea of home."

He followed her out of the car. As both doors slammed, a dog barked. The mobile home door shivered as the animal inside crashed against it.

"I knew it. You and Roger had something going."

"He's company for Momma."

She opened the door, bracing herself against the dog's rush. The dog leaped up and she grabbed his paws. For a moment they did seem to Jack like a parody of long-lost lovers. With a shiver, he remembered her photos.

"Roger. You disloyal son of a bitch."

Jack could have sworn the dog flinched. Dropping to all fours, Roger slunk over to him and dropped to his stomach, rolling up against his legs. Freeing a foot, Jack massaged the dog's stomach with his toe, though he told himself it was not in his heart to forgive.

Evie held the door open. He motioned her in, then followed Roger inside. The interior was cluttered with pine furniture that had seen better days. Roger dropped to the floor next to a wrinkled woman with dyed-pink hair and blue-penciled eyebrows. Wrapped in a quilted bathrobe, she was slumped in a wheelchair staring fixedly at a TV with a rolling screen and no sound. Evie, not bothering to adjust it, blocked the screen and spoke loudly into the woman's ear.

"Momma. This's a friend from Los Angeles. Wants me to come with him on business. I wanted you to meet him so you could see for yourself how nice he is. So you won't worry about anything nasty happening to your virginal little girl."

The woman's eyes glittered. Her lips moved but no sound came.

"What do you think Momma? Isn't he a handsome devil? Just the kind you always warned me to avoid—too good-lookin' and too young to have money or sense. But this one's got possibilities, Momma. He'd just learn to use the brains God gave him, he could start rock and rolling big time."

The woman's head began to shake. Evie glanced at Jack. "I know she can hear me. Right, Momma? You'd take my side if you could. Try to convince this sweet boy your little girl was too naive to see just how Sam Harris's jealousy was twisting him. When he learned this handsome boy had won her heart, he unbeknownst to her adjusted the clock so the timer didn't match the dial."

A coated tongue slid out to catch saliva forming in the corner of the old woman's slack mouth. Her rheumy eyes shifted to Jack. He turned away uneasily.

"Weren't you going to make arrangements?"

"Park manager's due to feed Momma at noon."

Jack checked his watch. Eleven-fifty. "Noon on the dot? Or

when she doesn't show, you going to tell me she's sometimes ten, fifteen minutes late? Leave a note!"

She stared at him, biting her lip, then picked up a pad and pencil from the table next to her mother.

"You're allowing your lust for revenge to overcome your reasoning abilities—"

"My reasoning abilities tell me that if I don't get you out of here fast we're sitting ducks for Harris."

"Sam's up to his ears in L.A."

"When's the last time you checked? Before or after he killed your father? Twenty'll get you fifty you're next on his list."

He was watching Evie. But a sound that raised the hair on Jack's neck came from the woman in the wheelchair.

"I'm sorry." The dismayed Jack leaned close to the old woman, trying not to recoil from her odor. "I thought you already knew."

"He brought it on himself." Evie's voice trembled, but more with anger than grief. "The sonofabitch was greedy. He told Sam he wouldn't deliver Mrs. Harris unless his share was doubled. Don't act so surprised. Blackmail wasn't part of Sam's original plan—it just turned out to be useful. . . . Shit."

Tears were welling out of her mother's eyes. Finding a Kleenex, Evie leaned over the wheelchair to blot the moisture out of the old woman's wrinkled cheeks.

"You're not grieving, are you, Momma? Didn't you drag me to the purifying desert to get me away from that sick sonofabitch?"

To Jack's horror, Evie was weeping too. He hardened his heart. "Finish the instructions."

Blinking hard, Evie picked up the pad again. "You're wrong about Sam's going after me. He wouldn't dare. Not here. Not anywhere. Angelo's got a long reach."

"Angelo."

"My boss."

"The guy Sam's laundering money for?"

Evie hesitated, then reluctantly nodded. "Sam was a big shooter. He lost everything he owned at poker, and then was stupid enough to tap into his wife's trust. When she found out, she threatened to get him fired from the bank. When he begged me to introduce him to Angelo, I made the mistake of feeling sorry for him. Sam offered a trade—he'd launder money for Angelo's people if Angelo would arrange for his wife to be hit. Angelo said no. Sam had to do his own dirty work. Then Sam, who'd always told me how much I looked like his wife on her better days, came up with the idea of me making

[207]

the switch. I wouldn't have done it, except Angelo convinced me it was in my own best interests."

Every instinct Jack had warned him to be wary of whatever she said. But though he knew she might be stalling in hopes the casino people would start wondering about her absence, his curiosity as to how far she would go got the best of him.

"And you couldn't say no to Angelo."

"No one says no to Angelo. But nothing that happened was my doing. I was only bait."

"That so? Whose idea was it to have you pretend to drown yourself?"

"It got out of hand. After I met you, I wanted out of what I was doing, out of my life — "

"Save it!" He was almost sure she was lying. "And who brought your father into the act?"

If there was any hesitation it was imperceptible. "Angelo knew Al."

He had to admit it was possible. "And how'd I get picked for the starring role?"

"Sam's almost as good with a computer as you are, did you know that? He kept sweeping the bank's data banks, looking for a fish — there's always some poor schnook, Sam said, who thinks he can beat the system. The problem was you turned out to be smarter than Sam gave you credit for. Not only were you frustrating Sam when he tried to nail you for the money drain, but he'd got to liking the idea of my being his wife so much that when he saw I'd fallen for you he lost his reason."

Jack didn't like it that he remembered how it felt drowning in those mountain-pool eyes. "What part did Sam like most about your being his wife?"

"That's unfair. In the beginning he was nice to me. Polite as could be. I have needs, like everybody else. And I hadn't met you yet, had I?"

Jack, knowing that he needed anger, not compassion, to survive, forced himself not to respond. Then he noticed the old woman, who seemed to have shrunk even further into her chair, staring at him. Was that malevolence, or fear? Now that she had his attention, she managed to lift her penciled brows and shifted her yellowing eyes from him to the table beside her and back.

But the table was empty. His imagination was running away from him, fueled by his own apprehensions. "Say good-bye to your mother and let's go!"

Evie glared. Ripping the sheet she'd written instructions on from the pad, she slammed pad and pencil down. As she angrily folded the note, her mother, taking advantage of Evie's inattention, inched her hand out of her sleeve and fastened her fingers, clawlike, around the pencil.

Jack pretended not to have seen. He reached his hand out to Evie. "Let me see that."

"That's an awful way to live, never trusting anybody."

He grabbed the note:

Dear Mrs. Bachardt, I've been called away on business. Could you make sure my mother takes her medication, and gets to the doctor Friday? If too much trouble, the Bide-A-Wee nursing home will take her. Any bills, call Angelo at the Taj Mahal. Thanks a million, Evie

"There's no secret code, if that's what you're studying on."

The reference to the nursing home had made him think of his father. He was afraid if he looked up she'd interpret his distress as weakness. He glanced at the old woman. She was slumped in the chair, exhausted.

Jack picked up the pad. *r i l a* was what she had somehow managed to scrawl.

"Poor thing." Evie was close enough he could again smell her perfume. "The stroke's messed up her mind. Anything she tries to communicate comes out upside down and sideways."

Though it made no sense, Jack put the note in his pocket. "Let's go."

Evie, making a face, pecked her mother on the cheek. "Try to bear up without me, Momma. No telling how long I'll be gone."

THIRTY-FIVE

Evie began weeping again as she Scotch-taped her note to the manager on the mobile home door. Jack was touched in spite of himself. "If your testimony convicts him you'll get off light."

"We'll never make it that far."

He shrugged. "Never know till we try."

She whirled on him. "What's galling you? Say you do manage to send Sam up. What's in it for you? Revenge is a sucker's game. You think you're going to come out of this looking like a hero? Think again. The very least you'll be nailed for embezzling funds. Who's going to hire you then? You'll be lucky to get a job unplugging sewers."

"Get in the car." It was difficult keeping his voice even. Sliding in beside her, he slammed the door shut. But he was shaken. He hadn't thought past bringing Evie to the police. "At least people will know I'm not a murderer."

"Oh, nice. Take that to the bank when you're ready to build your dream house, see how far you get. Explain to your old man why it is he has to rot in a nursing home."

"Let's hit the road, whattya say?"

"Jack, listen to me. You're a certified computer genius. Angelo trusts me. I tell Angelo you're the perfect man to computerize his operations, all over the world, he'll jump at it, make any kind of deal you'd want to make, including throwing Sam to the wolves, that's what you want. He'll give you a new identity, relocate you in a way you won't even remember anything bad in your life. . . . Oh, Jackie, just once can't you recognize a main chance? Don't you see how wonderful it could be? Rio. You'd like Rio. Carnival. Food almost as good as sex. Music that gets into your blood . . . or maybe you'd prefer the West Indies? The Cayman Islands? Air that should be bottled, a life-style that takes a dozen years off your life — Angelo'll send us wherever your idea of paradise is. You can set computers up any-where there are phone lines, can't you? And once we're settled in we'll send for your father—"

Jack scowled, angry at himself for even listening. But she could be persuasive, no denying it. Stronger men than he was would be tempted, he was sure. And the hell of it was he could picture island beaches, his father having dreamed over the four-color brochures of-ten enough, trade winds carrying the perfume of coconut and mango, the three of them in a secluded beachhouse overlooking a powdered sand cove, and while the old man drowsed on the mahog-any-planked, palm-shaded veranda, he and Evie would be making love in setting-sun-tinted water so clear it made your heart ache. . . .

". . . at least talk to the man you don't believe me. Tell him your requirements, what you'd need to organize his data bank, tie in a worldwide system to a state-of-the-art communications system. . . ."

Air-conditioned. The equipment, state-of-the-art, just as she said, mainframe and workstations, powerful enough to run govern-ments, videophones for conference calls, control panels as elaborate as a Pentagon war room, sited in a humidity-free environment to protect its calibrated workings from mildew and mold . . .

"There's a pay phone in the laundry room."

Jack blinked. The vision disappeared. She was leaning so close he could feel her breath—how could a woman who lived lies so much of her life exude a fragrance of pear blossom?

"You can't actually believe I'd be stupid enough to put myself in the hands of someone like Angelo?"

Evie closed her eyes and took in a shuddering breath. "I was hoping you'd be smart enough . . . but it's hopeless, I can see that—" She opened her eyes, turned on the ignition, started the mo-tor with a roar.

"Maybe not. Maybe we could make a deal."

She'd been about to engage the gear. Now she hesitated, staring fixedly ahead, as if afraid the least movement he'd change his mind.

"I'd have to have a guarantee up front that Sam gets busted first."

"How can anyone guarantee that?"

Those lines at the corner of her mouth were deeper than he re-membered, giving her a vulnerability that touched and confused him, making him unsure whether what he was doing was unspeak-ably clever, or a perennial loser's untenable gamble. "You make a confession, in writing, and we fax it to the authorities in Los Ange-les."

She looked at him then, giving him the full benefit of the limpid gaze that had so often melted his resolve. "How clever of you. Making sure if I wanted to change my mind, which I wouldn't, I couldn't." She sighed. "But if that's what it takes to eliminate any foolish worry you've got that I'm not playing straight, I'm happy to go along with it."

"When that's done I'll meet with Angelo."

She was uneasy. He met her suspicious gaze unflinchingly.

"Don't you think you should at least talk with him first? Not in person. By phone. He's on the coast—"

"You have his out-of-town number?"

"He has call-forwarding."

"What's the rush? With your confession in the bank I'm sure it'll all work out the way you said."

She grimaced. "I appreciate your trust."

"You've earned it. Got a credit card?"

"I'd rather use cash."

"You won't have enough."

"To buy what?"

"A laptop and a fax machine. We'll get a motel room and you can start typing out your confession. . . ."

"I know a place where we can be absolutely private, and has every piece of equipment you could want."

"No thanks."

"The place is shut tight." She hesitated. "It's Angelo's local hideaway, where he goes to unwind."

"And you have a key?"

She shrugged apologetically. Jack thought about it for a while. He didn't see that he had many options. And now that he'd brought her this far, he was anxious to get her confession on record. "As long as we take a pass at it first to make sure no one's there."

The house was ten miles outside Reno, over the river and past a housing development that looked as if it'd been created by architects who designed restaurants. She took an asphalted, two-lane road off the highway that snaked between red-dirt embankments into the purple-hazed foothills. An occasional mailbox, and momentary glimpses of large houses behind thick pink walls, were the only signs of life. She turned into a narrow, brick-topped lane that led to an electronic gate, where she stopped. He took her purse before she could.

"Allow me." He fumbled through the items of makeup, packets of Kleenex, travel perfume, and Binaca—that, he told himself, chagrined, accounted for her Arabian Nights breath—and found the electronic opener. He aimed it at the gate, thumbing the button. Silently, the gate slid open.

"Come here often?"

"Not after I met you."

The gate slid shut behind them, giving him a momentary shiver. The house, recessed into the earth, was shuttered. Nevertheless, Jack reached into the kit bag and gripped the shotgun. "Show me the grounds."

The sparse planting, between the bleached gravel and granite boulders laid out in geometric patterns, was all succulents. A sudden sound caused him to jump and whirl, shotgun out of the bag. A sprinkler had turned on. He crept to the corner of the house, looking for the gardener.

"No one's here. Watering's done by automatic timer."

Feeling foolish, he followed her up a crushed-stone path to the heavy front door, which had two locks in a vertical alignment. She produced keys for both.

Just inside the doorjamb was a numbered security alarm keyboard. A red light blinked.

"What're you waiting for? Punch in the code!"

"I'm trying to remember it."

She thought for a moment longer, then punched in numbers. The red light kept blinking. Frowning prettily, she shook her head, thought some more, and tried a different sequence. Still the red light blinked.

"How much time they give you, a minute?"

"At least."

"Ten seconds more and we're outta here!"

Biting her lip, she fumbled through her purse and pulled out a business card. Numbers had been written on the back. Reading from the card, she punched in those numbers. The light changed to green.

He was furious. "Why didn't you do that in the first place?"

She glanced at him, shamefaced. "I didn't realize I'd forgotten the code. I'm sure I was in time. But if you're nervous about it, I'll call the security people. . . ."

He was past trying to hide how jittery he was. "Do that."

She picked up the wall phone and dialed the number from memory. "Hi. I'm calling from Mr. DeAngelo's house on Southwick Lane? Evie Peers. I was late turning the system off, just wanted to make sure you didn't get an alarm signal. . . . You're welcome." She pressed the cradle down just as he was reaching for the receiver.

Had that been deliberate? Not hiding his displeasure, he slammed the humming receiver down. "Show me the equipment."

She led him through a modern, marble-countered kitchen with gleaming-white Formica cabinets that looked, in spite of an array of complicated gadgetry, as if it had never been used. They walked through a small dining room that had a table elegantly set for two, its candles partially used, past a well-stocked bar complete with blender and a variety of stemware, and into a small windowless room. He stopped, transfixed.

An L-shaped workstation counter held a Sony color monitor, a Compaq keyboard, a commerical-quality HP Laserjet printer, and the latest-model fax machine.

He looked at Evie. She shrugged, anticipating his question.

"Angelo doesn't understand computers. But he loves playing with them. He's actually all thumbs. Probably want you to teach him things."

"Least I can do, money he's going to pay me." He put the bag down and sat in the most expensive office chair he'd ever seen, adjusting the knob for varying tension in the seat and back cushions. Then he switched the computer system on and sat for a moment with fingers poised over the keyboard, feeling like a pianist must before his valedictory concert. Almost reluctantly, he booted up the word-processing program, then stood and wheeled the seat over to her.

"Ready?"

"I could use a drink."

"I'll get it for you."

"Vodka rocks."

Jack went to the bar. He found ice in the fridge under the counter, and poured her a generous portion from a half-empty bottle of Absolut. He resisted the temptation to make another for himself, certain that if there were ever a time to keep a clear head it was now, and poured a sparkling water into a wine glass. He'd taken long enough, he told himself then, and returned to the other room.

She was sitting with her back to the keyboard, his bag containing the shotgun in her lap.

He stopped for one breath, and then two, not allowing himself to consider why he'd allowed that relentlessly curious, malevolent imp inside himself to take one last and perhaps terminal risk on how much, or whether, she'd cared for him at all.

But did this prove anything either way? he asked himself. Puzzled as to why she hadn't got the drop on him when she could, he continued walking forward. He offered her the vodka. She took it, not resisting as he lifted the bag from her lap.

She was watching him closely. "It's not like you to be careless."

"Maybe I was testing you."

"Do I pass?"

"Looks that way, doesn't it."

"Aren't you going to check?"

"What's the point? You could've killed me if you'd wanted."

She lifted her glass. "Happy days, lover."

"*Salud, querida.*"

They drank.

"Better get started."

She nodded, but made no move to begin.

"Know how to type?"

She shook her head.

"You want to dictate. . . ."

"I'll manage." She snapped the seat around. Before he could caution her about her drink, liquid had slopped out of her glass. He grabbed for the keyboard. She pulled the Kleenex from her purse and began sopping up what liquid she could.

But when he depressed the keys only garbage appeared on the screen.

"You can't think I did that on purpose?"

"The thought crossed my mind." He unplugged the keyboard and held it at an angle. Moisture seeped from under the keys. "There a hair dryer in this place?"

She led him down a hallway to the largest bathroom he'd seen outside a health club. Vapors steamed from a recessed Jacuzzi in the room's center. A counter with toilet articles ran waist-high just below a mirror along one hand-tiled wall.

A hair dryer hung from aluminum brackets. Plugging it in, Jack moved the nozzle back and forth along the keyboard, aiming the hot air at every aperture he could find.

"I swear it wasn't deliberate. On my mother's soul."

He kept on working. "This doesn't do the trick, you can write what you have to say in longhand." When she didn't respond, he glanced up at her — then stared, transfixed.

"Thought I'd take a five-minute soak."

She was already half-undressed, stepping out of her skirt as she tossed her vest and blouse onto a marble bench. Her breasts, unconstrained by a brassiere, lifted under his scrutiny. To his surprise, her panties were sensible white cotton. This hidden modesty tore at his heart. No hint of the seductress there. Until those too were discarded.

"Maybe you should join me. You're awfully tense."

She arched her back, to remind him, he assumed, of how sinuous she could be, and then she walked, one foot placed precisely in front of the other, down to the tub, those superb cheeks, a matchless pair, sliding seductively side to side.

He caught his breath as she leaned over to check the temperature. Flicking a switch she stepped into the roiling water and sank in to her stiffening nipples, then, smiling under his mesmerized gaze, to her chin.

"Come on in, Jackie. The water's fine. Forget you were an altar boy. Why deprive yourself of pleasure? I can see you're tempted."

He looked down at himself. Even now, when his mind should be preoccupied with the danger he'd become increasingly certain he was in, his sexual longings had taken precedence. Seeing his blush, she laughed, that low, tremulous chuckle that promised so much, that he knew from past experience would deny him nothing.

He didn't know what he might have done next if he hadn't heard the noise. It wasn't much of a noise, not quite identifiable. It could have been a hummingbird hovering outside a transparently clear window, or a wary mouse in the walls. . . .

Or, he thought, a not entirely unexpected visitor.

THIRTY-SIX

Jack didn't bother with explanations or instructions. He simply picked up his kit bag and left the room.

Once he reached the protection of the hallway, however, he paused. He wasn't in so much of a hurry he wouldn't take time to check his weapon. Careful to make as little noise as possible, he pulled out the shotgun and broke it open. To his surprise, it was still loaded.

Was it possible he'd misjudged her? Confused by contradictory feelings of wariness and affection, Jack pulled the shells out and examined them. They didn't seem to have been tampered with. All the same, it might be wise to replace them, he told himself, and fumbling in the bag for replacements, he discovered that two of the shells were missing!

Had he miscounted? Or had she taken them? What could she be up to? Sweating, Jack replaced the loaded birdshot shells with two marked double-aught buckshot, and eased the shotgun back together. The click as the barrels snapped into place was distressingly loud.

Trying not to think about either the weapon's destructive nature or her capacity for treachery, he tucked the wooden stock firmly under his bicep. Laying the cold barrels over his raised forearm, he hooked a nervous finger inside the trigger guard, and began tiptoeing down the polished-oak corridor.

At each doorway he eased the shotgun into the room, then, jumping inside, agitatedly swept the barrels from wall to wall. Each room was empty. He was strangely disappointed.

In the living room, he was startled by droplets splattering the outside of the sliding glass doors. A different set of sprinklers were on. His paranoia had gotten out of hand, he thought. It was possible he'd completely misread the situation.

Jack felt the notepaper in his shirt pocket. *r i l a,* Evie's mother had scrawled, her brain too scrambled to make it come out right. What was she trying to tell him? How many different words could be made by recombining the letters?

Just as he formed a word — *rail* — out of the letters, his concentration suddenly left him. Something had disturbed the quiet. He felt, rather than heard, a hum like that of a drowsing fly. Or perhaps some appliance, the refrigerator, say, murmuring on.

He became extraordinarily conscious of his own breathing. Wood creaked. He froze. But it was only the floor. Carefully stepping out of his shoes, Jack skated his stockinged feet along the floorboards, keeping his weight moving so that he wouldn't settle long enough in one spot to produce any noise. All was silent except for the hiss of his socks along the wood.

At the doorway to the computer room, Jack became even more cautious. Dropping to his haunches, he frog-walked into the room, shotgun thrusting forward.

No one was there. The hum, however, was louder. His eye settled on the computer. Jack hastened to the workbench. He didn't remember having left it on. He was about to shut the system down when he spotted the words on the monitor screen:

`Attn MetroBank Central Data Processing:`
`Government auditors need totals Noble embezzlement`
`A.S.A.P. Will brook no further delay. SJH`

"Looking for me, Rooster?"

Jack whirled. Harris had risen from behind the printer. Unshaven, still wearing the satin warm-up suit, he was pointing a very large pistol at Jack.

Jack fought to control himself. If he was to get out of this whole, he couldn't allow himself the luxury of rage.

"That was you she telephoned. Not the security people."

"Don't take it so hard. You didn't really think when the dust settled she was going off into the sunset with you?"

Jack trembled with fury. Every instinct he possessed was screaming at him to use this heaven-sent opportunity to blow that smirking, malevolent SOB to the outermost reaches of hell. His finger tightened, and stopped. Why couldn't he pull the trigger? He cleared his throat. "Matter of fact, I never believed it for a minute."

Startled, Harris considered this, losing his smile.

"Get it over with, Sam, for Christ sake!" Clothes clinging to her damp body, Evie had glided barefoot into the room.

Jack was confused. What was she doing? "Better not, Sam. This beauty's loaded with double-aught buckshot. It'll take you and half the wall with it!"

"It's birdshot, not double-aught." Evie opened her palm. She was holding the two missing shotgun shells.

Harris laughed. "Wrong again, genius. Just hold that pose. Perfect for a plea of self-defense. We'll slip the shells back into your gun after, of course."

Jack felt cold sweat beading along his hairline. "She's lying to you, Sam. This gun is loaded. Believe me!"

Sam's gaze wavered.

Evie's did not. "He's bluffing. I took the shells out of his gun when he wasn't looking. And I made sure he didn't have extras."

Harris's eyes glittered as he lifted the pistol.

"Don't do it, Sam." Jack was pleading as much for his own life as the other's, guessing that whether he could pull the trigger or not his future, should he have any, was about to become irrevocably changed. "You'll be making a terrible mistake."

Harris's eyes contracted. Jack dropped to his knees as the pistol cracked, then felt himself lifted and flung backward to the floor. The thunderclap a split second later deafened him. Both shotgun barrels had gone off simultaneously.

Why hadn't buckshot spotted the ceiling? Fighting for breath, Jack felt over his body, searching for the mortal wound. Not feeling any blood, he tentatively raised his head, shrinking from what he might see. The wall behind Harris had exploded outward. Harris was nowhere to be seen.

In a panic, Jack scrambled to his feet. He took several halting steps forward, and stopped. Features unrecognizable, a cavity where his chest had been, Harris was sprawled against the broken wall with hands upflung.

Jack closed his eyes, giddied by a feeling he hadn't expected. For a wonderful instant he felt triumphant, made whole. His humiliation overcome, he was hard put to keep from crowing aloud. And then he shuddered at the feeling of shame washing over him.

Opening his eyes, he saw that Evie had crept forward and was looking down at Harris with an unreadable expression.

His voice was strangely distant. "You set us both up."

Her voice seemed remote as well. "Not both. Him. I loathed that SOB."

Jack swallowed hard. His ears popped. His voice became stridently loud. "What if I hadn't checked out the shotgun? What if I'd believed the shotgun was unloaded and didn't even try to pull the trigger? What if I *couldn't* pull the trigger?"

"You could be dead too! But you're not, are you? And neither am I. I counted on you not trusting me. I put all my chips on your having grown up enough to be able to kill someone trying to kill you."

"If I hadn't ducked he'd have blown my head off."

"You always had great reflexes."

"It's cold-blooded murder."

Evie stared. Her eyes suddenly pooled. "Why are you doing this? I put myself on the line for you!"

Jack looked away. "I wish I could feel grateful."

"You're upset." Evie sniffed back her tears. "I can understand that. When you've had time to think things through you'll come to your senses. You'll realize that what happened here was inevitable if the two of us were going to get a running start. You'll see. I'll make it up to you. I'll make you forget. . . ."

Jack couldn't stand listening to any more. He reached into his shirt pocket and pulled out her mother's note.

Evie examined the scrawl. She looked up. "I don't get it."

"It's like scrabble. You have to play with the letters. Guess the magic word. Your mother was trying to tell me what a *l-i-a-r* you are!"

Evie crushed the note in her fist. "That silly old bitch. You're not going to believe her? She hated me the day I was born! And when my dad—"

A bell dinged. The computer was on. Paper rose in the printer as words appeared on the page. Jack hastened to the machine.

The message read: MetroBank Central Data Processing On Line.

He took a moment to absorb this, then leaned to the keyboard and typed: Nancy there? He was so engrossed in what he was doing that he was only dimly aware that she had crossed the room.

"Don't you turn your back on me, damn you!"

Evie had picked up Harris's pistol. She didn't seem bothered by its weight.

Jack took in a ragged breath. How could he have been so careless? He was tempting fate once too often, daring this woman to punish him for the ultimate sin.

"That supposed to make me believe in your sincerity?"

"What is it you want from me? You want me to admit I lied? All right. I admit it. I lied. I did take a chance with your life. I'm guilty, your honor—but with an explanation. I did what I had to do to survive. I know the chances that a man would understand are slim, but maybe, if you tried real hard, you could get a glimmer of what it's like to be female in a world run by men, what it's like to be an overdeveloped thirteen-year-old and have your weeping father slipping into your bedroom in the middle of the night, begging to be held, crying into your nightgown about the knot in his groin, about the pain of living with a frigid, unloving wife — is there a dutiful daughter anywhere that could deny him?"

Jack's mouth went dry. He could barely manage to speak. "Al did that?"

"Al did that. And did that. And did that." She shivered. "He stank of formaldehyde. No wonder Momma couldn't stand him to touch her. And then one night she caught us. He convinced her I had enticed him. God, it was awful. She beat me up and dragged me to the middle of nowhere and set me up in that cruddy trailer. Said if I was going to whore I should get paid for it."

Jack blinked back the emotion that was threatening to betray him.

Her lip curled. "What bothers you most? The whoring? Or me being fucked by my dad?"

He hardened his heart against her. "I think what really sticks in my throat is you getting it on with my dog."

Evie approached him until they were separated only by the length of the pistol. "Isn't there anything you won't make a joke about?"

"What makes you think I'm joking?"

Her expression softened. "You're really pissed off, aren't you? I guess I can't really blame you." She touched him and he shivered. "I want to confess something to you. Nothing I just told you was true. When you showed me my mother's note, it pissed me off. I thought if you wanted to believe the worst I'd make up something that would really curl your hair. I mean my dad did try to molest me but I kicked and yelled and my mother got there in the nick of time. But she did drag me to the godforsaken desert. And I might have wound up a whore except that my very first customer was so knocked out by my legs he got me an audition for a casino show."

"You're going to tell me that was Angelo."

"Someone who worked for Angelo."

"And just like that you became a showgirl."

"It wasn't any cakewalk. I had to stand there bare-ass naked while the lights cooked my flesh — you could hear every man in the audience sucking it in, watching the sweat trickle down from my armpits and crotch. . . ."

"You hated it so much why didn't you quit?"

"And do what? Every woman goes through the same shit. It's

just a matter of degree. At least I was somebody. My face was on the posters and on the souvenir playing cards. . . ."

"And who are you now?"

"More than I was. Before I agreed to do what they asked, I said they had to teach me how to deal, put me on track for management. But they'd never let a woman be top dog. I know that. Jack, throw in with me. I'm smart. And you're smarter. In five years the two of us could be running the whole shebang!" The pistol was now all that kept them apart. Her pelvis was up against his. She began grinding her hips. "What we had is nothing compared to what we could have!"

"How many people would we have to kill?"

She took a step back, face working, pistol rising until he was looking down the barrel, which seemed enormous.

Jack raised his eyes to hers. They were blazing with rage. When her pupils started to contract, he told himself that unless he could get them to enlarge he was dead.

"Go ahead. Finish the job." He crossed himself, looking sky-ward. "Forgive me, Father, for all my sins." He braced himself against the expected impact. "You will remember I loved you?"

For the briefest moment, the pupils of her eyes stilled. He grabbed for the barrel. The wind of the shot blistered his cheek. Both of them clung to the pistol. Strength multiplied by the surge of adrenaline, he whipped her off her feet. She struck the wall.

She cried out and let go. The pistol was his.

Whimpering softly, she slid down the wall to the floor. "Bastard. Like every man I ever met, all of you tricky, lying bastards!"

This time there was no feeling of triumph. But none of shame, either. Only a deep, abiding pity.

He shrugged. 'That's the nature of the beast."

From the computer, a bell dinged. He walked to the machine and read: Here's Nancy. Who's there?

He typed with one hand, keeping the pistol at the ready with the other, determined not to put himself at risk again. Jack here. Forgive me. Call Harry, my lawyer. Have woman in custody who posed as Harris's wife. Send cops . . . strike that, make that Feds, repeat Feds, to South-wick Lane off Sand Canyon Road outside Reno. Crime syndicate involved. Got that?

He glanced over to make sure she wasn't going to try anything. She'd stopped snuffling, and was sitting up against the wall, mouth sullen, reddened eyes observing him. But all the fight seemed drained from her.

The bell dinged. Got it. My word. Anything else? Jack
hesitated a moment, then again typed: Forgive me?

After an interminable wait, the answer came: No.

He was turning away, suddenly weary and depressed to his soul,
when the bell dinged once more.

The word appeared, as if by magic, one slow letter at a time:
Maybe.

EPILOGUE

Two rawboned county deputy sheriffs, called in by the estate's security patrol, arrived first, followed soon after by thick-necked detectives of the Reno police, who'd been alerted by casino employees. Minutes later a half-dozen vulture-eyed federal agents in gray tropical suits poured out of two helicopters, jostling each other in their eagerness to make a bust they knew would produce nationwide headlines.

There was a heated jurisdictional quarrel, resolved by a phone call to the U.S. attorney. Jack B. Noble, accused of crossing state lines to commit murder, as well as money laundering, wire fraud, embezzlement, and kidnapping, all federal crimes, was roughly handcuffed and hustled to one of the waiting helicopters.

Evelyn Peers, aka Jennifer Harris, though insisting she was a victim of near-incredible misunderstandings, was politely informed that she was to be held as a key witness to, and possible complicity in, the various charges, then led, somewhat more gently, but also in handcuffs, to the other helicopter.

At the federal building in Reno, Jack and Evie were interrogated separately. Jack waived his right to a telephone call, or to have a lawyer present, anxious to get the proceedings over with. Hours later, mentally and physically exhausted, he slid off the metal folding chair, asleep before he reached the floor.

Evie, whose questioning was conducted by a soft-voiced but steel-hard female agent, professed bewilderment and anguish that she was even under suspicion. Under the silky guidance of an attorney, one of Reno's most prominent, who had arrived at the behest of parties unknown, she denied as preposterous every charge Jack had leveled against her. It was only after the agent suggested bringing her mother in to identify the body of Al Peers that Evie suddenly broke down. Over the furious objections of her attorney, Evie confessed all.

In the investigation that resulted, Jack, as key witness, accepted the offer of protective custody. It wasn't that he was fearful of attempts on his life so much as that he was emotionally unable even to think about trying to pick up where he had left off. The idea of returning to face those he loved or who had once loved him made him almost physically ill.

The sleek young government lawyers in J. Press and Brooks Bros. suits provided him with the transcripts of Evie's testimony. Jack read the pages with growing horror and shame. The lawyers, though professing sympathetic understanding, watched his reaction with barely submerged fury, that mixture of jealousy and contempt felt by those who never take risks for those who do.

Jack assumed that charges would eventually be brought against him for tampering with bank funds. He looked forward to being tried, believing with all of his Catholic heart that for each of his transgressions a punishment must be exacted. But the government lawyers, not bothering to hide disappointment, told him that not only was MetroBank dropping all charges, but they had rewarded him for his help in plugging the leak, with a CD in his name for $100,000.

Evie received twenty years to life. Jack was released without so much as an admonition by the judge. Evie refused to meet Jack's eye as court bailiffs led her away. He walked hesitantly out into the blinding, smog-ridden sunlight, uncomfortable in the button-down white shirt, rep tie, gray tropical suit, and cordovan wing tips provided by the government.

From the federal courthouse building he walked through the crowd of indigents, government workers, attorneys, and litigants toward Sunset Boulevard. Outside a small pink adobe chapel near Olivera Street he paused. Finally going inside, he crossed himself, then entered the handcrafted rosewood confessional, kneeling in the cramped space, mouth next to latticework whose lacquer finish had been dulled by the anxious breath of countless sinners.

"Bless me, Father, for I have sinned. It's been more than twenty years since I've been to confession."

"*Continue, mi hijo.*" The priest was Latino.

"You understand English?"

"*Dios* will understand what I do not."

"I have stolen from my place of employment. I have debased myself with sins of the flesh."

"Yes?"

"That's pretty much it."

"*Dice* twenty Hail Marys and a dozen Our Fathers."

[225]

"That's it?"

"Try your best not to sin anymore."

Outside again, theoretically absolved by the spirit of Christ as well as the letter of the law, Jack did not experience that longed-for sense of relief and uplift his schooling had led him to expect. Disappointed, he boarded the Sunset bus heading west, not looking forward to the long-postponed meeting with his father, which he'd managed to put off until the court proceedings had been resolved.

The old man wanted to meet up at Jack's lot for reasons he'd refused to go into. Maybe he'd finally found a buyer. Jack had asked Harry to transfer title, so his father could sell the property and use the proceeds to rent an apartment.

At the corner of Canyon Road and Sunset, Jack descended from the hot and smelly bus. Loosening his tie and removing his jacket, he started up the hill toward his lot. Behind him he heard a trumpet. A moment later a dusty BMW with a grinning Harry at the wheel pulled up alongside.

"Jericho horn. Hop in."

Jack barely got his seat belt strapped before Harry, dressed in sawdust-flecked Levis and a work shirt, floored the accelerator.

"What's the rush?"

"Transmission's dicey. Need speed to get up the hill."

"My father ask you to come?"

"Wants me to help kill the fatted calf."

"You don't mean to tell me . . ."

They were turning into the lot before Jack could finish. And then he couldn't believe his eyes: on-site stood the completed framework of his house. He recognized that slanted roof and arched window as his own design.

"Listen. It's one thing to sell the land. But I never said to include my building plans. . . ."

From a tent pitched in a corner of the lot, next to a portable outdoor toilet, his father appeared. He was wearing a Raiders warm-up jacket, and carrying a hammer.

"Welcome home, son."

Jack, overwhelmed, stepped forward into the old man's embrace. "Dad, I—"

A sudden report emanated from the tent. Startled, Jack dropped his arms. "What—?"

Nancy ducked past the tent flap carrying a foaming bottle of champagne and four glasses. Though she was dressed in carpenter's overalls, they could not disguise that she was female. Her eyes slid past his, giving him a momentary jolt.

"Don't everybody just stand there. Somebody give me a hand with this."

A grinning Harry passed around the glasses as Nancy poured. They lifted their glasses to him.

"*Salud.*" His father was teary.

"*Pesetas.*" Harry couldn't seem to stop grinning.

"*Y fuerte de su canoe.*" Nancy was now staring at him boldly.

Dazzled, Jack, lifted his own glass, puzzling over the translation of what Nancy had said. Strength in his *what*?

They watched, grinning, as he inspected the house frame they had worked so hard to complete. And there, on a plank in the dirt where the computer room would be, lay his beat-up laptop.

Jack opened the case. All his disks were stacked neatly inside. Pulling out the disk containing the football program, Jack stood and walked to the edge of the berm.

Hesitating only a moment, he drew back his arm and sailed the disk out over the brush-covered hillside. It soared, dropped, and finally disappeared into an inaccessible cleft of the canyon below.

Any feeling of regret was at a level so deep Jack was hardly aware of it.